NEW FIC EVE

The Open Curtain

A NOVEL

BRIAN EVENSON

COFFEE HOUSE PRESS

MINNEAPOLIS

2006

#23

Coffee House Press books are available to the trade through our primary distributor, Consortium Book Sales & Distribution, 1045 Westgate Drive, Saint Paul, MN 55114. For personal orders, catalogs, or other information, write to: Coffee House Press, 27 North Fourth Street, Suite 400, Minneapolis, MN 55401.
 Coffee House Press is a nonprofit literary publishing house. Support from private foundations, corporate giving programs, government programs, and generous individuals helps make the publication of our books possible. We gratefully acknowledge their support in detail in the back of this book.

Good books are brewing at coffeehousepress.org

LIBRARY OF CONGRESS CATALOGING-IN-PUBLICATION DATA
Evenson, Brian, 1966–
The open curtain : a novel / by Brian Evenson ; afterword by the author.
p. cm.
ISBN-13: 978-1-56689-188-2 (alk. paper)
ISBN-10: 1-56689-188-4 (alk. paper)
1. Teenage boys—Fiction. 2. Problem youth—Fiction.
3. Mormon Church—History—20th century—Fiction.
4. Blood accusation—Fiction.
5. Mormons—Fiction. 6. Murder—Fiction.
I. Title.
PS3555.V326O64 2006
813'.54DC22
2006012060

FIRST EDITION | FIRST PRINTING
1 3 5 7 9 8 6 4 2
Printed in Canada

Beside myself, separated, I tried to annihilate myself,
but I remained, and felt myself to be immortal.

—BONAVENTURE

These perfect and private things, walling us in, have
    imperfect and public endings—
Water and wind and flight, remembered words and the
    act of love
Are but interruptions. And the world, like a beast,
    impatient and quick,
Waits only for those that are dead. No death for you.
    You are involved.

—WELDON KEES

PART I

RUDD, PARSED

I

Rudd found the letters early one Saturday morning among his dead father's dead things, kept in five collapsing boxes his mother had been meaning to throw out. He had gone down to the basement for some other reason, but by the time he had trailed his hand down the pocked concrete wall and reached the bottom of the stairs he had forgotten what it was. As he held himself still, gaze flicking about, he noticed, beside the water heater, the boxes. He opened one.

It was filled with clothing packed in thin dry-cleaner's plastic—things he never remembered his father wearing. He removed three carefully pressed and flattened white shirts, a cardigan, a tie folded once and smoothed along the box's diagonal, two pairs of creased slacks, a thick woolen sweater, and a tightly rolled black belt.

At the bottom was a 1954 Western States road map, attached to the bottom of the box with yellowed, brittle tape. A route was traced on it in red pencil, from Utah south into Mexico. Removing the tape, he lifted it out.

He had been looking at the map for some time before he noticed the envelopes the map had been hiding. There were three of them: two addressed to his father from an A. Korth, their tops slit open, the other addressed by his father to Miss Anne Korth—posted but marked *Return to Sender,* unopened.

He blew one of the slit envelopes open, removed the single-page letter. It was brittle along the creases; he opened it slowly, smoothing each crease flat with his thumb.

The handwriting was looped and difficult to make out, leaning off-plumb and slightly forward, the ink faded into near illegibility.

Dear Gyle, it began—his father's name—

Why have you not [then a word he couldn't read. A question mark. An entire line in the middle of the first crease, absolutely illegible] *Lael grows, is heavy* [or perhaps *healthy*] *and has asked after his father. Will you acknowledge him? I* [two words scratched out then three illegible words written above them] *tell him.* [The second crease, illegible again] *duty to your flesh,* [illegible]

    All my Love,
    Anne

He took up Anne Korth's second letter, opened the envelope, but found it empty save for a single photograph of a child, four or five years old, awkwardly seated on a photo studio's blue shag before a mottled screen. He held the image up to the light, tried to see his own face in the photo, but could not.

Setting the photograph aside, he opened the returned letter. Inside was a single three-by-five card, a short typewritten message on it:

> *Miss Korth:*
>   *I reluctantly acknowledge the receipt of your recent letters. I am convinced I am not the father of this boy. I believe you are mistaken in the man, and know enough of your true character to argue convincingly as much in a legal setting.*
>   *I shall not reply to any more of your letters. Do not write again.*

His mother had begun to pile the counter's dishes into the sink. He looked at her back, watched the knitting-needle twitch of her shoulder blades as she turned off the water, began to scrub.

"Mother," he asked, "who was Anne Korth?"

"When did you come in?" she asked, turning about, her hands dripping and held away from her body. She dried them on a corner of her apron. "Anne who?" she asked.

"Korth."

"I don't know any Anne Korth, do I?"

He shrugged.

"What do you have?" she asked. "What are you holding?"

"These?" he said. "Nothing. Old letters."

"Of your father's?"

"Yes."

She held out one chapped hand. "Come on," she said when he hesitated. "They're not yours to begin with, are they?"

"I don't think you should look at them," he said.

She kept her hand out until he surrendered them. He watched her take the photograph out from one envelope, look at it, put it back. She unfolded the letter from Anne Korth, puzzled through it without comment or response save for a tightening of the lips.

"Well," she said, after reading the three-by-five card, her voice still strong. "There it is, just as your father said. She was mistaken in the man."

"But—"

"No buts," she said. "It's simple truth." Putting the letters together, she set them beside the sink. "We know the truth. There's no reason to speak of this again."

2

For the moment, he just forgot it. That was the way he had been raised. He had always stood by his mother, obeyed her. He was her only child, she reminded him often, and the man of the house now that his father was gone. She counted on him. His father had become for him no more than a pair of dark shoes, a featureless face, an absence no longer palpable. It did not matter what he had done or been. It made no difference to Rudd's life.

He grew older, his glasses thickening and beginning to sit too heavily on his nose. He asked his mother for contacts and she said *no, darling,* and pressed her hand to her forehead in a way that made it clear he shouldn't have asked. Everybody has to make sacrifices, she told him.

He was in junior high and came home two hours before she did. While she was gone, he wasn't allowed to have friends in the house, not that he had any friends to speak of. He would stay in his room and assemble models and sometimes, out of curiosity, sniff the glue. It made his head ache. Once, some got on his wrist and it burned, his skin quickly blistering as he tried to rub it off first with water then with turpentine. After that, his mother reclaimed the house key. He could either go to the library after school or wait on the porch, but if she found him hoodlumming around, by God he would never hear the end of it.

On Sundays they went to church, his mother sitting beside him through the sacrament service. When it was over, she walked out and down the hall with him, pretending to be friendly and loving though he knew she was simply making sure he went to Sunday school and not out into the fields behind the church, as some of the other boys did, to smoke. In the class-room, he sat on one of the folding gray-brown chairs, tipping on two legs and looking at the words *Edgemont 3rd Ward* stenciled in a hazy orange on the back of the chair before him, waiting for his classmates to arrive and for the teacher to huff in ten minutes late, loaded with pictures and paraphernalia she had amassed from the church library that seemed to have no connection to the lesson. Her favorite lesson taught that if you listened to the Lord and followed the Commandments you would be blessed. It was bolstered by tales of Church leaders and members who had done good and were blessed. There was something about a boy with a crippled foot and a baseball (she spoke rapturously of the crippled foot), something about obeying your mother and later becoming a prophet. He had learned by this time not to raise his hand and ask, "If people who are good are blessed, why was The Prophet Joseph Smith shot to death?" He knew the answer, which was, "He wasn't shot to death, he was martyred." When Robert Talbot, who had loaned him two dollars once at school, was killed when his bike was hit by a car, he posed a similar question, and she answered with, "That poor child will have his reward in Heaven." Loopholes like that made the whole thing fall apart for him. He wasn't sure what to do about the two dollars, who should get them. If Robert Talbot were still alive, Rudd would probably never have bothered to pay him back. He spent weeks in his bed alternately feeling guilty and thinking of ways to do good with the two dollars, ensuring his own place in Heaven. Then he forgot about them, went on to borrow other people's money.

He would spend most of Sunday school tipping his chair back and trying to balance on two legs, clattering down and up, up and down. The other children were nervous and excited, waiting to see if the teacher would tolerate it stoically until the end of class or if she would jerk him out of the chair and pull him by the ear to his mother's Sunday school class. There, his mother would pinch the skin on the back of his arm and pull him out to the car. "Your father is rolling in his grave," she would tell him. That was the only time she ever acknowledged his father's death, and she never did acknowledge it had been suicide. Rudd heard about that from the other children, who had heard their parents whispering about it. A knife was involved, he knew, but little more. "You're my cross to bear," his mother would tell him, "A heavy cross." *Likewise,* he wanted to answer her, but never did.

He was not the only troublemaker. There was David Nimblett and Paul Boeglin and Kathleen Dunbar. All of them had their moments and could be as bad as he was or even worse, though they would always stay away from him. He took the brunt of the blame, stood out that way somehow. They were all in seventh grade except for Nan Lutz who had skipped a grade in school and would have been in a higher Sunday school class except that, as the bishop often said, the schools don't control the Church. *No such thing as "gifted" in church.* Church stuck to the natural order of things—God went by age, not brains or brownnosing.

In twelve months they went through six teachers, including Sister Thomas who began to weep one day at the beginning of class and couldn't stop even though they became saintly the second she began. Eventually Nan led her to the bathroom and left her there. There was Brother Worster, Pamela Worster's father, who as his last act shouted to them all to *hold their tongues* and when they literally did told them solemnly and with a shaking voice that he had done his best by them but that they were determined to go to Hell. If he had his way, he said, raising his arm to the square, they'd be in Hell right now. Near the end was Dan Jarman, just back from his mission, young and sleek in a way all the girls in the class admired, who suddenly stopped showing up. For three weeks they had no teacher. When the bishop found out, he took over, though he did not teach them exactly, but just sat with them as they went around one by one reading the scriptures, one verse each, round after round.

When reading aloud, he found, you couldn't pay attention to what you were reading; your jaws were too busy moving and slipping around the words and trying to make the archaic sentences sound like they made sense. You felt no substance, but there was a formal satisfaction to the act. When, at home, in his daily scripture study with his mother, he asked if he could be the one to read from then on, she was ecstatic, saw it as a sign that he'd finally taken an interest in the Church. But it wasn't that, not that at all.

He was starting to have an odd relation to words. Phrases from the Bible or elsewhere would catch in his head and keep circling round and about, digging a groove in his brain. The oddest little thing, just a phrase or two. "Lo, verily," it was for a while. He would be eating a sandwich or watching TV all the while thinking, *Lo, verily.*

Then it was high school, ninth grade. At school, in physiology, he was assigned a table with Blair Manning and T. J. Hobbs. Blair had long hair that she curled under. She always wore jeans and a T-shirt, a silver choker around her neck. Sometimes she sat on her hands. She had a pair of tortoiseshell combs, one small, the other large, that she would fidget with while Mr. Fresk was lecturing. Rudd tried to make it early to class so he could take the middle seat and be guaranteed a spot next to Blair. They started out dissecting a crawfish and by the end of the semester were all sharing a pig fetus.

He called her once after the class was over, at the beginning of the following semester, and waited on the phone until her mother found her.

"Hello?" she finally said.

"Hi," he said. "It's Rudd."

There was a long pause. "Rod who?"

Somehow he ended the conversation and hung up the phone without her quite figuring out who he was.

His hands seemed too big for his body. Sometimes he sat on them, but not the same way Blair did. He tugged on his fingers and thumbs, trying to make his hands look longer, until at church David Nimblett began calling him fish hand, a name that puzzled him more than wounded him. He felt a little sorry for Nimblett, who was nearly as awkward as he himself was, with even thicker glasses and fallen arches to boot.

Rudd's mother told him he was becoming a handsome man, but his body hung awkwardly around him. He began to live furtively, traveling from locker to classroom without looking up. He didn't want to be noticed, yet he wanted to be noticed. It was either too complicated or too easy. He was sure it was worse for him than for anyone else, though he couldn't explain why and knew he would be considered an idiot if he ever said this aloud. He was paralyzed. He gritted his teeth and decided to wait life out.

Blair Manning was walking down the hall and he was coming the other way and she was fiddling with her choker, looking at him. It was too late. There was nothing to do but keep walking forward. He would have to walk right past her. She joggled one finger toward him and said, "Hey, I know you." He nodded his head, smiling but trying to keep his teeth covered. Her face lit up and then she said, "Pig fetus, right?" and her friends tittered and then he was past, feeling ecstatic and insulted all at once.

That was the problem. Nothing came unmixed. He felt that it was his curse to realize this fact while not being able to do anything to make it more bearable. Everything was humiliating but desperately needed.

He decided to try out for a sport, knowing in advance that it would be disastrous. He was a week late for football, so they gave him a helmet that was too tight and inadequately padded and he stood on the sidelines during practice. His mother bought him wraparound sports goggles that, he found on the first day he came to practice, were several years out of style. After a while, the coach allowed him to run sprints. Then he stood on the sidelines some more. Someone, one of the seniors that the coach called Wile E. Coyote, kept sneaking up behind him and hitting the back of his helmet as hard as he could. It made his ears ring, sometimes knocked him down, once knocked him out. He woke up to the face of one of the assistant coaches. The coach was still running drills. The assistant coach suggested that maybe football wasn't the right sport for him, told him to take the rest of the day off and think it over. He went home vowing he would work as hard as he could, would prove to all of them he could do it. He would become a key player. They would eat their words. Instead, he shucked his uniform and never went back.

Serving him breakfast the next day, his mother said she hadn't thought she was raising a quitter. "How does the quitter like his eggs cooked?" she asked. "Runny?" And later, "The quitter's actually going to drink *all* his orange juice for once?" He kept nudging at his plate until it slipped off the table and shattered. She stared at him, her face going white then red. She turned away, steadied herself on the lip of the sink. He left the house.

He wandered for several hours, down the streets that went through the river bottoms, along the old dirt track beside the creek, watching the water-skeeters flit across the water's surface, passing from sun to shadow. He tried to hit them with pebbles, then skipped flat rocks upstream. He climbed an oak tree, sat in the crotch of the branch until his leg fell asleep, then jumped down, limped home.

When he was a sophomore, his English teacher, Mrs. Frohm, praised to the whole class a half-page essay he had written on an Emily Dickinson poem. He was pleased and embarrassed, instantly worried that the others would tease him about it afterwards, which they did. Two days later Mrs. Frohm was dead from an overdose of sleeping pills. He felt vaguely responsible. The principal, a hometown football hero now in his fifties who had a dour, droopy face, decided to have a serious talk with the class about death. Death was wrong, he told them, suicide especially. After closing the door, he brought out the Book of Mormon, telling them that normally school and religion didn't mix, but that this was a special case. The gist apparently was that Mrs. Frohm was going to Hell. Rudd's essay had been praised by someone going to Hell. Did that mean he was going to Hell too, or just his essay?

Rudd didn't know what to wear to the viewing, settled on a red tie and a white shirt, his church pants. He stood in line to get to the body, hands in pockets, wondering what he would feel when he saw her corpse. Her face was pale under the rouge. He got his head down close enough to see the pores of her skin. Her eyelid, he could see, was just slightly open, two or three strands of cotton visible between the lashes. If there hadn't been people behind him, he would have touched her skin. Just thinking about it made him feel lightheaded.

It suddenly became too much of a bother to get in trouble in Sunday school. Instead, he sat still in his chair, blanking it out, his arms crossed, answering only when he had no other choice. The answers were the same as they had been when he was six—each year they were taught the same things over and over again in a slightly different format. Even the objections that some of the students raised, he realized, were objections they had been preconditioned to raise for years, easy objections with pat solutions. He could rattle them out as easily as anyone:

TEACHER:	Does God answer prayers?
CLASS [in unison]:	Yes, of course.
TEACHER:	So, if I pray for a red corvette, I'll get it, right?
CLASS:	It's not a worthy prayer.
OBJECTOR:	What if you need the red corvette to convert someone?
TEACHER [solicitous]:	That would be a worthy purpose. But I can't possibly imagine a car is going to bring anyone closer to God.
OBJECTOR:	What if you pray for something that God knows will be bad for you?
TEACHER:	Like a red corvette? [Laughs.] Then if you're worthy, God gives you what you *really* need.
OBJECTOR:	So, if you're not worthy, you end up with the car?
TEACHER:	If you're not worthy, you end up with nothing. It's best to ask God to give you what you need to fulfill his will. There's no need to be too specific.

Perfect, thought Rudd, same technique fortune-tellers use.

One Sunday, their teacher passed out a slip of mimeographed paper, a genealogical tree on it in blue, slightly blurred ink.

"Today," he said, "we're going to learn about family history."

Rudd was instructed to write his parents' names in the first two slots. If you knew your parents' birthdays or—he suggested, looking at Rudd—death day, you should write that information in the half-slots below marked "b" and "d." The full slots on the next column were for your name and the names of your brothers and sisters.

Rudd looked at the form. He wrote his father's name in the first slot. *Gyle Theurer*. He wrote his mother's name in the second slot.

He crossed to the next column, wrote his name in the first slot. There were five other slots, all of them blank. He looked at the form. It seemed imbalanced, his name crowded at the top as it was.

He began to write his name again in the second slot, then stopped. Crossing out the "R" and the "u," he wrote instead, *Lael Korth*. Next to "b" he wrote a "?" and then, in parentheses, *bastard*. Beside his father's name, he drew in another line and wrote, *Anne Korth*. It had been four or five years since he had read the letters. He was surprised he still remembered the names.

He stayed staring at the tree, trying to figure out what it meant. Then suddenly the teacher was behind him, staring down at the paper.

"What's this?" the teacher asked.

Rudd smiled weakly, turned the paper over.

"You have a brother? Really?"

"A half-brother."

"Your mother's never said anything about it."

Rudd shrugged. "It's a little complicated," he said.

Later, when the teacher wasn't looking, he folded the paper once, then again, and slipped it into his pocket.

That evening, at supper, his mother brought it up. He denied everything.

"Brother Meyers told me all about it," she said. "He said you even wrote the word *bastard*. What kind of hellion writes the word *bastard* in church? Don't lie to me."

He just looked at her, then looked at his fork.

"You don't have a half-brother," she said. "I've never been with any man but your father."

"I'm not saying—"

"To be vulgar, I've never had intercourse with anyone but your father."

"But—"

"Are you accusing me of being a whore?"

He shut up. He looked at his hand, saw he was holding the fork tightly, fingers whitening around it. He let go, watched it clatter onto the plate.

"Mind the china," she said.

"It's Dad I'm—"

"There are certain rules in this house—"

"Goddam!" he shouted. "I read the letters. I know."

"What letters?" she said. "I don't see any letters." She snorted. "You and your 'goddam,'" she said. "The only bastard around here is you, and you weren't born that way. You had to grow into it."

"I know—"

"There are rules in this house," she said. "One of them is to treat the china with care. You know that. You know what the other rules are as well. I don't have to state them. If you don't care for them, there's the door."

He was shaking but he stayed seated. Later that night, his mother in bed with a headache, he took the telephone book out. He looked through the Provo listings, went on to Mapleton, Orem, Spanish Fork. In Springville he found an A. Korth.

He dialed the number, listened to it ring.

It clicked on, a woman's voice at the other end.

"Mrs. Korth? Anne Korth?"

There was a long static moment.

"Hello?" he said. "Please," he said. "Can you help me?"

"You must have the wrong number," the voice said, and hung up.

3

H e asked around at school, trying to figure out which school bus would get him to South Provo and closest to Springville. He stumbled up onto it after the last bell. The driver looked at him suspiciously.

"I don't recognize you," he said.

"I don't recognize you, either," said Rudd, and blushed.

"You're sure it's my bus you want?"

Rudd nodded and passed into the back. There was a group of boys in the last seats playing five card stud for nickels across the aisle, one of them keeping a running tally on the inside cover of a geometry textbook. Howard somebody, Rudd heard announced, was "kicking our asses." He squeezed into a seat between two students he half-knew. "Dickwipe," said one, punching him in the shoulder. He tried to hold his face neutral, looking straight ahead at the neck of the girl in front of him.

He stayed on the bus as it went south, then east, students filing off. The bench in front of him opened and he struggled out from between his half-acquaintances to take it. "Motherfucker," the boy on the outer edge suggested as he struggled to force his legs past.

The bus turned north. He stood up and moved toward the front, swaying against the rhythm. When it stopped, he got off, looked around for a city bus marker. The kid who had called him *motherfucker* was out and near him and prancing about, asking Rudd if he wanted to fight.

"I don't want to fight," Rudd told him without looking at him, which the boy took as his cue to shove him in the back. Rudd tumbled down, scraping his palms, dropping his books.

Rudd stood up, straightened his glasses, licked his palms, rubbed them against his jeans. He slowly gathered his books.

"Do you want to fight now?" the boy asked.

Rudd shook his head.

"What's wrong with you?" the boy asked.

"Nothing," said Rudd. "I just don't want to fight."

He started walking south. There was no city bus marker that he could see. The other boy pushed Rudd from behind again and he felt his head jerk and snap. It made a muscle in his neck ache. He kept walking. A few steps later the boy pushed him again.

He stopped and put his books down.

"I want to fight now," he said, and held his fists awkwardly out.

The other boy skittered a few steps back, smiled broadly. "Fuck all," he said. "You're not worth my time."

He was walking backwards on the side of the state route, his thumb out, books awkward under the other arm, slowly passing the cement works, when he saw the police car. He pulled his hand in, swiveled around. Putting his head down, he concentrated on walking forward.

He heard the police car pull up beside him.

"Hey," the officer said.

He stopped, looked up.

"Come over here," the officer said.

He hitched his books higher under his arm. Walking over, he stood beside the car's open window.

"What's your name?"

"Rudd," he said, his voice wavering, breaking.

"What's your first name?"

"That is my first name."

When the officer implied that he was a liar, Rudd showed him the name written inside the cover of a schoolbook.

"I'll be damned," the officer said. "What the Hell kind of name is that?" He pushed his hat back a little on his head to reveal a damp clump of hair.

"You hitchhiking?" he asked.

Rudd hesitated, nodded.

"Don't you know that's illegal?"

Rudd nodded again.

The police officer looked up at him. "Didn't nobody ever teach you to lie?"

Rudd shook his head.

"Not yet anyway. Get in," the officer said, and when Rudd tried to climb into the front, "the back."

Rudd got in, pushing himself over onto the seat, staring at the grille between himself and the officer. He reached out and touched it. Putting his books down on the seat, he carefully wrapped his fingers around the door handle. As the officer began to drive, Rudd pulled the handle, pushed on the door slightly. It didn't open.

"Suppose you tell me where you were heading?"

"Springville."

"I can see that. Where in Springville?"

Rudd watched him through the grille.

"I'm meeting my brother."

"You live in Springville?"

"No."

"And your brother doesn't either, is my guess. You're going to Springville to raise Hell."

"No, he lives there. Half-brother. It's kind of complicated."

"It's always kind of complicated," said the officer, smiling. "That's what they all tell me right before I take them down to the station and book them."

Rudd looked out the window. They would give him some change for a phone call. He would have to call his mother. If she was in a good mood, she would come down to the police station, drag him home, yell at him a few hours. If not, anything could happen. He watched the trees flick by, then the county country-western bar, the turnoff to reach the freeway. *Welcome to Springville.*

"Aren't you taking me the wrong way?"

"You said Springville, right?"

"But I—," said Rudd. "I mean I thought—"

"I figure a boy roped with a first name like Rudd already has about as much punishment as he can take."

They came to the middle of the town and the officer asked him where to go. He stuttered, started leafing through his books looking for the scrap of paper with the address on it.

"Unless you were lying to me after all," said the officer when after a moment Rudd still hadn't answered. "I don't cut slack to liars."

Rudd kept looking through the books.

"You could have just written the name in those books without it being your name. How do I know they're your books?"

"Here it is," he said, and read the address.

They drove to Third, turned, drove east a few blocks. It was a corner house in the middle of a square plot, the house itself squarish and small, thrown together with red brick, gray shingles.

"That's it?" asked the officer.

"I think so."

"You think so?"

He thanked the officer, tried again to get out of the car. The door wouldn't open. The officer, he saw, was out of the car, walking back. Rudd rearranged his books, moved them to his other hand. When the door was opened for him, he stepped out.

He was halfway to the front door before he realized the officer was following him. He turned slightly.

"Thanks for the ride," he said.

"You're welcome."

"You don't have to stay."

The officer smiled wryly. "I'd just like to see how the complications unravel."

"What do you mean?"

"It means I want to see if you were telling the truth."

Rudd turned slowly back. The door was a textured yellow, the paint puckering and flaking to reveal a gray-green undercoat. He looked at it, then at the doorbell beside. He reached out, pressed it.

He could hear from within the house the chime strike the first eight notes of some tune that seemed familiar. He couldn't place what it was before the door itself was flung open and standing before him was a boy much his own age, slightly blonder, slightly bigger.

"This is my brother," Rudd told the policeman, looking all the while steadily at the boy. "Lael."

"Lyle," the boy said.

"Lael," said Rudd to the policeman, "his name is Lael."

The boy looked at him, opened and closed his mouth.

The officer took off his hat and held it by the visor, knocked the brim against his thigh.

"This is your brother?" the officer asked the boy.

"You can see the resemblance," said Rudd.

"I want to hear it from his own lips."

The boy licked his lips, shrugged. "Yeah, sure," he said. "He's my brother."

The officer picked his way down the path, through the dandelion-ridden lawn and back to the cruiser. Rudd lifted his hand, smiled, waved as the cruiser pulled away.

Before he could lower his arm, he was spun about, the boy's knuckles backhanding his face. He stumbled off the porch and into the hedge, his books scattering. He was still struggling to catch himself when Lael's foot struck him hard in the stomach and sent him lurching onto the damp grass. Somehow before he hit the ground Lael was already atop him, straddling his hips, knees pinning down his arms.

"Now tell me who you really are," Lael said.

"I'm sorry," Rudd said.

"The world is full of sorry people," said Lael. "What's your game?"

"Game?"

Lael drew his arm back, slapped him. Rudd's cheek began to throb.

"Nobody uses me," said Lael. "Never. Start talking."

4

It wasn't until the next year, when Rudd had his driver's license and had saved enough money to buy a used scooter, that he began to see more of his half-brother, always at Rudd's initiative. It was a Vespa, white, very stylish as it turned out, though Rudd hadn't realized this when he bought it. He, in any case, was incapable of remodeling himself to fit the scooter, and thus always felt slightly humiliated riding it. Lael fit no better, he knew. He looked at least as out of place, maybe more, but he didn't seem to care.

On a Friday or Saturday Rudd would ride the scooter down Ninth East, toward Springville. He kept the scooter close to the side of the road, cars passing him or sometimes pressing close behind. He would stop halfway, at the cement plant, to use the pay phone. If Lael was home, he kept going; if not, he sometimes kept going, sometimes went home.

He thought of calling earlier—from his house if he could get his mother off the telephone long enough, or from the gas station a few blocks away from home. Yet there was satisfaction in the half trip, in turning around at the cement plant with his brother unseen, as well as in the full trip. He had come to think of both as something he needed.

Besides, mostly Lael was there.

It was better when Lael was out in front waiting for him when he arrived. Once he called, Lael always said he would be sitting on the curb, waiting, but he rarely was. Rudd would wait, balanced on his scooter, finally blowing his horn. Lael, when he came out, came slowly, maddeningly, as if disinterested.

"I'm driving," he always said, and Rudd let him, not knowing where he would take them.

They hardly talked, just drove. The rare moments when Rudd broke the silence, Lael answered succinctly, no wasted words. He gave away nothing. Weeks passed with Rudd learning very little of Lael.

"Who are your friends?" he asked one day, holding on to the back of the seat as Lael labored the scooter up Spanish Fork Canyon.

Lael flicked his head back slightly. "You wouldn't know them," he said.

"Just give me some names."

Taking the scooter off the highway, Lael slipped carefully down a gravel access road and parked near the railroad line. They walked onto the tracks, skipping rocks down the ties, then walked over the trestle and down to the riverbank.

"Come on," said Rudd. "Tell me something."

Lael shrugged. "I don't think so," he said. When Rudd kept pushing, Lael took the scooter keys out of this pocket, threatened to throw them into the river.

Rudd told his mother nothing anymore, certainly nothing about Lael. When she asked where he went each week, he made things up, mentioned the names of people at school he wanted to be friends with but wasn't. Blair Manning, for instance, who he pretended to her was a boy. He asked himself if it felt different having a half-brother, was certain it did but couldn't quite say how.

Each weekend passed quickly. During the week he woke up at seven each morning to go to school. His mother, perhaps feeling she was losing him, finally bought him contact lenses. She began to hover uneasily around him in the evening. He started to resent her, succeeded in doing so until the weekend came and he drove off to see Lael again, then came back and lied to her. He would feel guilty and tender for a day, then start hating her again. They gradually adjusted to become tired of one another at approximately the same instant: by the weekend he was ready to go and she seemed glad— though she would never admit to it aloud—to have him gone. He rolled the scooter out of the garage and out into the street and started off.

He stopped at the cement plant and telephoned but nobody answered. He kept driving anyway. Lael was not waiting outside. He parked outside the house, blew his horn, waited straddling the Vespa's saddle to see if he would come out. When he did not, Rudd kicked the scooter onto its stand, slipped off the back, picked his way across the lawn and to the door.

Lael's mother was already opening the door by the time he reached out to ring the doorbell.

"Don't walk across the lawn," she said through the screen. "How many times do I have to tell you?"

She had never spoken to him before, at least not face-to-face. He had only seen her peering through the drapes and, once, on the front porch with her arms folded across her front. "Sorry," he said.

"What do you want here? Why do you come around here?"

"To see Lael."

"To see what?" she said.

"Lael," he said.

"Lyle?" she said.

"Uh," he said. *Your son,* he was about to say, but she was already shutting the door.

He stood on the concrete porch. After a while he walked back to his scooter, sat on it. Putting his hands on the grips, he twisted the rubber. He could see Lael's mother still looking at him through the window from behind the curtains.

He got off the scooter, started across the lawn toward the door, then doubled back and went up the walk. He rang the doorbell, was surprised when she opened it.

"What is it?" she said. But before he could answer she'd turned, was walking slowly back down the hall, away from him. Then she was gone. He stepped into the house and stood just inside the door. He didn't know what to do with his hands. After a while, he stepped out again.

Five minutes later he could see her coming down the hall again, toward him. Her hair was wet now, mascara streaking her face. And there was Lael suddenly behind her, gliding past. He came past her and onto the porch and past Rudd and across the lawn to the scooter. In the house Lael's mother kept coming slowly toward Rudd, arms out. Rudd stood hesitating at the doorway, watching her. Her wrists, pushed in front of her, seemed thick, almost swollen. Behind him, he heard Lael kick the scooter to life.

"Come on," Lael called, cupping his hands around his mouth. "Come on."

Rudd turned to go and left the porch, trying not to look behind him. He ran out to the street, climbed on.

"What was that all about?" Rudd asked.

Lael shook his head, laughed. "Welcome to my world," he said, and drove.

It was a phrase that for a time was caught in his head. *Welcome to my world.* He heard it for hours at a time, over and over again, always in Lael's voice.

Sometimes, he realized, his own lips were moving. It was like a virus, as if a part of Lael, translated into speech, had penetrated his skull. As it cycled, he waited to see if it would take hold of a portion of his head completely or fade into the babble of borrowed and now indecipherable voices upon which the whole anxious and tenuous surface of his thought was awash.

At night, in bed, he stared up at the ceiling and thought of Lael. It had taken Rudd weeks to tell him what he knew, to reveal to Lael that they were half-brothers. Yet when he had, there had been no shock, no surprise.

"Tell me something I don't know," Lael had said.

"You already knew? Why didn't you tell me?"

"I could ask the same of you."

He always had a sense that at any moment Lael would be willing to walk away and never see him again, that the only reason Lael saw him now was out of a kind of indulgence—whether of Rudd or of himself was hard to say. He was little more than tolerated, Rudd felt, and the closer he grew to Lael the more he felt how much he held himself apart. It made him wish that Lael's voice saying *welcome to my world* would swell and expand and take him and consume him.

And then in his worry he forgot the phrase for a time before it sprang on him again unawares, a static vision of Lael flashing up before his eyes in accompaniment.

5

Things began to go odd on one of their many long rides, this one up Provo Canyon, to the picnic tables at the foot of the mountain and beside the railroad trestle that crossed the river. They were sitting there, beside the scooter they had driven past the chains and over the gravel paths, watching the swirl of the water, the motor ticking as it cooled, when Rudd realized Lael was staring at him.

"What is it?" Rudd asked.

Lael shrugged, kept staring.

Rudd made a point of looking away, down at the water. He kept his eyes there, then followed the trestle up to the top, to where some kids were drinking beer from Seven-Up bottles and sunning themselves, sometimes jumping into the pool below. When he allowed himself to flick his gaze back, Lael was still looking at him.

"What?"

"You really don't hide anything, do you?"

"What do I have to hide?"

"Nothing," said Lael. "Not yet."

Rudd tried to press him but he would speak no further. They stayed idly near the river another half hour, then wandered across the trestle and climbed a shale draw to the dull hospital-green water pipe winding along the mountainside.

Rudd watched Lael put his feet on the bolts at a joint, climb up the side and onto the top. He stood balanced atop the pipe.

"Come on up," he said.

"No," said Rudd.

"What?" said Lael, suddenly interested. "Don't you love your brother enough to join him?"

"It's got nothing to do with you," Rudd said. "I can't stand heights."

"Hell, Rudd," said Lael. "You just climbed the side of a mountain."

"That's different," said Rudd. "There's no drop, just a steady slope."

"Could kill you either way. Come up."

"No."

Lael danced atop the pipe. "Come on," he said. "It's perfectly safe." He squatted, reached his hand down. "If you can't trust your brother, who can you trust?"

"It isn't that," said Rudd.

"Trust me. Prove you're my brother. Trust me."

Later Rudd thought, *I am only his half-brother, I can only trust him halfway*. But at the time he did not think it. Instead, he reached out and took his half-brother's proffered hand, put his foot on a bolt, and let himself be drawn up. He was on his hands and knees atop the warm pipe, not moving, the world slowly swaying around him. He felt Lael drag him up, felt his brother's hands pushing him, the world slowly yawing and turning. Things were going dim. After that, he remembered nothing.

He awoke in the hospital, his mother beside him. His arm was broken, in a cast to the elbow, his head wrapped in gauze. There were cuts up and down his arm.

"What happened?" he asked.

"You're awake," said his mother, then slapped him hard. "Don't you ever," she said. "You're lucky I came at all."

"Lael brought me?"

"What?" she said. "You brought yourself in."

"Where's Lael?"

"Lyle who?"

"No," he said. "There's—"

"Listen to me," she said. "It was just you."

He was given pills. He listened to her talk, her voice blurring and growing faint. He closed his eyes. When he opened them again, she was gone, Lael occupying her place, exactly.

"Why did you do it?" he asked Lael.

"Do what?"

"Push me."

"I didn't push you," Lael said. "You let yourself go."

Rudd went home, asking the desk on the way out who had admitted him. They looked up the file. He had driven himself in, broken arm and all, on his scooter.

Each day, his mother changed the dressing on his head, bathing his cuts with lukewarm water. The arm began to itch in the cast, and he scratched inside of it first with a pen and then with a bent coat hanger. At school, the novelty of a cast got a few people to talk to him who normally didn't acknowledge him. He invited them to sign his cast. *Get well,* most wrote. David Nimblett wrote, *Injured in the Line of Duty* and drew a saluting stick figure. Bryan King, smirking, wrote, *Break a leg.* Then the doctor cut the cast off and his life went back to normal, only his forearm was smaller and lumped in the middle.

He would not see Lael, he told himself the first weekend his cast was off, but by noon he was sick to death of his mother and changed his mind. He drove with one hand, precariously, the injured arm resting against his thigh.

He saw Lael once a week after that. He knew immediately something was different, yet it took days for him to realize Lael had started making a game out of everything, testing him. Lael offered the oddest appeals to brotherhood, at the oddest possible moments. Outside of these moments he did not mention their being brothers at all—as if brotherhood were a kind of bond activated only *in extremis.* Most of the time, Lael was detached, hardly present. Only at those moments when he dared Rudd to do what he would otherwise have avoided did Lael turn fully toward him. This turning was unpredictable, hardly encouraged by the same thing twice. It could come in his trying to convince Rudd to turn around and lie down while the scooter was in mid-flight, to put his chest on the back rack and hang his fingers down close enough to the ground to brush against the asphalt. Or in suggesting that Rudd throw a rock at a dog or at a window. But it could be something simpler, like forcing Rudd to ask a question of an attractive girl working at JCPenney. Indeed, Lael always had an ability to single out from very different situations what would make Rudd most uncomfortable. Rudd himself never could guess when his half-brother would turn toward him, call him brother, try to coax him into a painful fellowship.

Three months later, cruising south on farm roads near Spanish Fork, Rudd looked over Lael's shoulder, saw the gas gauge near empty.

"We have to get back to town," he said, speaking loud against the wind.

Lael slowed, then sped up again.

Rudd leaned forward, putting his mouth near Lael's ear. "Turn around," he said.

31

Lael didn't look back, didn't slow down. Rudd pushed up against him, reached past to tap the gas gauge.

"We're almost out of gas."

"Just a mile more," said Lael. "Then I'll turn around."

"Where are we going?"

"Nowhere."

They drove past a farmhouse, then a whitewashed barn, lines of fences with cattle scattered behind them. A drainage pipe appeared, opened into a narrow, slow-moving creek.

"Lael," he said.

"Just a little more."

They went through a crossing, past an old rusted-out tractor that was rolled off the road, nose-first into a ditch. The barbed-wire fencing gave way to simple split-rail, the pasture to an organized field, thick with the crenate leaves of a plant he couldn't identify, then another field, this one corn. A feed truck rattled past, flecks of hay swirling across their windscreen and over their faces, tufting on Lael's shirt and in his hair. An old man in a red Chevy two-ton waved slowly, as if underwater.

"Lael, now," Rudd said.

"No," said Lael.

"What?"

"I'm not turning back."

"What do you mean?"

"Let's see how far we can go."

"But we won't get back," Rudd shouted.

"Who cares if we get back?"

"I do," he said, and then, when Lael did not answer, again, "I do."

Rudd reached forward, tried to pry Lael's hands off the grips. Lael held fast, the scooter swerving slightly.

"Swear to God," said Lael. "Keep that up and I'll kill us both."

Rudd let go, gave up. He leaned back, kept silent until he heard the engine sputter and surge, then die. As they coasted to a stop, he got the sense somehow, through the back of Lael's head, that his half-brother was smiling.

6

It was essential, Rudd's senior English teacher, Mrs. Madison, insisted, that they learn how to do research. Whether they were going on to college or planning to work in the common sector, researching was a useful skill. For several days, attempting to convince herself as much as the students, Mrs. Madison kept repeating the words *common sector* until Rudd found them lodged in his own head.

On the third day Jenny Kindt, a pale and freckled redhead whose cheeriness had suffered a setback after her sister's drug overdose and subsequent death the year before, called the bluff and asked how research could possibly be important in the *common sector*. Mrs. Madison made the mistake of resorting to day-to-day, hands-on examples.

"Say you're working in a grocery story and a customer asks you a fact about broccoli. You've got to know how to research it."

"I'd tell her to ask the manager," said Jenny. The class laughed.

Mrs. Madison shook her head. She stood before the class looking somewhat bedraggled. She hooked her stringy hair behind an ear.

"No," she said. "Say it's not something the grocery store manager would know offhand. Something else."

"Like what?"

"What culture was the first to use broccoli as a food?"

"I don't want to know that." Laughter again.

"But what if a customer wants to know?"

"I'd tell her to go ask the manager. If the manager doesn't know, that's his problem, not mine."

"Look," said Mrs. Madison, her voice rising. "Research is just important. It just is."

Rudd found himself on both sides, sympathizing with Mrs. Madison, whom he liked, who seemed to like him, yet wanting to laugh. It was not as simple as feeling torn, for while at one moment he was torn, in the next he found himself at a cold remove, the people and the room as a whole crystalline and distinct.

Common sector, he heard in his head, the speech in the room and the laughter coming to him as though swaddled in cotton. *Common sector.* This coldness was, he felt he knew somehow, the way that Lael must feel all the time. He felt that if he had been before a mirror he would see not his own face but the face of his half-brother. He tried to catch his reflection in Mrs. Madison's glasses, but she was too far away. And almost immediately the vibratory moment passed.

There were strange spattered moments like that, where he felt he had understood something about his half-brother, something he could never quite verify and which he could hardly ask Lael about. As if the weekly proximity to Lael had weakened his skin and let his brother leak in. As he rode on the back of the scooter, his face pressed against Lael's back, he felt that even once he was separated from him he would be joined to him still.

Lael did not seem to feel this. It was as if Lael remained always unscathed, self-contained. Lael could leak into him but not he into Lael. What he felt only rarely and infrequently—the cold remove—seemed to him, at least as far as he could tell, Lael's dominant state. For if Lael felt anything, he rarely expressed it, and anything Lael did express toward Rudd felt pasted on, not so much an actual feeling as a kind of taunt or dare.

Yet perhaps he had gotten his half-brother all wrong.

Rudd stared at a blank sheet of paper. He was asked to write down *ideas.*

"Ideas for what?" he said.

"For the research topic, stupid," Steve Kilpatrick told him.

On the blackboard, overlaying a haze of chalk dust, had been written:

> *Start simple:*
> *Where would you like to live?*
> *What is your heritage?*
> *What decade fascinates you?*
> *Who is your hero?*

He did not have any heros, he told himself. None at all. In Sunday school when he was twelve they had asked him the same question, some strategy for an object lesson, and he sat there holding his pencil trying to come up with something. When they went around the circle giving their responses he hadn't known what to say, so remained silent until they passed him by. *Jesus,* the others had said, except for one who said *Rush Limbaugh.*

He copied the questions off the blackboard and onto his paper, leaving four blank lines between each.

Where would you like to live?

Springville, he wrote, then crossed it out and wrote, *Anywhere but here.* But on reflection it seemed like the sort of response likely to get him into trouble. Debbie White, seated next to him, had written California. He knew that he wanted to be as far from Debbie White as possible. He crossed his phrase out and wrote, *New York.*

What is your heritage?

He did not know what to say. His father was dead and his mother, he felt, had reduced him in memory to a nonspecific and general figure of good, a sort of vague and lifeless avatar of Mormon ideals. Yet his father, he knew, had slept with Anne Korth—had perhaps even been secretly and polygamously married to her or perhaps simply had no qualms, despite being an avatar of Mormonism, about committing adultery. But for the purpose of a school assignment, he would give both his father and mother the benefit of the doubt.

Mormonism, he wrote. *In the classical sense.*

What decade fascinates you?

What was this about? What did Mrs. Madison want to hear? He looked up and judged her hairstyle, the cut of her white dress, then wrote, *1900s.*

Mrs. Madison was in the front of the class, hands behind her back, step-ping tentatively from one end of the blackboard to the other. When he capped his pen, she hurried to his desk.

"Finished?" she asked. "May I?"

She took the sheet of paper off his desk, read through it quickly.

"Surely you have a hero."

"Not really."

"It doesn't have to be someone famous, Rudd," she said. "It can be any-one. Your father, say."

"My father's dead," he said.

"I'm sorry," she said, and pretended to be reading the list again.

He died in the *common sector,* Rudd thought to himself, though he knew this was not precisely true.

"So what do we have?" she said. "New York, Mormonism, 1900s. What's at the intersection of those words?"

"Nothing," he said.

"Now, Rudd," she said, pursing her lips. "If you start with that attitude you're already beaten. Is your glass half-empty or half-full?"

I don't have a fucking glass, Rudd thought, then thought, *That's Lael thinking.* "Half-full," he said. And then added, "Maybe even three-fourths full."

"That's the spirit," she said. "Now you're talking." Holding his paper in her hand, she walked to the front of the class, began to speak about what they should do next. He noticed as she spoke that people all around him were crossing out what they had written, quickly creating better combinations.

"We will be going to the university library," he heard Mrs. Madison tell the class. "I've made the arrangements. There, you will find a newspaper or magazine of national repute and look through it to find a news item that combines as many of your four answers as possible. So, for instance . . . " she said.

And then she held up Rudd's paper. He tried to look nonchalant, but he could feel his ears start to burn and he knew they had gone red at the tips.

Fuck them, thought Rudd. *Fuck all.*

But he knew he didn't mean it.

At least the field trip to the university library meant a few missed classes. She stood them all outside the doors, beside the frieze—a Utah artisan's approximation of Mayan culture. He could also see, from where he stood, the dark bronze figure of an eight-foot Indian. *What tribe?* he wondered.

They were to stay in the periodicals/microfilm area. They were not, under any circumstances, to leave the periodicals/microfilm area. A field trip of this sort was a *privilege*. If they needed something that was not in the periodicals/microfilm area they must request the "library pass." He watched Mrs. Madison hold up the hall pass she had brought with her from school.

They were herded through the doors and then through clicking dull green turnstiles. He stared at Ellen Barlow's bare neck, just inches away, shuffling his feet so as not to step on her heels. Directly behind him, someone was popping gum.

They went through and he looked behind him. Mark Pollard was the one with the gum. He blew another bubble as Rudd watched, popped it sharply.

"What?" asked Mark.

"Nothing," said Rudd and turned back around. He could feel Mark's hand even before it was on his shoulder, tugging at him, pulling him around. He felt himself growing distant.

"Why did you look at me like that?" Mark asked.

"Like what?"

"You know what," said Mark. "Want to fight or something?"

Rudd shook his head no, then, as Mark started to look away, slung his forehead down hard into Mark's mouth and nose. It hurt like hell. When he brought his face away he could feel the gum sticky and webbed all through his bangs. Mark was gasping, covering his mouth.

Immediately there was a hand pinching his neck from behind, hard, a second hand on Mark's neck.

"Rudd," Mrs. Madison said. "Suppose you tell me what's going on here."

"I don't exactly know," he said. "I have his gum in my hair."

"And why exactly is his gum in your hair? And why is his nose bleeding?"

He looked at her in a way he hoped was innocent. "We must have collided?"

She looked at Mark who, blood dripping down his chin, just nodded. Mrs. Madison took her hands off their necks. "Go wash up," she said. "I know you're both lying, but at the moment I'm too busy to care. Once more and I'll see you both suspended."

He splashed water through his hair, trying to rake the gum out with his fingers. It came out first in bits, then stopped coming out at all, tightening into clumps.

"You're going to have to cut it out," Mark said, patting his face and nose with a tan, coarse paper towel.

He nodded. He looked around for something to cut it with. There was nothing, unless he wanted to try sawing it off with the triangular teeth of the paper towel dispenser. He heard a click and when he turned, Mark held a pearl-handled stiletto in his hand. The blade was dull and oily, longer than his middle finger, twice as thick.

"Why did you do it?" Mark asked.

Rudd looked at the knife, shrugged. "I don't know," he said. He really did not know, he realized. He had still been shaking his head no, he didn't want to fight, when his head had struck forward and through Mark's face of its own accord. It had surprised him almost as much as it had Mark. "Why do you have a knife?" he asked.

"Don't you like me?" asked Mark.

Rudd shrugged again. "I never thought about it much," he said. "I like you good enough."

Mark made a slow and awkward pass with the knife, forcing Rudd back a step. He smiled. "Just kidding," he said, and handed the knife, haft first, to Rudd.

Rudd took the knife and held it, the light winking off the blade's edge and into his eye. Lael, he knew, in his place, would probably stab Mark. *I am different from my half-brother. I am my own person.* He lifted the knife, began to hack off clumps of his own hair.

1903 sounded like a slow news year. The 1903 *New York Times* came month by month in a faded yellow box on an open-centered spool, just like every other year, but he couldn't remember having heard the year mentioned in Ms. Stahl's The American Tradition class. Perhaps the paper would be stretching for stories and would report on minor human interest sorts of things, something that would come at least marginally close to the parameters forced upon him.

He put the microfilm in wrong and everything was sideways and backwards, the letters turned inside out. The spindle had not gone through the center hole, and the spool inscribed an oval as it turned. The harried reference librarian fixed it for him quickly, casting looks of hatred all the while at Mrs. Madison, who either remained oblivious or was exceptionally skilled at appearing so.

He began to crank the reel forward. When he got to the first page on the first day of January, everything was still sideways and it took him some time to figure out how to rotate the projecting apparatus to get the text to project correctly. Even then it was still in indifferent focus, strands of the page sharp, the remainder slightly fuzzy and blotted.

He started scanning titles. *Girl Met Polite Burglar,* something about iron and steel. Polite? he wondered. *Taylor to Be Hanged,* but no relation to Former Mormon Church President John Taylor as far as he could tell, then a flash of black and January 2 where *Boy Accidentally Kills His Brother With Rifle.* Directly below, *Ball Given in Barn.* The boy's murder in the present tense, the ball in the past, though both had already occured. Some significance there, he was willing to bet, but not enough to keep him from cranking through advertisements and on to the next day. *Horses Tortured in Trench* and *Got Carving Knife By Mail. French Painters Here.* He began cranking faster, flashed past an ad for muslin underclothing. *Sultan Rewards Spies* (perhaps by giving them muslin underclothing?), *Congo Raiding to Be Stopped, Activity in Billiards.* Does the *New York Times* still list billiard activity? he wondered. *French in an Amiable Mood* (perhaps because their painters are out of the country), and a few columns later, *French Murderer Not to Die* (just one more reason for the French amiability). More billiards, *Moving Day for Jesuits, Brought Dead Dog to Life,* "survived with adrenalin injections ten hours without a head." *Holy Hell.*

He wound the reel back up and took it off, packing it into its box, then went to retrieve the February reel from the pull-out cabinets.

He got the reel on and threaded right. *Typhoid Spreads at Ithaca, The Cake Walk in Vienna, Mr. Morgan Burlesqued, A New Kind of Orchid. Horse Kicked and Many Died. MERIT is what sells, OLD CROW RYE. It is a straight whiskey and cannot be equalled.* Just below, *The Frisky Mrs. Johnson. Large Oysters Scarce This Year.* Uncle Sam holding up some men and rockets wrapped in tape—a political cartoon that made no sense to him. *Rev. Robert Street Burned to Death.* "Daughter only injured, she will survive." At least this one's related to religion, he thought. He could ask Mrs. Madison if, since he couldn't find anything Mormon, Rev. Robert was close enough. He knew she would acquiesce, but would also tell him he needed in future to persist, because *Good Things Come to Those Who Wait.* She was always saying crap like that, and pronouncing it like a headline. *The Plague in Mexico. Body Discovered by Divers.*

He came to February third. *Billiard Championship.* He could ask to change his topic to billiards, list his hero as "a billiard player." *Anthracite at Retail* right next to *Easy Divorce. Men's $5 shoes for $3.50,* then, turning to February fourth, *Men's Shoes for $2.25. Match Caused Explosion, Shot Woman and Self. Important to Every Home—Silks. Billiard Champion Lost. Chorus Favorite Dead.*

He read about *Her 102d Anniversary,* flashed past the article just below it, registered it only a few pages later. He wheeled back:

Hooper Young's Trial To-Day

His Lawyer Will Ask Further Delay—
Prosecution Blames Mormon
Friends and Relatives

Jesus, he thought. He had managed three out of the four categories, purely by hazard. He was a believer now, but in what he did not know. Research, maybe. Or blind chance. He began to read:

> William Hooper Young, grandson of Brigham Young, will go on trial this morning before Justice D. Cady Herrick, in the Criminal Branch of the Supreme Court, on the charge of having murdered Mrs. Anna Nilsen Pulitzer last November. The trial may not proceed, however, for W. F. S. Hart, Young's counsel, will ask for delay on a number of grounds, one of them being that his client is physically unable to withstand the strain of trial.
>
> Assistant District Attorney Studin reiterated yesterday his statement regarding the disappearance of several witnesses, but said that nevertheless Young would be convicted. While Mr. Studin did not lay the disappearance of these witnesses directly at the door of the Mormon Church, he declared emphatically that the Mormon friends and relatives of the defendant were putting forth efforts to defeat the case of the prosecution. Mr. Studin pointed to an article which appeared over Young's name in the October number of *The Crusader,* the magazine edited in Hoboken by the prisoner and his friend Dixie Anzer. The article was headed "Sunrise in Hell," and in it, Mr. Studin said, there appeared more or less vague references to the "blood atonement" doctrine.
>
> It was learned yesterday that, while the prosecution would not assume this doctrine had any direct relation to the motive for the murder, it might be used to throw additional light on the tragedy. The "blood atonement" doctrine teaches that the soul of any Mormon who has gone back on his or her faith may be saved by the shedding of the blood of such a person as was the woman, and that the blessing thus conferred would reflect credit in the other world on the person who commits the deed.

Damon Philips was punching him between the shoulderblades, calling him punkass, telling Rudd he had to have the microfilm machine.

"Just a minute," Rudd said. "I've found something."

"What happened to your hair, punkass?"

"Mind your own business," said Rudd.

"Man, what's wrong with you? You're not usually like this."

"Like what?"

"Usually you're normal."

"What do you mean, normal?"

Damon shrugged. "You know, normal."

He didn't know what to say. *I never know what to say,* he told himself. Getting up, he surrendered the machine.

He stood leaning against the microfiche cabinets. The *Crusader,* he thought. *Sunrise in Hell.* Hardly building blocks from the *common sector.* Looking through the card catalog, he found no mention of a magazine called the *Crusader.* He went back to leaning.

"Well, Rudd," said Mrs. Madison. "Did you find anything?"

"Yes," he said.

"Congratulations," she said. "I guess that old glass was half-full after all."

His father's books were in a small slope-ceilinged demi-room halfway up the stairs to the attic. They were in stacks against the walls, empty boxes scattering the space between.

He began to look through them, sorting the church books out of the stacks, brushing the dust off of them, stacking them near the door. As he worked, dust spun slowly in the air. When he licked his lips, he tasted dust.

Carrying some books down to his bedroom, he spread them on his bed. *Mormon Doctrine,* one was called, a dictionary of sorts. He opened it, leafed through the A's to the B's, stopped at a section called "Blood Atonement Doctrine."

> (See *Atonement of Christ, Calling and Election Sure, Christ, Flesh and Blood.*)
> From the days of Joseph Smith to the present, wickedly and evilly-disposed persons have fabricated false and slanderous stories to the effect that the Church, in the early days of this dispensation, engaged in a practice of blood atonement whereunder the blood of apostates and others was shed by the Church as an atonement

for their sins. These claims are false and were known by
their originators to be false. There is not one historical
instance of so-called blood atonement in this dispensa-
tion, nor has there been one event or occurrence whatever, of any nature, from which the slightest inference
arises that any such practice either existed or was taught.

Next to the passage someone—probably his father—had written

Untenable. c.f. *Confessions of John D. Lee* or even the
practice of swearing, upon pain of death, not to reveal
the ceremonies of the Mormon temple.

He skipped down a few lines:

. . . the true doctrine of blood atonement is simply
this:

1. Jesus Christ worked out the infinite and eternal
atonement by the shedding of his own blood. He came
into the world for the purpose of dying on the cross for
the sins of the world. By virtue of that atoning sacrifice
immortality came as a free gift to all men, and all who
would believe and obey his laws would in addition be
cleansed from sin through his blood. . . .

2. But under certain circumstances there are some
serious sins for which the cleansing of Christ does not
operate, and the law of God is that men must then have
their own blood shed to atone for their sins. Murder,
for instance, is one of these sins; hence we find the Lord
commanding capital punishment. Thus, also, if a person has so progressed in righteousness that his calling
and election has been made sure, if he has come to that
position where he knows "by revelation and the spirit of
prophecy, through the power of the Holy Priesthood"
that he is sealed up unto eternal life (D. & C. 131:19-5.),
then if he gains forgiveness for certain grievous sins, he
must "be destroyed in the flesh," and "delivered unto
the buffetings of Satan unto the day of redemption,
saith the Lord God." (D. & C. 132:19-27.)

President Joseph Fielding Smith has written: "Man
may commit certain grievous sins—according to his light
and knowledge—that will place him beyond the reach of
the atoning blood of Christ. If then he would be saved, he
must make sacrifice of his own life to atone—so far as in
his power lies—for that sin, for the blood of Christ alone

under certain circumstances will not avail. . . . Joseph
Smith taught that there were certain sins so grievous that
man may commit, that they will place the transgressors
beyond the power of the atonement of Christ. If these
offenses are committed, then the blood of Christ will not
cleanse them from their sins even though they repent.
Therefore their only hope is to have their own blood shed
to atone, as far as possible, in their behalf."

Next to the last sentence, his father had marked an asterisk.

He heard noise from the hallway, turned the book face down. It was his
mother. When she saw the books spread around him, she smiled.

"You're finding your faith at last," she said, moving forward to embrace
him. "You've returned to the fold."

It was all he and Lael spoke of the next time they met, Lael at first feign-
ing lack of interest then gradually coming around. He had not heard of
Hooper Young, he admitted, but he did know something of blood
sacrifice. He told Rudd about the Laffertys. Two brothers, a few years earlier, one a bishop or a former bishop, he couldn't remember which, who
sacrificed one of their wives and her child at a makeshift altar and slit her
throat so the blood would run out over the altar to baptize it, and the
words *blood sacrifice* were used, but there had been nothing as flagrant as
writing about it in advance. "Sunrise in Hell," was it?

"There are a lot of fucked up people in the world," said Lael, and then
leaned forward. "What else do you know about him?"

"Not much," he said.

"Isn't there more?"

"I didn't have time to check."

"And by the way," said Lael. "What happened to your hair?"

He reached up to feel his hair, his bangs still uneven though he had tried to
cut them straight. It surprised him that Lael had noticed his hair at all. Perhaps
Lael was paying more attention than he had realized. He was mulling this over
when Lael stood and climbed onto the scooter, and before Rudd knew it they
were on their way down from the canyon and back to the library, Lael taking
the curves and slopes quickly as Rudd slid on the seat, trying to hang on.

There was a lot to it, more than Rudd had first guessed. The *Times,* Lael
found through a guide the reference librarian recommended, had reported

copiously on the crime, on Hooper Young's identification and capture and then, almost five months later, the trial.

He sat cranking the records up one by one, reading the articles as Lael peered over his shoulder. Only months later was he able to think it into coherent form. At first glance it all washed over him without really sinking in, and he left the library with names and places churning through his mind. But eventually, though he never articulated it as clearly as he wanted, it all came together:

On September 19, 1902, a woman's body was found in a mud ditch between New York and Jersey City, nude and lying in slime. A leather strap was wound about her waist, knotted at the back, and affixed to a twenty-pound hitch weight, of a peculiar make. The woman's skull had been fractured in two places—once just above the right eye, again a few inches above the left temple. A smoothly cut gash, about six inches long, extended diagonally downward from her left side through her belly.

Autopsy reports indicated that it was this gash that killed her, despite there being no interior hemorrhage, nor any punctured or slit internal organs. "The incision was made either by a knife with blunt and ragged edge or by a knife in the hand of a nervous person." The blows to the head, because of the absence of cerebral hemorrhaging, were thought to "have been dealt by a man of no extraordinary strength, and might have been caused by a fist or a sand bag, but not by any blunt or hard weapon."

Though at high tide the ditch was full and the body thus covered, at low tide the ditch drained to about six inches of water. The murderer was apparently either unfamiliar with the area or was in such hurry to dispose of the body that he was imprudent. The body was seen at one in the afternoon by the motorman of a passing trolley car, who notified the inspector at a nearby drawbridge, who in turn notified the police.

According to that first report, it was "beyond a doubt that two men were concerned with the disposition of the body, if not in the murder itself." A bridgeman spoke of a closed cab passing at eleven p.m. on the night before the discovery of the body—a quite uncommon occurrence—driven by two "rather young and well-dressed men" who kept their heads averted when the bridgeman stopped them and held up his lantern. The cab's curtains were tightly drawn. The vehicle went through the bridge and along the road that paralleled the ditch in which the body was discovered, but no other bridgeman could recall it coming out.

The corpse was Mrs. Anna Pulitzer, wife of tailor Joseph Pulitzer. Her husband, reading of the body's discovery in the morning papers, called police and asked to see the body, which he immediately identified as his wife of five years. A civil-minded citizen, Pulitzer had worked as an election captain on the day the murder was thought to have occurred, arriving home shortly before eleven p.m. "His wife, who had not gone to bed at that hour, said she wanted to buy some fruit, and started out to buy some. She took off all her rings except her wedding ring, and left them at the house. Then she went out, and was never seen again by him alive." She was last seen in a bakery at 11:40 at night, where she bought some rolls. When Pulitzer identified the body, he was immediately locked up until his story was investigated and, to the degree it could be, corroborated.

By the next day, the paper announced, *Slayer of Mrs. Anna Pulitzer Is Known*. It identified him as "William Hooper Young, grandson of Mormon leader Brigham Young." Young was described as "extremely dark, with a sallow complexion, a slender figure, and bushy eyebrows that stand out conspicuously over small black eyes." He was between thirty and thirty-five years old, weighed 130 pounds. He had worked for newspapers on both coasts, was known as "a reckless character and a debauchee." He was described as "half-adventurer, half-newspaperman." He was the son of John W. Young, a financier. One of Young's coworkers on the *Weekly Crusader,* a fellow named Anzer, had heard Young speak of returning a borrowed horse and rig to a particular stable. Anzer, having read of the murder, felt the fact worth mentioning to police. Police approached the liveryman, who positively identified Young as the man who had taken the rig and returned it without either weight or leather strap. When they went to Young's father's apartments, where Young had been staying while his father was in Europe, "Evidences of a most repulsive murder were discovered":

> In the first bedroom of the apartment were bloody sheets, pools of blood in a closet, and a large knife. Capt. Schmittberger said he believed the murderers gave the woman knockout drops and lured her to the place, intending at first to cut up the body and get rid of the pieces. From the blood stains under the kitchen sink and in the bedroom closet it is inferred that the body might have been concealed in either one of those places.

Two days earlier, Young had left the house with a steamer trunk, which the bellboy had helped him load into the rented rig. The following day the trunk had been brought back to the house, then had been shipped, according to the bellboy, to Chicago.

Yet, despite declaring Young guilty, the *Times* in the same article pointed to other details that seemed to implicate another man, an unidentified gentleman described as "very stout" who called upon Mrs. Pulitzer the afternoon of her disappearance, rushing upstairs saying "She expects me." He was described as "a clean-shaven man, very heavy, dark, and rather Jewish or German in appearance," with a "heavy gold watch chain and a gold cigar cutter hanging to his vest."

On Sunday, September 21, Young's "arrest is expected hourly"—the police believed he had not yet been apprehended because he was being protected by Mormons, for according to the New York police captain:

> There was once in this city a secret society of Mormons. I believe it still exists. It was broken up once by the United States Secret Service Bureau, but it is going along on the quiet, I believe. Although the members of his former church say he is a recreant member and a villain, they will stick to him. He was once sanctified, so he must be protected.

The steamer trunk that Young had had shipped to Chicago arrived and was seized by the Chicago police, who sent a dispatch indicating that it "contained woman's dress, underclothes, hat, shoes, men's clothing, dirk knife, all smeared with blood . . ." and "nearly 100 letters addressed to William Hooper Young." The articles of feminine apparel were marked with the name or initial of Mrs. Anna Pulitzer.

In addition, the "trunk contained memorandum book containing name William Hooper Young. . . ." On the first page of another memorandum book found in Young's father's apartment itself were written the words "Blood Atonement," followed by half a dozen scriptural references that, when examined, seemed related to the Mormon doctrine of blood atonement.

The local Mormon authority denied the existence of blood atonement, declaring there to be "no such thing in the religion." He "denied absolutely that there was any doctrine of the Mormon Church which demanded the shedding of blood as an atonement of sin. He said that there was not one of the doctrines of the Church which would give even a man partially deranged the idea that in killing a woman his own sins would be forgiven."

"My father," said Rudd, "our father, I mean, wrote that it did exist."

"What did?"

"Aren't you here?" said Rudd, pointing to the subtitle, *Blood Atonement Denied.*

"Why would I be there?"

"That Hooper Young might have discussed the idea of blood atonement is possible. He had erroneous ideas on many subjects. This idea did not prompt his terrible crime," Rudd read.

Lael shrugged.

"No comment?" asked Rudd.

"What else could a Mormon, speaking on behalf of the Church, possibly say? Yes, we do kill people?"

Both the police and reporters had begun to speak with confidence that Young was the murderer. Despite the belief of both parties several days before that there had been two men involved in the disposal of the body and perhaps in the murder itself, Young was declared the sole and singular murderer.

The Captain of Police received a letter as well from "H. Young" stating that he intended to commit suicide:

Search in vain; have killed myself. H. Young.

The letter was written on a scrap of cheap white paper and "inclosed [sic] in a small envelope such as are used for visiting cards." The Captain believed it was a letter from "some crank" though he decided to have experts compare the handwriting to that of Hooper Young.

One of the most startling developments of yesterday was the discovery by Capt. Titus that a murder bearing much similarity to this one was committed in Salt Lake City, Utah, in 1893.

"A Frenchman was murdered there in that year," he said. "And this Young was living in Salt Lake City at the time. No one could find the Frenchman's body, nor could they trace the murderer. A long time afterward the body was found in a trunk that had been shipped to Chicago."

"I do not say that Young committed this murder out West, but it seems highly probable, that his mind was affected by it. Of course, the two cases differ, but still they are similar. A trunk was sent to Chicago in each case, and in both the trunks was evidence that the murderer was attempting to conceal."

•

47

"Why Chicago?" asked Rudd.

Lael read the paragraphs Rudd pointed to, shrugged. "Copycat," he said. "Unless he killed the Frenchman too."

"Do you think he did?"

"It's more interesting if he didn't," said Lael. "That he had in his head from the first killing the idea that all murdered bodies should be shipped to Chicago."

"You think he was crazy?"

"Crazy's not the right word," said Lael. "Possessed, maybe."

"You think that happens? Someone goes to see a movie about murderers and then they go out and kill people?"

Lael shrugged. "Sure," he said, "but the person has to want it to happen first. Some people are just aching for an excuse."

The "Chief Detective said that he had found letters in Young's flat that proved the man to be a moral pervert." In addition, "he had a very peculiar walk, as though something was the matter with his legs, and I think anybody who ever saw him could identify him by his gait among a million men." Other tenants in his father's building described him as "a dope and a vagabond. He had gone to the roof often and acted queerly. When anybody saw him there he would dodge behind chimneys." "He was a cigarette fiend." "He was a brilliant talker." ". . . haggard." "He was the most attractive fellow you ever saw. He was well educated, perfectly honest and seemingly well-balanced." "He was quiet and did not seem freakish in any way."

By Monday, September 22, a man disguised as a tramp but matching Hooper Young's description was picked up in Derby, Connecticut, after a scuffle. The man refused to give his name or account for his whereabouts. His face resembled Young's. Upon being apprehended, his clothing, though trampish in appearance, proved to be new. He was said to have "a look of refinement about him which does not become the clothes he wears." "The nervous condition of the man is such that it would appear that he is on the verge of collapse, and he is restless in a most exaggerated degree." It was thought by the arresting officers that Young had a gold tooth, which they looked for, but "instead was a hole in the gum where a tooth had been extracted quite recently." In the same article, Captain Titus insisted that in the police descriptions of Young "no mention of a gold tooth was made. Young has no gold teeth." His pockets were full of red pepper. A packet of red pepper, it was discovered, was found in the trunk sent to Chicago as well.

As more details surfaced about how Young spent his time after the murder, the motivation for the crime began to seem more complex to Captain Titus:

"All this is certain. After buying the clothes in which he was clad when he hired the rig in Hoboken, he must have spent some more money, including what he paid the liveryman. While he was pawning the jewelry and getting the buggy, the body of his victim was resting in his bedroom closet, covered with blood. By all who saw him during his preparations for the disposal of the body, it is stated that he was very calm and collected. A man who could stroll around without excitement while the woman he had killed lay in his apartment must have been a hardened and deliberate criminal."

THE CRIME DELIBERATE

Capt. Titus said he had come to the conclusion that not only the motive of robbery entered into the crime, but that the murder had been deliberate.

"I argue," said the Captain, "that, if robbery had been the only motive, Young might just as well have carried the woman into insensibility. When he carried her to his flat, he knew he would have to kill as well as rob. . . ."

Joseph Pulitzer insisted, though it had not been mentioned in earlier interviews, that just a few hours prior to her disappearance, his wife had been accosted by a man resembling Young who proposed that she visit his apartment. How Pulitzer knew this or why he wasn't troubled by it remained unclear.

More importantly, according to Mrs. Pulitzer's parents, the murdered woman had known Young for nine years. There were some hints made suggesting that she had followed Young north to Jersey City and then to New York.

The man disguised as the tramp at first denied he was Hooper Young, claiming instead to be Bert Edwards until the police brought him into contact with an athletic instructor who knew Young, Mac Levy:

"Hello, Hooper!"

There was no response. Young turned his eyes on
the speaker deliberately and looked hard at him with no
sign of recognition. If there was any effort in his
assumption of indifference it was not visible. There was
a long pause. Finally, as if he thought he was expected
to say something, he answered.

"I don't know you."

"Of course, you know me," said Levy, placing his
hand on his former friend's shoulder.

Young without a trace of emotion, responded:

"You should be sure of your identification. This is a
terrible crime for which I am held."

After this, at the command of the officers, the prisoner divested himself of his clothing, so that Levy
might make the identification more certain. . . . It was
then that the man admitted for the first time that he
was William Hooper Young.

When questioned about his guilt, Young answered cryptically, "Yes and
No," and "hinted at the existence of an accomplice in the murder," though
at this stage he would not identify an accomplice by name, nor would he
quite admit to having been involved in the crime. He failed to give any
account for his movements since leaving his flat after the murder, nor would
he give the police any information as to his whereabouts during the time
the body of the woman remained in his room.

Once Young was caught, the full and complete contents of the trunk
sent to Chicago could be revealed.

When they raised the lid the first thing that came in
sight was a sword-shaped stiletto, with a blade several
inches long and an ivory handle. The blade was covered
with bloodstains.

In a paper bag touching the knife were half a dozen
mixed cakes, the same which the murdered woman
had bought in the bakery at Seventh Avenue and
Forty-eighth Street ten minutes after she left her husband last Tuesday night, and a few minutes before she
was lured or consented to go to the place where death
awaited her. The next thing to come in sight was her
set of false teeth, one of which was missing, and under
them, covered with blood stains, were skirts and
underwear. A switch of false hair and a pair of gloves
were sandwiched in with the other articles. The sides

of the trunk were streaked with blood. In one corner was a big splotch.

Besides the things already mentioned there were found in the trunk the missing bedclothes from the Young apartment . . . three pairs of men's old shoes, Young's trousers and coat, vest, and undershirt . . . some red pepper, a hairpin, a bent safety pin . . . Some of the clothing was torn. There were also stains on the man's clothing and on a broken comb and pocketbook found at the very bottom of the trunk.

Young's father, in Paris, sent a cable urging Young to cooperate, promising to stand by him if he did so. He engaged a lawyer, William F. S. Hart, who expressed the opinion that if Young were guilty he "was certainly insane. He did not think him guilty, however. . . ."

A newspaper from Portland, where Young had once lived, suggested, "Young seemed to be a man who was easily influenced, and his friends say it was always possible for him to be led into anything, if inducements were offered. He was very studious and carried a Bible with him all the time. He was very fond of discussing religious topics and, when not at work, was to be found reading Biblical literature." The Seattle Chief of Police telegraphed New York, saying that Young was wanted on two charges of forgery.

Rudd's eyes had begun to hurt. He stood up, stretched his arms, headed for the door. Lael kept reading, paying no attention to where Rudd was going. Rudd left the reading room, walked down the hallway until he found a drinking fountain. He stood pressing the button, the water bubbling out, waiting for it to get cold.

When he got back, Lael had taken his chair. He had flipped forward to the next day, the next article. Rudd sat behind him, read over his shoulder, squinting sometimes to make out the words.

Young Says Another
Did Actual Murder

Protests He Tried to Revive Mrs.
Pulitzer After Crime

. . . "About three weeks ago I met a man named Charles Elling in Central Park. He accosted me. We talked and got acquainted, though he was a degenerate. After that he called on me several times in my flat. On the night Mrs. Pulitzer died Elling and I met her at Broadway and Forty-sixth Street by an appointment I had made. We went to the flat together. I went out for some whiskey after we got there, leaving Elling and the woman alone. When I got back I found Mrs. Pulitzer lying across the bed with a gag in her mouth. Elling had gone.

"I ripped open her clothing and moved her hands back and forth over her head to induce respiration. When she didn't breathe I put my hand under her waist and felt her heart. It was not beating. Then I decided to notify the police, but thought I would go to Police Headquarters instead of calling a policeman. I thought Police Headquarters was in the City Hall. I got on a train and started downtown, and on the way I got to thinking what a lot of disgrace the affair would bring on me and my father. That made me decide to get rid of the body.

"I took a long knife and cut into the body, intending to cut it up so that I could get it into a trunk, but after I had made the first cut my courage failed and I could go no farther. . . ."

Mrs. Pulitzer's murder has not lost all its mystery, as the police had expected it would as soon as Young was caught. The prisoner told them that he could not remember where he had been since he left New York. Nor did he explain the injuries to the head and face of the dead woman.

Captain Schmittberger was eager to point out the similarities between the murder of Anna Pulitzer and the 1900 murder of Kate Feeley in New York. Feeley disappeared after speaking to someone of Young's appearance. Her body was spread throughout the city, dismembered, though the head itself was never found. Schmittberger felt that Young's indication that he wanted to dismember the body linked the murders.

Young, sleeping in jail, took an "unflagging interest in newspaper reports of the murder." Police, searching for someone matching Elling's description, discovered nobody. They continued to claim that no such person existed. There was a man of similar description who had checked himself into Harlem Hospital, suffering from a dose of muriatic acid, under the name of Charles Garnett, hinting he was from Bridgeport, Connecticut, the town Young claimed Elling was from.

> "I want to die," Garnett suggested as he checked himself in.
>
> "What have you done?" asked a surgeon.
>
> "I know what I've done," he said, "and I want to die."
>
> He declined to say anything about himself. Later when told that he would die, he answered: "All right." Then he was asked if he came from Bridgeport.
>
> "If I tell you where I came from," he said, "you'll hang me."

Yet, police continued to claim that 1) Elling did not exist and that 2) Garnett was certainly not Elling even if he did exist.

It was discovered who Young had purchased his trunk from, though this raised certain complications. The trunk dealer insisted Young had no mustache when he purchased the trunk, though numerous people had seen him with a mustache on that day and on the day before and after. "He didn't have a mustache, but he looked like the pictures of Young." This led some to believe that Young had an accomplice after all.

In October of 1902, a coroner's jury declared that "from the evidence adduced we find she came to her death by violence at the hands of William Hooper Young." Seven days later a grand jury indicted Young for murder in the first degree. Mention of Young disappeared from the paper for more than three months, reappearing in February, as his trial approached and as several of the witnesses against him disappeared, the district attorney placing the blame for their disappearance on the Mormon Church. On February 4 was the article that Rudd had first seen. He read it through again, then watched Lael's eyes flick back and forth until he had finished as well. He cranked forward a day.

Young, unable to face the trial, had managed to have proceedings delayed a day, and sought to have them delayed further. Hart, his lawyer, begged for delay "on the grounds that his client was physically unable to stand the strain of the trial." The Court Coroner, recruited as a physician, examined Young and declared him too ill to leave his cell. Justice Herrick, after another examination by another doctor, ordered Young to attend.

> Young was literally dragged into court, between two Deputy Sheriffs. He appeared to be in a state of great physical weakness, and seemed to have aged at least twenty years since the time of his arrest last September. The deathly pallor of his features was in pronounced

contrast to the long, shaggy black beard which he had grown while in prison. Had it not been for his luminous brown eyes the face would have resembled a death mask more than anything else. He wore no collar, and his linen and other clothing were in a state of neglect. When he was taken to the chair at the table of his counsel, he collapsed and fell forward.

After a further examination by eight physicians, the Justice decided the trial would proceed. At first Young "sat in various attitudes of dejection and at times his head swayed weakly from side to side. But after the proceedings began in earnest, he seemed to brighten up and take interest in what was going on about him. . . . He scanned each talisman called with manifest care and regarded each juror sworn intensely."

By the following day, his appearance seemed further improved. "His hair was combed, his beard had been trimmed, and he wore a collar. But he still shows signs of great weakness," and "Once in the afternoon session he wept."

Yet the reason he looked good was only because he had been dressed by the combined efforts of three prison guards. Indeed, when they first arrived he had not been dressed at all; "they found him crawling about his cell on all fours," searching for a rabbit's foot.

By the following day he had assumed "an attitude of dull dejection . . . his head resting on the table before him and his face buried in his hands."

On February 10, only six days after his trial had begun, it was over.

YOUNG ADMITS HIS GUILT

Confesses Murder in the Second Degree and Gets Life Sentence

Justice Herrick Advised his Counsel to Enter That Plea—Man Medically, But Not Legally, Insane

William Hooper Young, who has been on trial before Justice Herrick in the Criminal Branch of the Supreme Court for the murder of Mrs. Anna Pulitzer, yesterday pleaded guilty to murder in the second degree. [. . .]

Young looked like a changed man when he entered court yesterday morning. For the first time he walked by himself up to the table of his counsel, where he pulled his chair into position and sat down. His eye was clear, he bore his head erect, and he looked like a man from whose mind a great burden had been rolled. All in the court room wondered over his altered appearance. [. . .]

After the whispered conference, Clerk Penny of the court called the defendant to the bar. There was a brief silence when he entered the room and then Justice Herrick ordered the prisoner to stand up.

"Young," said Justice Herrick, "I understand that you want to recall your plea of not guilty and enter a plea of guilty of murder in the second degree?"

Young stood up, clutching the railing in front of him with both hands. He seemed calm and unperturbed. Prompted by Mr. Hart, he said something which the Justice construed into an assent.

"Do you desire to be sentenced now?" asked the Justice.

"There is no occasion to comment on the heinousness of the crime you have committed," said Justice Herrick then.

"You are aware of the penalty for your crime. The sentence of the Court is that you be taken and confined to State prison at hard labor for the term of your natural life."

Young sank back in his chair. There was an expression of relief on his face. He soon was taken away, and as soon as the doors leading to the prison pen had closed on him, Justice Herrick made his explanation to the jury.

"It is only right," said Justice Herrick, "to tell you gentlemen that the court advised the defendant's counsel to tender this plea, and that the court also advised the District Attorney to accept it. The man's mental condition was the cause for the action taken. You are aware that this man has been under medical observation. The experts reported this man legally sane, but insane from a medical point of view. He therefore is supposed to know the difference between right and wrong and should be held responsible. But as his insanity has been reported to me as being of the progressive order, it is difficult to tell where one line merges into the other."

7

Elling, Hooper Young had named his accomplice. Lael believed Elling existed, so he now claimed, but Rudd still did not: Elling was a figment or an excuse—there was only Hooper Young.

"If he existed, they would have found him," said Rudd.

"They found Young only by luck. Besides, if you have one man in custody, certainly involved, why admit to the press a second man, not in custody, is also involved? It just complicates matters."

"Hooper Young was avoiding responsibility for—"

"—he was trying to share responsibility with the other person involved. People never act alone. They always drag others along with them."

"You have no evidence—"

"—neither do you."

"I've got the district attorney."

"I've got Hooper Young."

"He's biased."

"So's the attorney. And both of them are not only biased: they're dead."

They had hardly argued before, Rudd always giving in, but now for some reason he found himself unwilling to back down. Thinking it over later, he couldn't understand why it mattered to him to insist that Young had acted alone. Even when, ten days after reading the articles, Lael claimed to have found among the microfiche of genealogical records at the church library one Charles Elling, of Connecticut, born 1840, excommunicated 1898, no death date recorded, he continued to argue.

"That would make Elling sixty-three at the time of the murder," Rudd said.

"It's still possible."

But Rudd would not admit it. He could not imagine Hooper Young being accosted in the park by a sixty-three-year-old deviant, then somehow, despite the difference in age and (at least putatively) in sexual orientation, making friends with the man. He could not see a rheumy-eyed sixty-three-year-old, his hand gnarled and liver-spotted, bashing Anna Pulitzer's skull hard enough to kill her.

"Sixty-three isn't so old," said Lael. "And the paper said the blows were weak."

"It's old."

"Depends on the man," said Lael. "At least admit it's possible."

But Rudd would not admit, and the more he refused to admit, the more interested Lael seemed to be in forcing an admission from him. Lael got closer and closer to Rudd, looking into his eyes steadily until Rudd broke the gaze.

"You'll admit," said Lael. "Sooner or later. You always do."

He started writing his research paper, despite Lael's warnings not to do so. According to Lael it was a mistake: Mrs. Madison would read Rudd into it.

"What do I have to fear?" asked Rudd. "She can read me into it all she wants: I'm not there."

She would treat him differently, Lael said, would ask him how things were at home, would look at him strangely. Eventually, he himself would become different as a result.

"You don't even know her," said Rudd.

Lael shook his head. He knew enough, he said. He knew how people were.

Rudd shook him off, wrote his pre-paper summary. He wanted to prove to Mrs. Madison that his glass was half-full. It was simple, a research paper, all he had to do was develop a topic, formulate a few questions, let words accrue. He did not have to present conclusions, just summarize and, to a limited degree, interpret. It was just to prove he could do research.

It took him a few hours to pull the summary together. As he did so, he felt he was somehow missing everything that had seemed so clear in his head when he had been reading the articles.

"The Murderous Existence of William Hooper Young"
by Rudd Theurer
For my decade I chose the 1900s and the year 1903 but

some of this happened in 1902 too. The most important part in fact (the murder). My heritage is Mormon (LDS) so I decided to research something LDS (Mormon). For a place I chose New York because that is a city with a lot of mystique to it. I did not choose a hero because I do not have a hero. I leave that kind of thing to others. I do not want you to think William Hooper Young is my hero because he is not.

In 1902 William Hooper Young was involved in killing a woman named Anna Pulitzer and dumping her body into a drainage canal. The body was "nude and lying in slime." I said "involved in killing" on purpose: certain people think that he might have had some help from someone named Charles Elling. I do not believe Charles Elling existed. Neither did the New York Police (the murder happened in New York even though the body was found in New Jersey). The whole story is described in the *New York Times* in 1902 and 1903. That is my source. (Mrs. Madison: If you would like dates and page numbers for this summary let me know. Otherwise I will save them for the paper.)

With the body was a hitching weight, something used on wagons with horses. It had a "curious" mark on it. The body had a bashed-in skull and a gash near the waist. The strap for the hitching weight was wrapped around the waist. The police started asking around at the rent-a-horse places to see if somebody had brought a horse back without a "peculiar" hitching weight. That was how they figured out who did it. The person who did it was William Hooper Young. He liked to go by Hooper Young. They searched his apartment and found bloody sheets and pools of blood in a closet. Young sent Anna Pulitzer's clothing to Chicago along with a bloody knife and some other stuff, some bloody, some not.

Hooper Young knew the police were looking for him so he hid up in Connecticut as a tramp. He got drunk and filled his pockets with red pepper, which he was planning to throw into the police's eyes if they ever came after him. He never did get a chance to throw that pepper. When the police caught him he pretended he was not Hooper Young. Even after people who knew him said he was, he still said he wasn't but then finally admitted he was.

In court, he kept breaking down. They said he was insane but not legally insane. Everybody was confused. He agreed to plead guilty to avoid the death penalty. Nobody knows what happened to him after he was put in prison.

Rudd read it over, made a few corrections.

"What are you writing?" his mother wanted to know.

"Nothing," he said. "It wouldn't interest you."

"Come on, darling," she said. "It wouldn't hurt you to share your life with me."

He stood and in a state of agitation began walking all about the room, the two loose pages pressed against his chest, words facing in. His mother stayed in the doorway, leaning slightly against the frame.

"It's a paper," he said, "for school. Satisfied?"

"That wasn't so bad now, was it?" she said. "Can I see it?"

"You mean, *may* you see it?" he said, and rushed past her and out.

He meant to recopy it but ran out of time and ended up turning in the rumpled handwritten sheets, smoothing them out by drawing them taut along the desk edge, as if they were the strop for a razor. When he finished they curled slightly. Mrs. Madison smiled when she took them.

Yet the next day as class was beginning, she asked if he would speak with her afterwards. There was a matter they needed to discuss.

"But I have wood shop," he said. "Rotkin. Can't be late."

"It won't take long," she suggested.

He sat through class, hardly listening. She was speaking about the next stage of the research paper, he vaguely gathered. Now that you had a summary you had to think about how to make an argument. What is an argument? she asked. An *argument* is where you *argue* for or against something. *Circular logic,* he thought, but even as he thought it she had begun to rephrase: An argument is where you are for or against something.

What am I for or against? Rudd asked himself. *What do I feel strongly about?* Nothing really, or not much. He felt strongly about his mother, but it is one thing to feel strongly about something and another thing to know *what* you actually feel. To say that feelings are strong says little about what the feelings are. He could not say that he hated his mother or that he loved her, the feelings were far too jumbled for him to be able to sort them out so easily. *This must be true,* he tried to convince himself, *with anything you care about.*

When the bell rang, he gathered his backpack and started to leave, and then remembered and waited fidgety near the door, ill at ease, not quite sure how to stand. He tried putting his backpack over one shoulder, then held it hanging from one hand near his waist. Mrs. Madison was talking to Jenny Kindt but seemed to be trying to break away from her.

I will give her until the count of ten, he told himself, *and then I will leave.*

But when he had finished counting he instead shifted his weight to the other leg, let his loose hand toy with the hem of his shirt. By twenty, Mrs. Madison had stopped talking, was moving things about on her desk, cheeks slightly flushed.

What would it be like, he wondered, *to be Hooper Young and look at a woman and know you intended to kill her?*

He looked immediately away from his teacher, searching for other objects to occupy his attention. A desk, the straps of the backpack biting into his hand, the weave of the puke-colored carpet, *What am I for or against?*

Unless Young didn't know, he thought. *Unless he didn't know he would kill her until she was already dead.*

He shook his head, dizzy. If you didn't know for certain what you might do in advance, you were capable of anything. There was nothing solid to you. He asked himself what he was for or against again and considered some tentative answers, but they were all so general and vague that they rang hollow. Hooper Young had not been for or against anything: he had been "easily influenced." *There was nothing to Hooper Young and nothing to me,* he thought, and knew that Lael's belief in an actual Elling was safer, less dizzying. But Rudd couldn't convince himself that Elling existed, not really, unless Elling was a part of Hooper Young. Which was at least as bad, for who was to say who else was hidden in the folds of your brain, waiting to worm their way out? Better at least to think there was volition, that Young had known beforehand, maybe even that he had killed her to prove something to himself. Better still: believe he had plotted and planned the killing for years.

But he could not believe it.

"I'm worried about you, Rudd," Mrs. Madison claimed. "Concerned."

He looked at her with dull eyes, stared at her prim mouth.

"This summary," she said. "You've not exactly chosen a savory topic."

Savory? he thought. "No," he said. "But I did get three of my four areas."

"Don't you have a hero, Rudd?" she asked, and he flicked his eyes up long enough to see her eyebrows crease with slight pity. It hurt him. "No one? Boys who don't have heroes end up in trouble."

"No," he said.

"Everybody needs a hero," she said.

"I'm sorry," he said.

"This," she said, and he realized she was waving his summary in his hand. "This, this Young fellow. What interests you about him?"

"I don't know," he said.

"I worry that he's becoming a hero of sorts for you."

"Look," he said. "It's just an assignment. I didn't even want to do it. I said in there he *wasn't* my hero. I didn't choose my topic, my topic chose me."

"Don't," she said. "Please. No need to get upset."

"I'm not upset," he said. "Or yes, I am, but it's just . . . I'm going to be late for Rotkin's class."

"Under the circumstances," she said. "You being from a troubled home and all—"

—*A troubled home?* he wondered. What did she mean, *a troubled home?* He and his mother were both smack dab in *the common sector,* no different from anyone else—

"—I think it would be better for you to choose another topic. One with a hero."

He shook his head.

"At least think it over," she said. "I'm not going to *force* you to change. I just want what's best for you. Just think it over."

"I'll think about it," he said.

She reached out and touched his shoulder. It made him flinch. He found himself out in the near-deserted hall, halfway to Rotkin's shop, before he realized he had forgotten to ask her for a late note.

He would give it up. He knew he would choose another topic, even before he made it to Rotkin's door and went in to be confronted with the greasy-haired, ovoid teacher standing in a blue smock and wearing horn-rimmed safety goggles, greeting Rudd with his perennial "About time you showed up, Mr. Tardy." He would choose something that was thoroughly grounded in the *common sector,* something that wouldn't allow him to be singled out, at least not in that way. He hated to be defined as worthy of pity. He wanted to be above the crowd, not below it, or if being above were not possible, just part of it, nameless and mixed in. By the next day he had a new summary, a benign topic, Reed Smoot, an early Mormon u.s. Senator, and it was all Mrs. Madison could do not to embrace him.

"I knew you could do it, Rudd," she said. "I just knew you could!"

When he told Lael about it the next Saturday, he just smirked.

"What did you think would happen?" Lael asked. "People don't want to face things."

"What things?"

"Things," said Lael. "It doesn't matter what."

"What's that supposed to mean?"

"Teaching's not about truth. It's about comfort."

"You don't even know her. How can you say that?" He was talking too loud, he knew.

"I was right about her before. I'm right now."

"Leave her alone," said Rudd.

"You're the same way," said Lael. "The truth's all around you yet you want no part of it. Why?"

Rudd got up from the grass and started pacing. "What the Hell do you know?" he said. "Motherfuck." The word came out singsongy and ridiculous, hardly a curse.

"Motherfuck yourself," said Lael calmly. "You want stability. You want to fit in. You don't want to see yourself as you really are."

"What's truth anyway?"

"Don't be clever."

"But—"

"Cut it out," said Lael. "Listen for once."

Rudd closed his mouth, opened it again. He walked over and stood by the scooter. He stared at it, one hand in his jacket pocket, then thumped the seat loudly with his other half-closed fist.

Maybe Lael was right, he told himself, then told himself no, not right at all. It was like that on the silent ride back home, then that evening, then as he lay in bed. He hated Lael and then a minute later loved him, no transition between the two emotions. A strange two-fold vibration between extremes, a leap between one extreme and another, no middle ground between.

It had been a stupid thing to argue about, he knew that, but he was angry. He resented Lael. His brother did not care about him, he told himself, that was something he had not wanted to face, but he would face it now. And how did he know Lael was his brother anyway? Nothing was certain. He had never spoken directly about it to Lael's mother, except for the first time he called. Then, while stuttering and confused he had tried to piece together the story, she had interrupted brightly and almost airily: "You're a boy, right? You must want to speak to my son," and then hung up. That was all she had said, and it was clear from the little he had seen of her since that she wasn't exactly sane. She had never said, "Your father is Lael's father." True, Lael hadn't denied it after listening to Rudd's story. But Lael was the type to go along with things just to see where they would lead.

Yet if Lael wasn't his brother, who did he have?

No one, he told himself, and then, *My mother.*

That was not much. He stood and went to the window, pushed the curtains apart with his hand. There was no moon. The streetlight had nearly gone out. It gave off only a pale orange glow that lit the top of its pole and little more. He could see through the streaked pane the Milky Way above, unless it was just streaks, and pale clumps of stars. Closing the curtains, he returned to bed.

What had Hooper Young wanted? he asked himself. *Certainly not the truth.*

I don't need anyone, he told himself. *Truth is overrated.* He lay in the dark, fingers softly rubbing the wool blanket. He could feel himself starting to fall asleep, his legs and face numbing until it seemed as if the sole thing that existed, suspended in a void, were his fingertips, and, around each, a few square inches of wool, his soul crowded into what little was left of him, then that fading too until it was gone.

He thought of nothing but Lael through the whole course of the week, but when Saturday arrived, he couldn't bring himself to call. He uncradled the telephone and held it in his hand, rubbed the earpiece against his scraggly chin, then replaced it.

He spent Saturday lolling around the house. He lay in bed until late, past noon, and when his mother called him lazybones—it indicated a good mood, for her—he said nothing and still didn't get up. He didn't wash and when he ran his hand through his hair felt the skin between his fingers go greasy.

He decided to look through his father's old books. He thumbed through them without reading them. In the rafters of the attic, there was a stack of gnawed newspapers bound in twine. He took them down, bringing down a slow sift of torn scraps and dust with them. Untying them, he discovered five tiny, eyeless, pink baby mice in a chewed-out space in the middle, their only movement a near-convulsive shuddering. He dropped them one by one through the dormer window, watched each roll down the black shingles into the gutter.

He spent the better part of the afternoon looking at his hands, nails flecked with white streaks, knuckles large probably from his having cracked them ever since he was a child. His mother caught him staring, asked if everything was O.K.

"Fine," he said.

"At church tomorrow—" she started.

"—I'm not going to church tomorrow," he said.

He could not look at her while he said it. He heard her wheeze. "Excuse me?" she said, her voice severe. His heart was beating terrifically, though he told himself that there was no reason to worry, that he was long past caring about what she thought, though he knew he did care, fuck all.

"Excuse me?" she said.

"You heard me," he said.

"I swear, your father would roll over in his grave."

"Let him roll."

For the rest of the day that phrase was stuck in his head, *Let him roll,* sliding around with a kind of mute doom that was hard to evade. His mother had stomped out. When, near evening, she came back, he made no attempt to reconcile with her. *Let him roll,* he thought from the doorway, watching her core and slice a head of lettuce at the sink, the dull knife bruising the edges of each leaf. She turned and looked at him and he fled.

She did not call him to dinner, and he told himself he wouldn't come if she did call. Before she went to bed, he heard her walking around the house turning off the lights. He thought she might stop outside his door, but she didn't. *I don't need anyone,* he thought, and snuck into the kitchen to find his plate cellophaned in the fridge. He ate it, he tried to believe, not for himself but for her benefit, to keep her from worrying. It was an act of kindness to her, though he had enough spite left to eat the food cold.

He spent the night wandering the darkened house, dragging his hand along the walls, imagining that he was establishing a tactile knowledge of the house that would come in handy if he went blind. Then she would be sorry. He awoke on the floor of the half-attic, dust drifting in the sunlight coming through the window. He couldn't remember falling asleep there. He went into the bathroom and splashed his face with water, then called for his mother. She didn't answer.

The car was gone, his mother already at church. She had left his black leatherbound scriptures on the kitchen table. Next to them was a crudely drawn map to the church, with just two squares indicated, one marked "House," the other marked "Church." An arrow pointed from the first to the second. "In case you forgot the way," was written on the bottom. On the table she had also spelled out the word HELL in white grains that he took for salt but which, tasting, he found to be sugar.

He took a paring knife from the counter, scraped the sugar into a pile, and began, carefully, to shape it into a series of concentric circles. As he worked, he imagined himself putting on his tie and button-down oxford and going to church, walking through the crowded pews and straight to the pulpit and from there publicly washing his hands of his religion for good. His mother would be in the audience, shocked, her mouth open. He would renounce Mormonism and then, baring his chest, would invite the devil to take his soul. Not that he believed in the devil, or God either, he told himself.

When he was done shaping the sugar, he had a target. He thrust the knife's tip down hard in the center, so it stuck.

On Monday it was as if nothing had happened. She woke him happily, served him breakfast, chattered at him as he ate. She fussed and preened as he was about to leave for school and he hoped for a moment she would say something conciliatory, but knew she wouldn't. If he brought it up she would say, *What fight?* And, if he insisted, *I don't recall a fight, dear, you must have been fighting with yourself.*

He went through the week. At school somebody pried his locker open. He returned from English to find his books scattered down the hall, his notebooks reduced to rumpled scraps of paper. Humiliated, he picked up what was salvageable, other passing students kicking his books farther away.

The next day he feigned illness until noon, staying home until his mother's attempts to baby him became too derisive. When he arrived at school his locker was fine, untouched. By the end of the week it hadn't been broken into again, and he began to suspect that he had left it ajar himself.

It wasn't until the next Saturday that he thought of Lael, and then only to marvel that he didn't miss seeing him. He didn't call, instead spent the rest of the weekend moving pieces about on a chessboard, reading, and watching TV.

The Hooper Young murder stuck with him. Even though he was no longer writing his paper on it, it continued to rustle about in his head. At night, he found aspects of the case wound into his dreams. He dreamed that he had a gold tooth that, if he were to escape the police, had to be removed. He tried knocking it out with a hammer. He awoke slightly nauseous, sticky and damp, his heart beating rapidly.

Saturday night he dreamed that it was 1903 and he himself was heading the investigation of the Young case and that they had somehow cornered Young's accomplice, Charles Elling, in an alley that resembled something from a Universal Studios back lot. Elling had turned and had covered his face with his hands and did not move when Rudd reached out to touch him. Indeed, Rudd had to put his hands on Elling's shoulder and physically force him to turn. He pried Elling's hands away from his face, which when uncovered proved not to be Elling's face at all, but a smooth, blank surface.

Suddenly he was awake, with no memory of having screamed, but someone was shaking him and asking him if he was all right, and he realized it was his mother.

"I'm fine," he said. He started to reach for the lamp to turn it on, but his hand was shaking so badly that he thought better of it.

"You're sure?" she said. "Who's Ellen?"

"There's no Ellen," he said. "Just a bad dream."

"If you're dating someone named Ellen, I demand to be introduced."

He moved to the far side of the bed, turning his face to the wall. His mother sat down, the springs of the bed squealing. Her hand brushed his ear, fell to his shoulder, slowly settling. She began to rub his back, rocking her body slightly forward as she did. He wriggled uncomfortably.

"Don't you like that?"

"I'm not five years old," he said.

"You'll always be my baby," she said.

"God, no."

She stopped rubbing, drew her hand away. He felt her weight leave the bed, her slippers brushing across the carpet. When she spoke again, it was from the doorway, her voice rampant with bitterness. "It's because you stopped going to church," she said shrilly. "God is punishing you." And then she was gone.

Early Sunday she was in his room, shaking his wadded shirt and tie in his face, telling him to get dressed and visit God, that it was for his own good, the only way to be free of bad dreams. He didn't say anything, just put the pillow over his head. She kept talking, her voice getting higher and higher until all she was saying was "Answer me! Answer me!" over and over, then she slammed the door. *I hate my life,* he thought, though he knew it wasn't as simple as that. And before he knew it, despite his anxiety, he drifted off to sleep.

He was awakened by the doorbell. He lay in bed, considering who it could be. Jehovah's Witnesses probably, but did they come on Sundays? He was already on his way back to sleep when it rang again. Maybe it was a friend of his mother's. It was certainly nobody he knew. He pulled the covers over his head.

It rang a third time. A moment later he heard the knob rattle. Maybe a thief, he thought, someone who knew his mother was at church and thought he would be too.

He sat up in bed and peeked out through the window. If he leaned just right, he could see the front porch. Nobody was there. He stood and pulled his shirt off the chair, found a pair of pants among the twist and curl of clothing on the floor. He was pulling them on when he heard the back door open.

Cursing softly he opened the closet as quietly as he could, looking for a weapon. All he could find was a wooden shoe tree, which he took and held in one hand like a prototype blackjack. He made his careful way out of the room and down the stairs. The back door was open slightly. He closed it, locked it.

"Mother?" he called, then regretted having said anything.

Going into the kitchen, he slid a long, thin boning knife out of the block, leaving the shoe tree on the counter. He went into the living room. Empty. He stood at the edge of the den.

"Anybody there?" he asked.

No answer. Probably, he thought, they had come in and gone back out again. Or maybe they had not come in at all, but only opened the door and then gone off, leaving the door ajar. He opened the door to the garage, flicked the light on and off. He searched the laundry room, the downstairs bathroom, then went up the stairs and into his mother's room, her bathroom, and out again. Last of all his own bedroom, his closet. Nobody, no one at all.

He had finished his report, now on politics and Mormonism. Mrs. Madison was pleased, told him he was making real progress. Yet he couldn't put

Hooper Young out of his head, and finally went back to the university library to sort through other newspapers, to see if there was more about the case, if it had ever been mentioned in the Utah papers.

He had affixed the reel of the Church-owned *Deseret News* to the machine when he realized someone was standing behind him. Turning, he saw Lael.

He did not know exactly what he felt. Guilt was involved, and anger at feeling guilt, as well as resentment. But mixed in with it was a weird burst of ecstasy, and immediate awareness of the power Lael still seemed to have over him.

"You stopped seeing me," said Lael.

"I can't explain," said Rudd.

"Try."

"It was all too much for me."

"What?"

"It," said Rudd. "Everything."

"Me, you mean."

Rudd shrugged. "I mean you didn't even . . ." he said, then stopped. "What are you doing here?"

"What do you think?" Lael said, and held up a microfilm spool. "Same as you. But don't try to change the subject."

"I wasn't," said Rudd, and then found he could not, somehow, meet Lael's eyes.

"So tell me," said Lael. "Go ahead. Tell me what's wrong with me."

"Nothing's wrong with you," said Rudd. "It's just—"

"Do you want to know what your problem is?"

"Not really," said Rudd.

"No? If you can't take advice from your brother, then who?"

"Half-brother," said Rudd. "And I'm not entirely sure you're that."

"Of course I am," said Lael. "You contacted *me*, remember? You'd figured it all out before we ever spoke."

"I was wrong, and you were a liar."

Then they were both pushing at each other, buttons popping off Lael's shirt. The heel of Lael's hand flashed past Rudd's head, clipped his ear, distracting him while the other hand struck him in the temple. Rudd fell, still grasping Lael's shirt.

"So we're brothers only when it's convenient?" asked Lael, crouching over him and trying to pry Rudd's hands loose.

"No, I—"

"Let go," said Lael. He slapped the back of Rudd's hand hard. "Let go!" he said, louder.

Rudd let go and scrambled up, stood breathing hard. He waited until Lael was playing with the buttonholes and the remaining buttons on his shirt, then punched him in the face.

Lael stumbled, woozy, steadying himself against the wall with one hand. He shook his head, his nose flicking blood across his cheekbones and onto the wall. Rudd watched him, his fists clumsily up. Lael looked at him and smiled slowly. Spreading his arms, he stepped forward and toward Rudd to embrace him. And this, to Rudd, was somehow more terrifying than if he had leaped forward swinging.

A few evenings later Lael called him at home for the first time. It was a school night, late in the evening, nearly dark. He begged Rudd to drive down. "Let bygones be bygones," he suggested. "This is important. Bring a light."

When he arrived, Lael was already waiting, sitting on the front porch, a shovel slung along his shoulder blades, a hand flopped over either end.

"What is it?" asked Rudd. "What are we doing?"

"Did you bring the light?" Lael asked. Rudd showed him the flashlight. Giving Rudd the shovel, Lael climbed on in front of him.

They drove, slowly, out of Springville. This time, instead of turning up the canyon, Lael kept north, toward Provo.

"Where are we going?" shouted Rudd over the hum and whine.

Lael shrugged.

"What are we going to do?"

"If you're asking if it's legal, it's not."

"That's not what I'm asking."

Lael half-turned, kept driving until they came to the fork that led to Ninth East. As they passed Beesley Stone and Monument, Lael slowed, parked the scooter in front of it.

"Why here?" asked Rudd.

Lael took the shovel from him. "We can hardly park in the cemetery, can we?"

They walked across the street and in through the main gates of the cemetery, following the circular road for about two hundred feet and then cutting away from it, stepping across the damp grass and graves, Lael leading. They passed a crypt and Lael asked Rudd for the flashlight. He turned it on, began to examine each headstone in turn.

Then there it was, a square and solid pillar of white marble, encrusted with dirt.

Gyle Theurer, beloved husband and father. No dates, simple.

"Now what?" asked Rudd.

Lael slung down the shovel, chunked it into the dirt. "What else?"

Rudd watched the shovel bite out the first chunk of earth. "No," he said. "Not such a good idea."

Lael sighed. He leaned forward, resting his weight on the shovel. "I wouldn't do this if it weren't absolutely necessary," he said.

"It's wrong," said Rudd.

"That doesn't make it less necessary."

"But—"

"Don't you want to know if we're brothers?"

Rudd swallowed, shook his head.

"Sure you do," said Lael. "You said so yourself. Come on, tell the truth." He brought his foot down on the shovel head, cut into the grave again. "This is the only way you'll ever know."

The shovel gnawed up hunks of grass and roots then began slicing through the loam below. Lael kept digging, speaking to Rudd in a low voice. Though Rudd did not answer back, he didn't leave, and eventually when Lael, winded, held out the shovel to him, he took it and held it and looked at the blade as if into a human face. Then he himself began to dig. After that they took turns digging or holding the flashlight, stopping and hiding behind the crypt when a carful of whooping teens pulled onto the cemetery drive and spun around the circle before pulling out again. Cheap thrill, Lael suggested, smirking. Across the street a drunk stopped and sat on Rudd's scooter, turning the wheel back and forth before getting off again.

"I don't feel good about this," said Rudd.

"I'm not asking you to feel good about it," said Lael. "I'm just asking you to do it."

Sometime well into the night they struck the casket lid. Standing on it, they managed to clear enough dirt to free it but they could not figure a way to heft the casket up and out of the grave.

Standing on the lid, Lael broke the latch open with the shovel blade. He climbed out, slid the shovel down until the blade's edge rested on the worn rubber between the lid and the box.

"We'll only have a few seconds to look," said Lael. "Shine the light directly into his face."

Rudd nodded, shaking slightly. He steadied the flashlight against the edge of the pit, played it over the reflectant surface.

"Ready?"

Rudd shook his head no.

Lael leaned the shaft of the shovel against the pit's edge, then stepped up and onto the end of the handle. The coffin lid cracked quickly up and open and Rudd shined his light onto his father's cut throat and into his face that, as he watched, collapsed, became inhuman. It was a terrible thing to see and he dropped the flashlight. It rattled down the pit and into the coffin to lie, shining, between the remnants of his father's legs. Lael's feet slipped off the shovel and the lid swung closed.

"There," said Lael. "Did you see?"

"See what?"

"His face," said Lael, triumphantly. "I'm in it. You're in it and so am I. Did you see us mixed in his face?"

Rudd tried to picture his father's face as it had been, for an instant, whole, before privately collapsing, but kept seeing only the collapse, the flashlight clattering down. There had not been in that any hint of either himself or his brother.

"Yes," Rudd lied. "I saw."

Lael moved forward, a blotted, shambling shape in the dark. "That's proof," he said. "We're brothers. Time to celebrate."

8

He did not remember how he got home after the grave digging; he remembered nothing other than Lael's darkened body coming toward him. He awoke in his bed, his hands sore, dirt under his fingernails. It worried him.

Later still, he could not remember how he had reached a point where he had begun to see some value—strictly theoretical, of course—in blood sacrifice. He was not sure whether he had convinced himself or whether Lael had convinced him. There was no sorting it out afterwards, though he knew this too tied back to the desecration of his father's grave. He supposed that once that taboo had collapsed between him and his half-brother, nothing else seemed insurmountable. It was as if they were capable of anything. He understood for the first time how Lael must have felt driving the scooter, knowing it would run out of gas but rejoicing precisely in that. It was perhaps Lael's voice, dim and quiet as they sat on a large iron-rich slab up the canyon, speaking slowly of the Lafferty brothers who had sacrificed one of their wives and her child, of Ervil LeBaron, who at God's command had two dozen people (including his own daughter) killed, of a man in Salt Lake City who had slit his child's throat and then hung the child from the laundry line by its feet to let the blood drain out.

"Morbid," said Rudd.

"Sure," said Lael. "But that doesn't make the act any less powerful. You do something like that and it takes you completely outside the world."

"Seems to me digging up a coffin does the same."

Lael shrugged. "It's not a bad start."

Rudd did not respond, but kept listening as Lael kept talking. There were people, Lael claimed, who had sinned so greatly it was a mercy to kill them. Killing them did them a favor.

"I'm just explaining the logic," said Lael, stretching indifferently.

Were there sins for which you could not be forgiven? Rudd wondered, late at night, alone. His thinking had become confused when he had met Lael, and he was not certain how to straighten it out again.

"Before the age of eight, what are you?" asked Lael.

"What?"

"Mormons don't get baptized until eight," said Lael. He stood up and brushed his pants off, then straddled the scooter. "Before eight you're not accountable for your actions. You can't sin. Why else would they wait to baptize you?"

"So?" said Rudd, taking his place behind him.

"So, it's better to die before you're eight. The biggest favor you can do for people is to kill them young."

"You're saying we should slaughter everybody under eight?"

"Theoretically speaking," Lael said. "Only in theory."

There were dreams in which Lael consumed him, chewing off pieces of his limbs. Rudd felt simultaneously disturbed and gratified. He day-dreamed of the Prophet bringing about the Millennium and the return of Christ Jesus by ordering all children under the age of eight slaughtered. It seemed sound in the abstract, as long as he could constantly envision a line of children streaming to heaven, but it started to break down when he started picturing the ax chunking through the back of each child's skull.

"No," said Lael, when Rudd mentioned the ax. "Knives. Slit throats, like a sacrifice." But that didn't seem to help much.

The traditional method, Rudd learned from one of his father's books, an old spiralbound typescript called *The Confessions of John D. Lee,* was to dig the grave and then slit the throat and hold the man up a moment so that, dying, he fell forward and into the grave already dampened by his own blood. This was described as baptizing the grave.

He became distracted. His grades slipped. Mrs. Madison had him stay after class, scolded him sternly about responsibility. Mr. Burnside told him that if things did not quickly improve, his mother would be receiving a telephone call. He found himself standing in the principal's office with no memory of how he had gotten there or what he was there for. Ever since the grave digging, there were gaps like that, odd moments when his body seemed to run on its own and he couldn't remember where he had been or what he had done. It all went back to the night in the graveyard, something that had happened or that he had done. He wanted to ask Lael about it but couldn't admit to another person, not even Lael, what was happening.

There were times, during the evening, when he became conscious and saw his mother regarding him strangely, her penciled eyebrows arched, waiting as if expecting something from him or waiting for the answer to a question. Strange minute drawings of disembodied human hands began to appear in the margins of his schoolbooks, and a series of lines that he recognized as the sacred marks on Mormon undergarments: a v and a right angle next to each other, a straight horizontal line centered beneath them, then below and slightly to the right another straight horizontal line. He did not know what they meant—their significance was never discussed with those too young to go to the temple. In his pockets and in the folds of his clothing were scraps of paper with words scribbled on them in a script that he couldn't read. In his drawer there appeared a burnished rudimentary brass pipe hardly longer than his thumb. There was an aching in his head almost all the time, his life was slipping away from him and what was left was blurred on the edges and fading, and the image of the coffin opening was always with him: the brief flash of his father's collapsing face.

He would go see someone, he would go talk to someone, he told himself. A counselor at school perhaps. Only he didn't go. What would he say? How would he explain it? It wasn't rational. There was his bishop at church, church wasn't rational: it appealed to other systems, other logics. Even though he hadn't been to church in months, he could go to his bishop, tell him the problem. Would he believe him?

Sometimes I am not in my body.

What do you mean?

I don't know.

Where do you go?

I don't know that either.

No, he realized, it was not a conversation it would be wise to have with a bishop. He thought about going to another faith, Catholicism perhaps, and confessing, but at least with his own Church he knew when to keep something hidden. In another religion, there would be no context. He could get himself into serious trouble.

Walking to school, walking home, he began to feel he should tell someone on the way, a stranger, someone he might never see again. He would employ some sort of disarming smile, sidle suavely close, take the stranger's arm and begin to talk as they walked, explain both to the stranger and himself his problem, letting go of the arm before he had given too much away, moving along to someone else.

Sometimes I am not in my body, he heard.

Just what I need, he thought, *to have that phrase stuck in my head.*

He woke in the middle of the night to find a blurred blue ink stamp on the back of his hand reading, "FDA approved Grade A Beef." He hadn't been near a grocery store or butcher's shop that he could remember.

"What's that?" his mother asked at breakfast.

"This?" he said, staring at the stamp on his hand. "I don't know. Some kind of joke."

"What makes it funny?"

"It's not the kind of joke that's meant to be funny."

The whole evening was lost. *Sometimes I am not in my body.* There was an element of panic to it all. He racked his brain to try to retrieve memories that seemed not to exist.

One minute he was riding on the scooter, down to Lael's house, the next moment, as if no time had passed, Lael was in front of him and they were halfway up the canyon, Lael's hair whipping back against his forehead. He would see a psychiatrist, he told himself, but did not, could not: had no money for it, and couldn't ask his mother. The last thing he needed was someone to confirm the seriousness of his condition. *So what?* he thought. So what? This probably happened to everybody, he was O.K., not crazy, fine, he would be O.K. So what? Everybody was walking around, furtive, with the same dilemma. Everyone was blacking out and thinking they were the only one.

There was no pattern or consistency to the blackouts. The blank spaces came sometimes several times a day for several days in a row, at other times not at all for as long as a week. Each time he grew concerned enough to bring himself to do something about them, they would temporarily stop.

"What happened to you?" Lael asked when Rudd arrived to pick him up.

"What do you mean?"

Lael tugged him down to one of the scooters' round mirrors. He saw his face, pale and flaccid, his eyes couched in dark circles.

"I haven't been sleeping well," Rudd said.

And then they got on, Lael driving. He could feel himself sliding out of consciousness, a strange disequilibrium. It was too late to do anything about it but close his eyes. When he opened them, he was sitting cross-legged on the grass of a park he didn't recognize, on a treeless hill. Lael was holding a small pipe to his mouth, and Rudd could smell the sweet thick smoke. Lael extended the pipe toward him and began to cough, smoke flooding out of his nostrils.

"No thanks," said Rudd. "I don't smoke."

Lael looked at him oddly, head cocked to one side. "You've been smoking it all afternoon."

And only then, suddenly, could he feel the numbness in his face, his dry mouth, a faint scratchiness in his throat. Confused, he stood, slightly woozy, then sat down again.

"It wasn't me," he claimed.

Lael watched him, cupping the pipe in one hand, smiling. There was a wrinkled and creased Ziploc bag at his feet and out of it Lael packed the pipe, pushing the marijuana tightly against the screen with the tip of his thumb. He held it out to Rudd, a lighter in his other hand.

"Then who was it?" he asked.

"It wasn't me," said Rudd again, dazed, but taking the pipe just the same. He took the lighter, flicked it on with his thumb, surprised he could manage so easily. He did not know what to do next but his hands knew and he watched them hold the lighter near the bowl of the pipe, the flame angling and then, when he sucked, striking downward, the green shreds glowing red and writhing, then running pale. He felt the smoke fill his lungs. He began to cough.

"No more excuses, brother," said Lael. "That was you."

What you do is you dig the grave first and then you lead the sacrifice to it and call upon it to confess and give itself over to God. You slit its throat from one side to the other so that the blood spills out and into the pit and baptizes the grave. Then the sacrifice is allowed to fall into the pit and is buried just as it falls, without being straightened or arranged. It has been baptized in its own blood along with the grave, and it will arise from the grave in the Millennium renewed.

But what, he wondered, if the victim is killed when he is not in his body? Then the wrong one is killed and arises refreshed. And where is the victim left then?

There were the notes in his pockets. He took them out to read them but still could not read the script. He had in his hands not notes at all, he saw, but a small blunt pipe and a lemon-yellow disposable lighter.

"This isn't just pot," he said. "There's something more in this." His voice sounded distant to him, more subdued somehow. Lael was looking at him, unblinking, from the other side, reaching for the pipe.

He dug his hands into his pockets again and felt paper there and pulled out some notes. They stayed notes this time. He unfolded them one by one, smoothing them flat on his thigh. He could not make them out, the hand too obscure and tortured. He kept turning them over and looking at them.

"What are those?" asked Lael.

He did not know how to respond. Finally he said, "Notes."

He expected Lael to ask what notes. Instead, Lael hesitated, nodded. The notes were still in Rudd's hands. He could feel them and he was looking down at them again, trying to remember what they were. He tried to read them but was quickly distracted. *But what,* he wondered, *if the victim is killed when he is not in his body? Where does the soul go then?* There should be a handbook on blood sacrifice, he thought, something to keep you from making mistakes. If you did it right, not in error, it was an act of mercy. *Where are these thoughts from?* Rudd wondered. *Who is crammed in here with me?* Within him someone was speaking, leading him further and further out. And there was, outside of him, his half-brother.

Lael gestured to him with the stubby stem of the pipe. Rudd stood up and stumbled about, then sat down again.

"What is it?" Lael asked, as if from a distance.

"I don't know," Rudd said. "Something's happening to me." He stopped and looked at Lael, expecting him to say something, but Lael said nothing. It was not just the drug, he felt, but something about Lael. He could feel his skull pressing against his skin. He felt desperate and missing, the gaps of the previous weeks threatening to unveil themselves. *Who is crammed in here with me?*

Lael was before him and he felt something in his hands, realized he was still holding the wrinkled and crumpled notes, and when he brought them closer to his face it was as if he had now a sense of the words though he couldn't exactly read them. And then, at the end of one, a single line, he picked up the letter "W" and next to it an "H," a "Y," all capitalized. William Hooper Young, he thought, the man's initials, but maybe it wasn't Young, maybe it was simply "why?" *W. H. Y.—why?* He had never made that connection before. And then, as he looked further, the letters themselves struck him as dubious, a function of the drug, and he was unsure of what he had actually seen.

Lael was using the tip of the pipe to draw a line in the dirt between them. "Cross the line," he said, smirking, "and step into Hell."

Rudd stared at the line a long moment. He watched as Lael, on his knees, extended it, threaded it in an irregular circle around him.

"Cross the line," Lael said, "and enter . . ."

Rudd stood. He wavered around the circle, his breath bruising out of him. He began to turn slowly, following the circle around, turning and turning until, nauseous, he pitched into Lael's arms.

It was nearly the last moment he would remember of that day. Already as Lael embraced him he felt his vision turn dark and fade. "We'll go out," Lael was saying, "All the way out," and then Lael led him toward the scooter.

Everything froze in an instant with a click and a flash, and all of it was wiped away, replaced by what looked like a bare, white wall. After a moment he realized he was lying on his back staring at his bedroom ceiling, not on the bed but on the floor.

He pulled himself up. He felt an ache in both legs. He got to his knees and stood, walking just long enough to fall onto the bed.

It was dark outside. He tried to sleep but couldn't, so got up and turned on the desk lamp.

There, on the door his mother had converted with the help of stacks of bricks into a desk, were his father's old books. He picked each of them up, turned them about in his hands, dropped them again. He opened his notebook, saw pages filled with the same illegible script as the notes. Other than that, the desk was empty except for a day calendar turned to a date a few months forward. May seventeenth. He turned it back to the current day.

He got up and went into the bathroom. Filling his cup with water, he drank fully, tasting the traces of toothpaste in the cup. He could see, in the darkness, the ghost of his face in the glass. He turned and flicked on the light and looked at himself in the mirror. Lifting the cup, he drank again, half-watching his reflection, and saw that the cuff of his sweater looked as though it had been dipped in blood.

The glass clinked against the counter as he put it down, distant, as if in another room. Up close, he stared at the dyed strip of fabric, his gaze falling from there to the back of his hand. He noticed now, in the deepest creases, slight traces of blood.

He looked at his hands for cuts, felt back along his arms under the fabric of the sweatshirt. There was nothing, no tender or painful spot.

He stripped off the sweatshirt, running water over the stained cuff, then rubbing the fabric against itself, then rubbing a cracking cake of soap into the stain, then running water over it again. It did not come clean. Balling it up, he hid it under the sink, among the pipes.

Going into his bedroom, he lay down on the bed and stared at the ceiling. After a while, he pulled the telephone over, dialed Lael's number.

It was Lael's mother who answered. At first she claimed to have no son. Then he thought she had hung up. Yet a moment later he was speaking to Lael.

"What happened?" asked Rudd.

"Good," said Lael. "You made it home."

"Home from where?"

"What do you mean?"

"I arrive home," said Rudd, "and the first thing I notice is blood on my sleeve."

"What did you expect?" asked Lael.

"Is it your blood?"

"Of course it's not my blood," said Lael. "What's wrong with you?"

"Whose blood is it?"

"Look," said Lael, his voice flattening out. "Stop messing with me."

"I'm not messing with you," said Rudd. "I really want to know."

For some time, as Rudd stood listening to the underplay of static, Lael didn't respond.

"You got me," said Lael finally, laughing quietly. "You really had me going, brother. See you Saturday." Rudd heard the line click dead.

A sort of frenzy, mixed with anxiety, rose in him when he thought about the missing hours. Yet there was nothing there, not even a scattered image. He felt almost as if his head had two brains, each entirely independent of the other, and that he clicked back and forth between them for reasons unknown to him. He was lodged entirely in one brain. He could not say who had taken up residence in the other.

What was the worst he could have done? he asked himself. He wasn't covered with blood, had blood only on the extreme of one sleeve. Whose blood was it? Not his, not Lael's. Not necessarily human. Perhaps they had struck a rabbit or a chipmunk riding the scooter and it had come somehow from that. No matter what had happened, it was not he anyway who had done it: only his body.

But could he be separated from his body? Wasn't there some responsibility, no matter what? And wasn't it his fault that he had said nothing about it, that knowing the hours were blank he continued to act as if he were still unified and whole?

•

Two days later, just below the fold on the front page: *Woman Found Dead at base of Squaw Peak.* She was young, around seventeen. In addition to the cuts from the fall, she had two lateral incisions, one just over her breast, one across her belly, clearly made (the paper said) not by the fall but by a man-made instrument, probably a small knife. And on her neck, just over her windpipe, were two round bruises where someone had choked her, perhaps enough to render her unconscious before her fall.

It wasn't him, he told himself. He was afraid of heights, he couldn't climb the cliffs, couldn't get anywhere near that sort of open space and slope without growing dizzy. He wouldn't even have been able to stand. It was impossible. Even blacked out he couldn't imagine his body able to negotiate such heights.

Yet there was always Lael. Perhaps it had been Lael.

There were tens of thousands of people in Utah valley, he told himself. There was no reason to believe that this had anything to do with him or his half-brother. They were good boys, both of them, he was not concerned, he had nothing to worry about.

Yet where was the time going? What had happened to him between climbing onto the scooter and arriving home? He would find a hypnotist, would get the memories back that way. No, he could not bring himself to find a hypnotist. In the course of sixty seconds he went from feeling he was terribly ill, that something was desperately wrong, to feeling that everything was all right, that he simply had a faulty memory. Another sixty seconds and he again felt something was desperately wrong. His opinions wouldn't settle long enough for him to take action. The one time he did pick up the telephone, intending to speak to a psychiatrist, he never managed to get the receiver to his mouth. One moment it was the bright of day and he was holding the telephone receiver in one hand, the next he was crouching behind bushes, in the dark, behind a house he didn't know. Confused, he pulled himself up, brushed his knees off, walked casually home.

For a month he looked at each day's paper carefully, looking for something further about the murder of the young woman. Most days there was nothing. Days when there was news, it was trivial: *Police Dub Murderer of Young Woman "Canyon Killer."* Leads were rapidly exhausted, no additional bodies appeared. One expert suggested it was the work of a cult. Another disputed the original findings, suggested the cuts might have come from razor-sharp rocks, that the girl might simply have fallen after all. There was talk of exhuming her body, but nothing was ever done. The police seemed to have no idea who the killer (if there was one) was.

He talked to Lael about the case and Lael listened to him attentively but had little to say. He would not join in the speculation, though he seemed to enjoy it well enough.

"Are you fascinated with murder?" Lael asked, in a voice Rudd couldn't determine to be mocking or not.

"What?" asked Rudd. "Why should I be?"

Lael shrugged. "First the Hooper Young case, now this."

"You were interested in Hooper Young too," said Rudd.

"Sure," said Lael, his lip half-curling. "But who was it that got me interested?"

Rudd stared at him a moment, then flicked his gaze in another direction.

"Do you want me to stop talking about it?" asked Rudd.

"All I'm asking is, What's next?"

"What do you mean, 'What's next?'"

"Just what it sounds like."

"It doesn't sound like anything."

Yet later he could not help asking himself the same question. What *was* next? Where was it leading? Where had it led already? He had known from the beginning that the Hooper Young case was unlikely to yield itself to analysis, no matter how often he went over the newspaper articles and constructed in his mind situations with or without Elling. There would always be uncertainty there. Young's initials—W. H. Y.—were exemplary; no matter how far he got they would be there, shimmering; Young's life itself was a continual and unending question. It did not lead him to answers, but to further questions, drawing him into the void, where he was afraid he would catch sight of his own reflection. The canyon killing was the same in substance—unresolved—but where Young's case was unresolved because of time and distance, the existence/absence of an Elling, this case offered only a corpse and an empty name: "Canyon Killer." There was nothing behind it, he realized, and he knew the killer would never be caught. It would remain a name that referred to no one, though the suspicion nagged him that if it was associated with anything, it was with his own body. *What's next?* Rudd wondered. He finally asked Lael, "What's going to happen?"

"Anything can happen," said Lael. "Absolutely anything."

9

Sometimes at night, drifting toward sleep, he would see, in the wrinkle of the curtains or the oak grain of his armoire, glimpses of Hooper Young. He did not know how he knew it was Young—he had never seen a picture of the man—but he was certain it was him. He had a dark complexion, a certain charisma. Rudd would flick his eyes away and when they flicked back, the face would have vanished. Sometimes, in the afterimage Hooper Young left, he thought he glimpsed something else, a different face. But this face did not give up its identity easily.

It made him reluctant to sleep. He would stay awake for hours, stumbling about or reading until he was falling asleep between lines, the plot of the book taking a hallucinatory turn as he slipped in and out. He didn't feel well, though it wasn't anything tangible or physical, nothing he could put a finger on.

He began doing well in school again, schoolwork distracting him at least for a time, keeping him from wondering if he were going mad. His neck ached; he tried not to read it as an indication of something seriously wrong—he had given up defining himself as ill. He tried too to continue ignoring the vanished hours, as well as the rips and tears that appeared in the same bloody-cuffed sweatshirt that he often found himself wearing, late at night, though he had no memory of putting it on.

His mother was there, knocking at his door, asking him if something was wrong. He tried to use his voice, but he couldn't—his mouth kept opening and shutting, only a hiss of air coming out. The handle rattled and his mother knocked again, demanding he unlock the door.

He stumbled from bed, made his way in darkness to the door, then stood there, trying to speak, only managing the low hissing, his chest and throat heaving.

"Rudd?" his mother said, her voice higher than normal.

He reached out and unlocked the door, pulled it open slightly, just enough for her to see his face. She was standing in her robe, one hand held out as if to knock again.

"Are you all right?" she asked.

He nodded slowly.

"I mean," she said, and half-glanced down the hall. "I heard shouting."

He shook his head.

"It wasn't your voice," she said. "It was another voice. Then, just a moment ago, a hiss."

He shrugged, slowly closing the door. She blocked the gap with her forearm.

"You're alone in there?" she asked.

He nodded again, trying gently to push her arm out.

"Nothing's wrong?" She was staring at his face, trying to smile. "Why aren't you saying anything?"

He opened his mouth wide, felt his tongue pulse, struggle to speak, but hissing instead. His mother's eyes rolled back and she collapsed.

By the time he had straightened her on the floor and rubbed her face, thinking that it might help somehow, he had his voice back. It was awkward at first, somewhat harsh, but it quickly got better and stronger. Her eyes fluttered open and she looked at him warily, without speaking or moving.

"You're all right?" he asked.

"You can speak?"

"Why shouldn't I?"

"You couldn't a moment ago."

"Of course I did," he said. "There's nothing wrong with me."

She stared up at him. He held his face lax hoping she would not know he was lying. Then he pulled her up.

"It's late," he said. "Go back to bed."

As he slept less and read the scriptures more, it began to seem as if they were speaking directly to him, encouraging him to do something he could never quite put his finger on, offering a kind of destiny. Everything he read, even his schoolwork, even a story problem in geometry, seemed to have a secret meaning cached just below the surface, but it was a meaning he was never quite able to uncover. He would see Young now not just at night and in dreams, finely controlled in the textures of a curtain or a blotch of paint, but everywhere, out of the corner of his eyes, gone when he tried to see him more clearly. The dark and undefinable Elling, if he was Elling, was there too. He could burrow into school or other pursuits and be briefly free of it, but he knew always in the back of his head that he would see them again. It was most frequent, he began to realize, as he neared a blackout.

The whole of his life began to resemble a hallucination, dark and folded inward as if assembled from his mind. There was a falsity to it, as if he were acting, and often he found himself having to hold himself back from laughter because everything seemed contrived. All that really mattered were the blotted hours, but they were the only things he had no access to. He borrowed a video camera, tried turning it on when he sensed a blackout coming, but when he came conscious again the cassette was removed, the tape spooled out into a loopy, shiny pile. On the wall was written a note in pencil, but again it was nothing he could make out. Perhaps it wasn't letters at all but some other system of symbols. From a certain angle, if he looked at the marks for only an instant, they resembled the sacred marks on his mother's temple garments, and once the idea was in his head he started to see the marks everywhere, on every surface, God's claim to all. He could do without sleep, he knew; all he had to do was close his eyes and he could rest, but he would go on thinking the whole time his eyes were closed, his eyes still closed but seeing the marks on the wall in his memory. Then, just as suddenly, the feeling left him and he was holding his pencil, trying to erase God's marks from everything, then knowing he had to get out. He was out in the hall and past his mother without speaking to her and down the hall and out the door. The whole world was running all awash with noise, too much noise for him to sort anything out. A voice was speaking, but it was not his voice, and how it had come to be in his head he didn't know. It was not to be believed. He was fine, healthy, the world had always been speaking to him, only he had never been able to hear it until now. Soon he would not only hear it but comprehend it, and then he would know what was expected of him, what he should do next.

"Rudd?" a voice was saying, "Rudd?" It took him a moment to realize the voice was not inside him but somewhere before him. A dark face, Elling. Only not Elling. A woman. Mrs. Madison.

"Is anything wrong, Rudd?" she asked.

He knew the right answer. He started to raise his hand, then realized it was not the sort of answer you raised your hand to give. "No," he said. "I'm fine." It was the truth, in a sense, and if it wasn't true exactly it was certainly necessary. One lived by necessary things and necessity—

"You're certain?"

Had the first answer been wrong? Was it the wrong voice he was listening to, or if not the wrong voice maybe he was mishearing the right one? He looked up and into her face again, saw her features shadowing, her voice growing dim.

"To tell the truth, I haven't been sleeping well lately," he mumbled, his vision dimming, blackout, blackout, blackout.

And then, just as Rudd had shown up at Lael's door for the first time, unannounced, in midafternoon, several years before, there was Lael, this time at Rudd's door.

"What are you doing here?" he asked.

"What?" asked Lael. "You asked me to come."

"I asked you?"

"Today's the day, May seventeenth, remember?"

He did not know what to say. "How did you get here?" he asked.

Lael looked at him, lips closed, head tilted slightly. "You loaned me your scooter."

"Oh," said Rudd. "Yes."

"Is anything wrong?"

"No," said Rudd, already seeing the patches starting to spread across Lael's face, the dark mask overlapping it. "Nothing," he said. "Nothing at all."

And then it was as if he blinked his eyes to find himself riding not on the back of the scooter this time but on the front, Lael hanging on to him from behind. He swerved a little, slowed down, realized he didn't even know where he was going. He kept going straight. It was the middle of the day, perhaps the same day, perhaps another day, and they were driving through fields on back roads, farms all around them, the mountains looming before them, rocky and scrub-covered and awkward. The scooter was whining and his hands tingled from the vibration as if coming asunder, and he realized he was holding the grips too tightly. He could see in the back of each of his hands the shadow of Elling's face, and had difficulty paying attention to the road. He kept looking at the faces on his hands and then glancing at the mirror, trying to catch Lael's reflection to compare, though he could see nothing of

Lael, felt only his chin pressing into Lael's back—or rather Lael's chin pressed into *his* back, Lael's head hidden behind his own body. Yet it was as if it were *Lael's* back and *his* chin because before it had always been that way; he felt for a moment that he had exchanged bodies with Lael. As he let the idea fill his head it was almost as if he couldn't see to drive because his face was pressed to his own back. He was trying to raise his head, but when he finally did, he was not on the scooter at all and Lael was not in front of him but beside him and they were both of them marching not along a road but up the slope of a hill. He felt himself growing dizzy, so to distract himself he tried to keep his eyes on Lael instead of the slope. He went stumbling upward, listening to a ragged wind that he came to realize was his own mutilated breathing. Or his own mixed with Lael's who, he now perceived, had in his hand a glinting object that he made out to be a knife.

"Why do you have your knife out?" he managed to ask.

Neither of them stopped climbing, though Lael leaned slightly toward him. "For the same reason yours is out," said Lael, and Rudd caught between steps the flash of the blade in his own hand. He wanted to close the knife and put it away but did not, nor could he think of a reason he should be holding it; indeed, all he could consider was his sheer stumbling dizziness. He reached out to steady himself on Lael and realized that his knife had torn through his half-brother's shirtsleeve, jabbing into his arm.

"Jesus!" said Lael, and stopped to examine his arm and shirt. Rudd could see a certain panic to him, perhaps even fear.

"Sorry," said Rudd. "I mean, I didn't—"

"I've trusted you," said Lael. "I've gone along with you in all of this. Was I wrong to do so?"

"In all of what?" asked Rudd.

Lael shook his head and continued climbing, muttering under his breath. Rudd took a step forward, the ground rolling under his feet, and collapsed.

Then just as quickly he was crouching on a hillock over a nearly deserted camping area, a green ranger's box at the end of a paved road, rutted dirt roads leading back to campsites. It was near sunset. Lael was holding onto his shoulder. The ground was steady for a moment though slowly starting to tilt and buckle again. He got down on his hands and knees and, as it grew worse, onto his belly.

"There," said Lael. Rudd blinked, tried to focus his eyes, saw only trees, grass, dirt, the scars of fire pits.

"What?" he asked. "Where?"

Lael pointed and Rudd tried to follow his finger out. There was something below them, through the trees, a car of some sort, a station wagon, and around it bustling shapes.

"That's it," said Lael. "They're the ones."

Rudd lowered his head, smelled the ground against his face. Then Lael pulled him up to his feet and they were off and stumbling, Lael still holding him and helping him stay upright. They skidded down a scattered flow of shale, crouched behind some old, withered sage, the slight smell of it clearing his head. There they were, a family, about a hundred yards distant, three of them in all, a tent set up, an unlit lantern standing on the table.

"What do we do now?" Rudd asked.

Lael half-turned. "We wait for dark," he said. He turned his knife around, beginning to strop it first against the side of his shoe then against a half-buried stone. Rudd didn't know the family at all. They were tossing a frisbee, two of them anyway, a man and a young girl. A woman watched from beside a fire pit, poking the fire with sticks.

The ground wasn't sloshing so much, and he thought at first it was because they had descended slightly and the ground had begun to level out. Then he realized it was because he was beginning to feel isolated, insulated, buried deeper inside his body. He was no longer so close to the outside. Even looking through his eyes it was as if he were looking from deeper within his head, his vision of the outside framed, a large darkness encroaching.

"What do we do?" he heard himself ask again.

"Be patient," said Lael. "Night is coming."

He took a deep breath, felt his vision grow dim. He felt himself slowly crowded out of his senses and into oblivion.

By scraps and bits I've in the past surrendered myself to strangers . . . but there he is with a dozen different faces moving down a hundred separate streets.

—TRUMAN CAPOTE, *The Grass Harp*

. . . people shouldn't ever look closely at one another, they're not like pictures.

—SHIRLEY JACKSON, *The Bird's Nest*

PART II

LYNDI, ADRIFT

They showed up at her door to warn her, but it was too late, it was already on the news, the hiker having called the press before the police. She was sprawled on the couch, idly watching TV while working through her algebra homework: *four bodies, not yet identified, a campsite, vicious slaying, three long and careful cuts across throat, breast, hips. Each body arranged on the ground to form a pattern: a V, a right angle, each next to each. And then, a little downslope, midway between the V'd body and the right-angled body, a corpse spread straight with hands to sides, a horizontal line; and another body, beneath the right angle but farther down the mountainside, spread straight as well:* so that from the air (according to the artist's graphic representation) it looked like:

$$V \qquad L$$

$$-$$

$$-$$

Suspiciously resembling, the reporter went on to say, *if you cared for an instant to block out the river disrupting the pattern, the distinctive markings of the Mormon temple garment.*

Weird, she thought, and turned the channel. But the story was on the next channel as well. When she switched again she saw neither mountainside nor reporters but an old picture of her father. It was as if something were wrong with the television. It took a moment for her to understand, switching back to where she had started and seeing the picture there too. It was her father's photograph, her mother's face beside. Two men wearing plastic gloves, zipping a body into a bag, the photographs of her parents again, the name of her sister as well, spelled incorrectly, no photograph. *We confirm, then, the names,* and a shot again of the reporter, shaking her head, *a tragedy, horrendous, no leads to speak of—one survivor.* The doorbell was ringing, had been ringing for some time she realized suddenly, and she was walking toward the door with the remote still in her hand, *once again we confirm the,* and then she was opening the door: two men dressed in street clothes brandishing badges that flashed with light. Behind them, along the property line, a cluster of reporters beginning to shout the moment she opened the door. The plainsclothesmen, badges still out, moving their lips without her hearing a word. Or hearing, rather, but unable to string meaning through their words. *I know,* she heard herself saying, the remote clattering from her hand, *I've just been watching.* She turned and took two steps back toward the couch, found instead her cheek pressed against the floor.

They wrapped her in a blanket, kept asking her how she felt. A man holding a camera high above his head shoved his way toward her, flash fluttering, and was pushed back.

"Is she all right?" they wanted to know. "Is she ready to talk?"

Four bodies, she thought she heard, low and behind her. *A ritual of some kind.* They were forcing a cup of something into her hands, but she couldn't unknot her hands from the blanket. Fluorescent lights, buzzing slightly. A desk, bare except for a pencil, another desk beside it, another desk beyond that.

"Perhaps we should take her to the hospital?"

"Linda, are you all right?"

"Is that her name?"

"Hell, I think so. Who's got the file?"

"Is there a file already?"

"Linda, are you there? Can you hear me?"

Surging up: two faces to either side of her, the strange melange of their various aftershaves and respective fleshes wafting around her like webbing. Then fingers biting into her arm, her body propelled out of the police station, the sun bright in her face, a camera held toward her, her body spinning, strapped down to something, on the move.

Light, dark. *Bring me my robe,* she was sure a voice said. Needle in her somewhere upon the back of her wrist, an opaque tube looping away from it to a pole-strung plastic bag, swollen with pale fluid.

"Lyndi?"

She opened her mouth, felt over her lips with her tongue. Dry, cracked. Someone shining light into her eye. A hand resting on one side of her face, fingers holding eyelids apart.

"Lyndi?"

The light in her eye flickered off, the afterburn a significant fist in her head. She hooded that eye, opened another. Two dim-featured heads, indistinguishable, then slowly taking form, congealing into a doctor and a second man whose professional role wasn't revealed through face or clothing.

Water, she managed. The second man left her sight, returned with a cup he held to her lips. Water trickling from the corners of her mouth, prickings of cold on her collarbone. He removed the cup, daubed her lips with the corner of her sheet.

"How do you feel?" the doctor asked.

"I'm going crazy," she said.

"Of course you are," the second man said, smiling. "Metaphorically, I mean."

"Now," said the doctor. "This is nothing extraordinary. We've experienced a severe shock, haven't we."

He began again to shine light into her eyes.

"There's a needle in me," she said.

"That's an I.V." said the doctor. "Nothing to worry over."

"I mean what's in it?"

"In it?" he said. "Something to stabilize us, fairly mild. Look left, please."

"Lyndi," said the second man.

She tried to turn her head to face him, but the doctor held it in place. "Look left," he suggested again.

"What is it?" she asked.

"Do you mind if I ask a few questions?" the second man asked.

"Questions?"

"Sure. You wouldn't mind that, would you?"

"A moment, officer," said the doctor. "Almost through here."

"Right," said the second man. "Beg pardon."

"Officer?" she asked.

"That's right," he said. "As in police. Detective, actually."

Then the calm voice of the doctor questioning her about things she didn't see the point of: what the date was, whether she preferred eggs or cheese, what portion of her forearm was he touching, whether she remembered how she had arrived there. She could not tell if she answered in a fashion he approved of. He kept posing the same questions and getting the same answers until finally he was stepping away from her, writing on his chart all the way out the door.

"Well," said the detective. "Just you and me now."

She regarded him a little more closely, his eyes unblinking. Pale face, dark hair, somewhat puffy-featured. "I guess so," she said.

"About those questions," he said. "Was there anyone who didn't care for your parents?"

"Enough to kill them?"

"Your father, did he have enemies?"

"I don't know."

"Why didn't you go camping with them?"

"I don't know. I'm in college."

He edged a little closer to the bed, regarded her closely. "Lyndi," he said. "What about you?"

"What about me?"

"Did you kill them?"

"What?"

"Or arrange for someone else to do it?"

"I can't believe," she said, "that you—"

"Just between you and me," he said, and muffled her hand within his larger own.

"No," she said. "Of course not."

He offered a flitting half-smile, patted her knee through the sheet. "I believe you. I'm glad we got that out of the way," he said. "Now let's see what we can figure out."

There was a police officer stationed at a door down the hall. Inside, a man in a bed, arms strapped down, i.v. plugged into the back of his hand, tube down his throat, neck packed in cotton. A heart monitor clicked beside him.

"What's he called?" she asked.

"Rudd something," the detective said. "Troyer, I think. Not that exactly, but it's in my notebook. I could look it up." He made no move to do so. "Only survivor. Recognize him?"

"No," she said. "Not like this anyway."

"Not a friend of the family? He wasn't with your parents?"

"No."

"You've never seen him before?"

"No."

The detective shook her hand, held out his card. "You're free to go."

Pocketing the card, she thanked him. Her head still felt thick. She started for the door, came back to look at the man again. She got close enough to see both sides of his face. Not a man really, a boy, her age or nearly. The detective was still there, behind her, asking was he familiar after all? No, she had never seen him before. Certain? Certain.

2

The bishop came by and tried to talk to her about what had happened, tried to comfort her. She was both grateful and resentful. Some ladies brought over casseroles, which she thanked them for but which she somehow couldn't eat. They sat on the counters until they fuzzed over with mold and she threw them away. She wasn't eating much of anything, she found.

For reasons she could not quite fathom, she began to clip out articles on the murders. She stored them in a shoebox beneath her bed until after the funeral and then taped them above the washer and dryer. The Devil's Kitchen killings they were calling it, though the bodies had been found east and south of Devil's Kitchen. The newspaper accounts contradicted each other. One article speculated that her father had been attacked first, others that Rudd Theurer had been the first, with his attack stumbled upon by one or more members of her family. Her family had been dead seven hours before their bodies were found, according to the *Daily Herald*. Or was it, as the *Salt Lake Tribune* suggested, twelve? The murder weapon was variously described as a knife, a razor, a sharpened rock, a shard of glass. In some accounts, they had died quickly; in others, they had suffered lingering, agonizing deaths.

As the dryer rumbled, she stood reading them, staring into the grainy pixilated photographs—the bodies from the air, the police rolling a body (her father, she was almost certain) onto a gurney. Rudd all but dead, a crowd of paramedics around him, only his hand and forearm visible.

What to make of it she didn't know. What she did know was that her parents had gone up to the mountains, had either had Rudd with them or had decided to pitch camp close to him. Then a person or several people had killed her parents and sister by slitting their throats and cutting deep incisions from breast to breast, hip to hip. Then a person or group of people had carefully bent the bodies, arranging them on the hillside in a pattern that resembled the markings of the Mormon temple garment: the square, the mark of the compass, the navel mark, the knee mark. Too young to be allowed to enter the Mormon temple, she didn't wear garments herself, and didn't know their full significance. The markings were something sacred. The Church-owned *Deseret News* said they could not publicly speak of the symbolism of the marks but did state that a Mormon investigator on the team had the matter *under consideration*. The victims had all bled to death save for this Rudd, whose windpipe had been gashed opened but none of his major arteries cut. Still, he had been lucky not to choke on his own blood. Perhaps, the *Tribune* speculated, the killer (or killers) had been interrupted before he (or they) could finish the task properly.

Mormons came to her door, encouraging her to put her life back together—first two women from the Relief Society, then the Relief Society President. *How was she?* they asked, and she sensed in them a kind of hunger for any details that hadn't been revealed in the papers. It showed as a gauntness to their faces, but yet they genuinely seemed to want to help her as well. Why wasn't anything simple? They spoke about healing and God's trials, and confessed their own trials to her. She both liked them and was repulsed by them. It was good she was going sometimes to church, Lyndi was told, but it would be even better if she attended every Sunday, especially at this time, especially now. There was comfort to be found there.

Most of the week, she was left alone to wander the empty house. She was drawn in particular, she found, to word of Rudd in the articles, since, though comatose, he was the only survivor. He was an only child, had lived alone with his mother until the accident. He was several months younger than she, still a senior in high school. He was described as solitary, as a reasonably good student with sometimes odd notions, afraid of heights, an unlucky boy who had apparently managed to be in the wrong place at the wrong time. The articles reproduced a yearbook photograph in which he was at once smiling and trying not to smile, his teeth hidden, the resulting strained expression having the character of a death rictus. When she took out her own high school yearbook, she realized Rudd's was the expression most students had. Her own photograph was the exception, all teeth. He was disturbed, his English teacher said of him, obsessed with death. *How ironic,* the teacher was quoted as saying, stepping exuberantly into a parody of her professional role, *that the one obsessed with death would be the only one to survive.*

Her aunt Debby from southern California showed up on the doorstep, sporting four designer suitcases. She had tried to call, she claimed: wasn't Lyndi answering the phone? She was concerned, she claimed. Sure, certainly Lyndi was of legal age, but with the shock and all perhaps she would like company for a few weeks, perhaps even longer?

"Uh, well," said Lyndi.

She knew how it was. Constant crying, state of shock, bags under the eyes, everything in disarray, feeling like you want to die, Valium. She was there to help her limp through the hard times. Lyndi could count on her.

Not knowing what else to do, Lyndi invited her in.

Her aunt entered, peeling off her gloves in the process, leaving her bags on the porch for Lyndi to lug in. She stood looking around the living room apprehensively.

"How delightfully quaint," she suggested.

Then she plunged through the entryway and fully into the house, up the stairs straight to Lyndi's parents' old room, pushing her parents' clothes all to one side of the closet and beginning, once Lyndi had brought up the suitcases, to unload her own things. She rearranged the drawers too, putting Lyndi's father's socks and underwear into the same drawer, then wedging all the rest of his things into her mother's armoire. When Lyndi protested:

"My dear, you'll have to face it sometime, you know. They're dead. They're not coming back."

It was not that Lyndi wasn't facing it, it was not that she didn't know they were dead. It was the lack of respect her aunt was showing, the way she dumped her parents' toothbrushes into the trash and emptied her parents' half-full bottle of shampoo into the toilet so that when the toilet was flushed it foamed up and over the rim. She rearranged all the drawers in the kitchen—*it'll be good for you, dear, you've got to let go*—so they matched her drawers in her house in California. But Lyndi had kept the drawers as they were, not as an homage to her parents but because she had grown up with them in a particular order. She could find things.

There her aunt was, peignoir-wrapped and sitting across the coffee table, or the *postum table* as she chose to call it in deference to Mormonism: *avoid the very appearance of evil,* her aunt would claim, *strong drinks should be banned even from the names of household furnishings.* They were having a *chat,* something her aunt liked to *schedule* from time to time and which Lyndi suffered through. The chats involved her aunt reciting gossip about people Lyndi had never met and whose names she could barely keep straight. There was Rod Fuller, a used car salesman who secretly drank. There was her aunt's next-door neighbor, accused of acting rudely, Lyndi's aunt carefully ticking off grievances against her: coming to the door with her hair in curlers, playing the radio in her garden, hanging her bras on the outside line to dry. There was Mrs. Miller down the street who had been married five times despite what her aunt called "a colostomy situation," and who was now sleeping with a boy half her age.

"I've got homework to do," said Lyndi. "May I be excused?"

"Homework, Hell," said her aunt. "You're in mourning."

She had been doing fine, Lyndi told herself. It wasn't easy, hadn't been, she loved her parents, she loved her sister, it had been difficult to lose them, but she had been wading through. Wading through her aunt, though, struck her as a more difficult proposition, one she shouldn't have to face.

"Half her age," her aunt was saying, "if even that. Some folk find a colostomy bag exciting, if you get my meaning, but I'm not one of those people. Still, it takes all kinds and thank God for that, else all the weirdos and sickos and nuts would be after you and me both."

Her aunt reached down to the coffee table, took a saltine from its plastic sleeve then commented on doing so, as if this act might be of interest to Lyndi, might even aid in her healing. She pronounced the last syllable like tines of a fork.

"You've got to go on," she said, munching as if tranquilized. "You can't let yourself fade from existence."

Whatever, thought Lyndi.

Her aunt tugged at the hem of her dress.

"I've been married twice," she said. "Actually three times, but the second one didn't count because there was hardly any sex to speak of. So I know a lot about wanting to die."

Then her aunt's eyes were tearing up, the last corner of the saltine slipping from her hand. Lyndi looked around for Kleenex. There wasn't any. Still crying, her aunt reached into the plastic sleeve for another saltine.

"Together we'll make it through," her aunt managed through tears, spitting cracker dust. "You and me against the world, kiddo."

Dear God, thought Lyndi, *kill me now.*

•

It was hard to stay clear of her aunt's chats, but once her aunt was chatted out, Lyndi was able to slip away. She would go to the library to read and do homework. She continued doing her homework though certain of her professors had suggested she'd done well enough so far; they were willing to just give her the grade she deserved to that point in the class, give her time to recover. This *was* recovering, she felt, doing things she would do if her parents were still alive, though her aunt claimed a better term for it was *denial*.

Whatever it was, she was doing it. Up at seven, showered, made up, making her own breakfast. Her aunt stumbled in to eat with her, rubbing her eyes, falling back on a terry-cloth robe once her peignoir was dirty. A glass of orange juice, and then her aunt would quiz her about the coming day. If she didn't have her schedule sufficiently full, that was grounds for scheduling a chat; if it was too full her aunt would rattle on about denial, threaten to set up an appointment with a *counselor*.

"Not a psychiatrist or a psychotherapist"—her aunt didn't believe in pseudo-scientific hoodoo—"but a good plain honest-to-goodness counselor, grain-fed on common sense."

"Grain-fed?" Lyndi asked.

"Don't you get smart with me, Missy," her aunt said, wagging her finger. "Turn me against you and who else you got in the world?"

No one, it was true, but she wasn't convinced that no one was a step down. Her aunt seemed more of a contradiction each day, an amalgam of many different anxieties in collision. Not a remarkable woman exactly, but a woman pieced together with more than a few visible seams. These seams all a result of *coming to terms* and *not fading out of existence*.

She placed egg, scrambled, on a plate.

Lyndi juggled the chats and the threats about counselors, walking a line that would allow her a minimum of the one and nothing more than the threat of the other. Her aunt seemed to regard Lyndi as an indentured servant, leaving all the meals to her niece, though Lyndi's experience with cooking was minimal. The grocery shopping, too, was left to Lyndi and that, along with school and cooking and laundry, kept her busy enough that she was barely lying when she told her aunt she had a full schedule. The one task Aunt Debby reserved for herself was to give Lyndi what she called *a complete fashion makeover*. "A new you for a new life," her aunt kept saying. As it turned out, Lyndi was an *autumn* and had been dressing all wrong for her coloration. Her whole wardrobe was *disastrous,* would have to be abandoned in favor of *muted tones*. Her makeup too wasn't quite right; surely an

Avon Lady lived in the neighborhood? *You know, Avon Calling?* When Lyndi claimed she didn't know, her aunt shook her head. "Not to speak ill of the dead," she claimed, "but your mother didn't teach you a damn thing about what it takes to be a woman."

There were trips to the mall, her aunt lamenting over Utah's lack of high-end boutiques. Clothing at Nordstrom and JCPenney, most of which made Lyndi look like she was eighteen going on forty-five. Professional outfits straight out of realty ads, business skirts that buzzed against her thighs when she walked, pastel twin sets, sweater dresses with fringed sleeve ends. Her aunt was there, beside her, each time holding up something new and even less to her taste. Lyndi was sent, laden down, to the fitting room, made to come out wearing each outfit, twirl, slide on to the next. Then on to the Brass Plum, more wearing, more whirling, bags slowly accumulating with clothing that had nothing to do with her and that, if she wore them at all, would feel imposed, borrowed. Ahead: a makeup counter garrisoned with stick-thin women plastered with artificial faces, accessories clicking against each other like mandibles. Two sturdy women wandering the lingerie section, a man watching them surreptitiously from across the aisle. A seeing-eye dog guiding a woman who was pale-eyed but who had none of the mannerisms of the blind. Lyndi's hand grabbed, tugged onto a counter, palm up. Escalator halfway across the store, three children running up and down, treads clanking. A faint sensation at the extreme of her arm. "Tell me what you think," a voice saying, but was it to her? An array of bottles, all hues. Light fixtures, circular, long broken lines. Aisles below, between sections and centers, jagged and strung about. "Do try, dear"—her aunt's voice, bored—"do make an effort." Near the escalator two children tipped over a mannequin, its grinning head rolling off. Watching her own hand coming off the counter and toward her face, as if propelled.

"Darling, whatever can be the matter? You're shaking."

"I'm fine," she said, hearing her voice resound from a distance. She could not bring anything quite into attention, her eyes flicking rapidly from one thing to the next. The perfume was too strong on her wrist. "I need air," she claimed.

"Shall I go with you, dear?" her aunt asked.

There were bags at her feet and she pushed through them, stumbled down the first aisle she came to. She half-turned and looked back, saw her aunt behind her smiling oddly, her mouth moving too slowly. The film of her life was running down. The aisle swerved abruptly out from under her feet and she found herself plunging through racks of clothing, hangers jangling, glints of light everywhere. An aisle again and she followed it around a curve to find herself at a perfume counter, staring at somebody's aunt.

"I thought you needed air," the aunt said.

"I," she said, then clamped her mouth shut and pushed off again, going the other way this time and keeping to one path until it led her round and about and out of the store into the mall proper. A larger interior courtyard with hundreds of people milling about, a fountain, kiosks strung in all directions with sunglasses and blown-glass animals and temple replicas, strange solitary plants scattered and dying in awkward pots, arranged without pattern across a faux-marble floor. Paths to either side, no sign of air. Somebody beside her, asking was she all right, but she could not see him precisely and then she was off and away again, sloping right. Shops everywhere, neon glaring, another fountain, a food court packed with tables and chairs, crowded with people and bags and babies and food. Through them and out the other side, past rows of identical shops, face wavering in the glassed fronts, and then, at last, the end of the path, a set of doors leading outside.

Open air, light. It was dizzying. Standing on the edge of the sidewalk, under an awning, the parking lot slick with rain now past, its smell still strong in the air. Walking, starting up one row, cutting between cars, cutting back again until she was near a car that looked like hers but wasn't. She looked around for her car, couldn't see it. She felt her pocket for the keys, realized her aunt still had them in her purse.

She found a lamppost, sat on its base with her back against it, and waited. At first she covered her face with her hands and then, when her breathing steadied, she uncovered her face and stood again to look for the car.

And then suddenly she saw, passing by her in slow procession, her family: her father, dull-eyed and pale, his keys out and held awkwardly, his skin hanging open and gaping at his throat. He stopped and turned his eyes upon her briefly, then continued on. Her sister, nervous and birdlike, then her mother, slightly behind, pale. Behind them, gaze averted from her, was Rudd, holding his throat, limping.

She waited for a glimpse of the killer. When he didn't come, she stood to look for them, saw them climb into a car that looked like hers but wasn't. It pulled away. Yet when she went to where the car had been, it was still there. She stood staring at it. When she tried the door, it was locked.

She walked back toward the mall, where a taxi was parked just outside the nearest entrance. She climbed in.

"I need to go home," she said.

"Where's home?" the driver asked.

She started to offer her address, trailed off. "The hospital," she said. "I want to go to the hospital."

"Anything you say," he said, looking at her in the rearview mirror. He started the cab, drove.

3

Her aunt returned to California, pronouncing Lyndi *hopelessly self-absorbed and wading neck-deep in denial,* threatening to come back at a moment's notice if Lyndi should prove healable after all. Lyndi, bored and alone, started going regularly to the hospital and sitting beside the comatose Rudd. His throat was unpacked, the stitching removed to reveal a dribbled red scar slowly fading pale. She would sit with her hands in her lap, near the head of the bed. Once she pulled his eyelids open with her fingers. She saw a thin slit of blue under one lid, what was visible of a rolled-up eye. Under the other lid she only saw white.

They fed him from tubes. As the days went by he grew thinner, his cheekbones becoming sharply defined, the skin settling on his face. Sometimes she helped the nurse move him and change the sheets, saw the sores beginning along his legs and back. Sometimes too she would speak to him, ask how, or if, he had known her mother and father and sister. What had it looked like, she asked him, a man coming at him, covered in her parents' blood, brandishing a knife or razor or sharpened rock or shard of glass? She imagined four men, one for each possible weapon, all of their faces obscured. Or perhaps the killer was a fifth man, with a different weapon, with no face at all. They all crowded in her head, jostling. Or perhaps the killer had approached from behind, she said, partly to Rudd, and he had had no warning—a sharp, hot pain at his throat and a rush of blood down his shirt.

He had survived, she told herself, and for that reason would have to stand in for father and mother and sister all at once. They were connected through violence.

Sometimes, if she was there still by early evening, Rudd's mother would come. Once Lyndi tried to introduce herself, but his mother merely regarded her oddly, half-smiled, and said nothing. *Are you deaf?* Lyndi almost said. Instead, she got up and left, and from then on departed quickly whenever his mother arrived, going to get some dinner and then coming back once she was certain his mother would be gone.

In her head and sometimes out loud she had conversations with him. What did he like to do, what TV shows had he grown up watching, who were his favorite movie stars? "No," she said, when he did not answer, "really? Me too." How was high school life? Was he sorry to miss graduation? "No friends? No girlfriend? No one to visit you? What? A nice looking boy like you?" The policeman at the door sometimes stared in, watching her. Sometimes she drew the curtain around herself and Rudd, but still felt the policeman staring at her feet and ankles. She started sitting on the edge of the bed, which was high enough to keep her feet above the bottom of the curtain. She told Rudd about her aunt, about her parents and sister. She talked until the policeman came in at the end of the night to usher her out—"my shift's over; nothing personal, but visiting hours are long gone"—locking the room door and going home himself. "My family didn't even *like* the mountains," she would tell Rudd the next day when she came back. "They hadn't been on a picnic in years. You wake up one morning," she said. "You decide to go to the mountains, on a whim, and you're killed. What about you?" she asked. "Was it a whim for you as well? I can say anything to you," she said. "Something utterly random. Pigskin," she said. "You're the only boy in the whole world I've ever been able to say pigskin to," she said, and then wondered why she had said that, of all things. She traced the pink scar across his throat with her finger, *pigskin,* let her hand glide along his jaw and up to cup his ear. She had already spoken hours to him, why should she not touch him? She ran her fingers into his hair. *What do you care about?* she wondered. *What do you believe in?* Perhaps, she thought, he is not so different from me.

A nurse came in and undid Rudd's restraints. She rolled his body to one side of the bed, the tube that ran down his throat tightening against his neck.

"Is that safe?" asked Lyndi, then held him steady as the nurse undid the sheets on the free side of the bed, pushed them over to bunch under Rudd's back. They rolled him back to the other side of the bed, over the hill of crumpled sheets, repeated the process to get the new sheets on.

"He's your boyfriend?" the nurse asked.

"No," she said. "Not exactly."

"A friend, then," the nurse said.

"No," Lyndi said. "Not quite that either, to be honest."

The nurse, smoothing the sheets, nodded slightly. "If you don't mind my asking," she said, "what exactly is he?"

What indeed? Lyndi wondered. She hardly knew him, knew only what she had read about him in the papers, most of which was contradictory. What was he to her? He had survived, he had distinguished himself in that way, and for that reason would have to stand in for her family. But in the light of the nurse's interest such reasoning seemed suspect. He had no obligation to her, didn't even know her, had never seen her. Her interest, she tried to tell herself, was only a function of finding who her family's killer was, of avenging them. He was useful to her. He could give her *closure*.

But she wanted more than that, she knew, realized that even though she did not know Rudd at all she felt closer to him than anyone else alive or dead. *The next time a nurse asks if he's my boyfriend,* she promised herself, *I'll say yes.*

She came one day, after algebra, and found the policeman gone. The door was open, the curtain drawn back. Rudd, hands still restrained, was lying as he always had.

She closed the curtain, pulled shut the door, went to the nurse's station.

"The guard's gone," she said to a ponderous pale man with frizzy blond hair, obviously dyed.

"Excuse me?"

"The guard," she said. "The policeman."

The nurse pursed his lips. "What room, please."

She gave him the room number, watched him scan down a chart in a crinkled plastic sleeve.

"Theurer?" he asked. He pronounced it with a soft "th" and an "ew." *Thewer.*

"Yes," said Lyndi.

"No guard listed today," he said.

"A policeman's been there every day," said Lyndi.

"No guard listed today," the nurse said again, and turned the chart facedown.

Lyndi hurried back to the room. She sat on the edge of the chair, regarding Rudd. She took from her wallet the card the detective had given her, picked up the telephone beside the bed. She tried dialing the number, but the line clicked after the first four digits, suddenly dialed.

"Podiatry," a voice said.

She hung up the phone quickly, stood looking at it. She went back to the nurse's station.

"Is there a phone I can use?" she asked.

The nurse reluctantly uncradled a receiver, handed it across the desk. He punched in a nine. "What number?" he asked.

Lyndi gave him the number. She held the receiver to her ear, staring down the hall where Rudd's door was, just out of vision.

"Lyndi," the detective said when he realized who it was. "I'm sorry. Still no leads."

"No," she said. "It's not about that. It's about Rudd."

"Rudd? What about him?"

"Where's the guard?"

"Lyndi, you have to understand there's only so much we can do. He may never wake up."

"But the killer," she said. "He's still loose."

"I'm sorry," he said.

"But there was always a guard here before," she said. "Just a few more days."

"Lyndi," he said. "I sympathize. I really do. But I answer to the taxpayers."

She took the brakes off the wheels of the bed's casters. With a case shucked off a pillow, she tied the i.v. stand to the bed rail. Pushing the bed close to the door, she left it there while she went out and scanned the hall.

Nothing there, no one coming. Dragging the bed down the hall, she wheeled it toward the elevator. She pushed the button and the elevator opened immediately and she wheeled the bed in.

An old woman was inside, in the corner, wearing a checkered bathrobe. Around her neck was a chain with glasses on them, no lenses in the frames.

"Johnny?" the woman said.

"What?" said Lyndi. "No, not Johnny. This is Rudd."

"Johnny?" the woman asked again.

"What floor do you want?" asked Lyndi. "This floor? Were you looking for this floor?"

The woman said nothing, stayed in her corner. Lyndi reached out to press a button, felt the elevator lurch upward before she could do so. The wound on Rudd's throat was wet with blood, weeping slightly. The doors opened, and she saw before her two white-suited interns.

"Johnny?" the woman asked.

"There you are Mrs. Baetz," one of them said. "We've been looking for you."

"Excuse me," said Lyndi. The interns moved aside without even looking at her, one of them holding the elevator door back with his hand as Lyndi pushed the bed out.

"Come on out, Mrs. Baetz," one of the interns said.

"Johnny?" she said.

"No, Mrs. Baetz, I'm not Johnny," Lyndi heard him say and then she was down the hall, around a corner. *Outpatient,* a sign read. She heard shouting behind her, a high pitched voice. She moved toward a set of double doors that swung open on their own accord. She passed a deserted nurse's station, kept on down the hall, looking into each room until she found an empty one. Wheeling the bed in, she shut the door.

She turned the light off. A streetlight outside gave a pale and brittle quality to what she could see of the room. She undid the i.v. stand, checked the tube for kinks. Putting down the rail and sitting on the edge of the bed, she undid the restraints on Rudd's hands as well. She folded his hands on his chest, the i.v. tube drawing tight, its terminating needle bulging slightly beneath his skin. She kept her hands on his hands.

She stroked his cheek. He was not unattractive, she told herself, though emaciated now. She was used to his face, at least. Her hand slid down his jaw and onto his throat, felt the smooth, dribbled scar, the dampness of the weeped blood. She could feel the slow pulse in his neck.

She got out of the bed and went to the other side, took down the rail. Slowly and carefully, she tugged him over, the bed sliding on its casters. She set the brakes, pulled him over until his shoulder hung off the edge.

Going to the other side of the bed she tucked herself under the i.v. tube and climbed in with him, stretching her body next to his. She carefully stretched her arm over him, letting her hand rest upon the sharp carriage of his hips. She stayed like that, listening to his shallow breathing, speaking softly to him. Soon she fell asleep.

When she awoke, she was uncertain of where she was. There was someone beside her and a hand on her shoulder. She shrugged and the hand slid off. She lifted her head and saw the face beside her in the dim light. Its eyes were fluttering open and closed.

"Rudd?" she said.

"No," he said, and closed his eyes.

She said his name again, but he said nothing. She wondered if she had dreamt it. She shook him, nothing happened.

"Rudd?" she said again.

She got up out of the bed, wandered the room. Maybe she should call someone, she thought. But if it were just a dream?

She went to the window, looked out. Below, the hospital parking lot was lit dimly by streetlamps. She found her car, parked near one of the lampposts. Perhaps it was nothing, she thought. Perhaps she had imagined it. She went back to the bed and climbed in. She looked into Rudd's face, waiting.

When she awoke again it was light, sun streaming into the room through the window, the fluorescent lights on above her as well. There was a doctor just beside her and a nurse too, and Rudd's mother as well, looking stricken.

"There you are," said the doctor. "We wondered what you'd done with him."

"I was saving him," she said. "The killer."

"She was kidnapping him. Call the police," said Rudd's mother.

"Now, let's think a minute," said the doctor, turning toward her. "There's no harm done, really. No need to bring the police in, is there?"

Lyndi climbed out of the bed. "I was protecting him," she said. "He woke up."

Rudd's mother looked at her. "I want her arrested."

"Now, now," said the doctor, smiling. "Let's have none of that." He reached out, took the boy's face in his hands, examining it by holding it still and moving his own face frenetically about. Rudd's eyelids fluttered.

"He was doing that before," said Lyndi.

"Was he now?" said the doctor. "Rudd, can you hear me?"

Rudd opened his eyes and looked up, looked at Lyndi. He held her gaze, quiet. His expression was placid, almost not an expression at all. He stayed looking at her, until his mother elbowed Lyndi aside, and, effusive and enveloping, embraced Rudd's suddenly terrified face.

4

After a while she was back to her real life—the end of classes, her few school acquaintances leaving for the holidays, scattered phone calls from her aunt, occasional visits from church members and neighbors, late night television until she fell asleep on the same couch she had been sitting on when she first received news of her family's deaths. She was alone.

Over break, she woke up in the early morning and pulled herself off the couch, turned off the TV, and stumbled upstairs to sleep a few more hours in her own bed. When she awoke, she showered in her parents' bathroom; afterwards, a towel wrapped around her head and another knotted just above her breasts, she went slowly through her parents' closet, just looking. She rearranged the drawers of the kitchen, put them back to how they had been before her aunt had arrived, and then spent four or five days opening the wrong drawers until her body was trained again.

A neighbor tried to set her up with her nephew, a pouting fraternity brat who had few interests outside of skiing and bubblegum rap. She started going to church again, made it through the immense pressure of attention on her first day back.

"Where are your parents?" Sister Woolsey, a cantankerous and catheterized widow in a wheelchair bellowed. "Why didn't you bring them along?"

"They're dead, Mother," Lyndi heard Sister Woolsey's granddaughter whisper.

"Good thing she didn't bring them, then."

She was going on, she was getting along. She took a job gift-wrapping for the university bookstore, found herself the only gift-wrapper under fifty. *Come out and visit for Christmas,* her aunt suggested to her answering machine, *if you can afford it.* She didn't bother to return the call. There was a singles congregation locally, the bishop let her know—*maybe you'd prefer to attend church there? Perhaps you'll find this book interesting?*, offering her *The Seven Habits of Highly Successful People*. There was a picture of a bald man on the front. She thanked him, and fled his office as soon as she could.

At first, through the windows, she could see a fine snow, tiny flakes drifting in the air without settling, the air bitter cold. Quarter to five. She tore another piece of tape off the roll, creased the paper, folded it. "Next," she said.

When she had finished wrapping—board games, scriptures, inspirational tapes, even a book or two, lines from nine in the morning until six when the bookstore closed—she walked out through the Wilkinson Center, past the theater, down the stairs and past the flower shop, under the awning and out into the open air.

She crossed the street to her car, one of the few left in the lot. She got in, turned on the car, then sat there. Snow was coming down quicker now and gathering on the glass. She could not bring herself to drive. *What's wrong with me?* she wondered. The snow gathered until she could see nothing, the car enclosed and silent, the whole of the world outside blotted out. There was nothing but herself and the interior of the car. She found the thought alarming and flicked the windshield wipers once, the snow scraping back. Yet the glass was so fogged within that it was still difficult to see. She brought her hand to the gear shift, but already the snow had begun to fill in the windshield and, as it did so, she was again unable to bring herself to drive.

Why is it? she thought. And then, *What is it about parking lots?*
And, *What if he comes after me?*
Who?
The one who came after my family.
And who was he?
I don't know.

She had been worried for Rudd because he had seen the killer. Rudd *knew*. Or might know. But what of her? She was the only member of her family left. If the killer had meant to kill her father and mother and sister, if this was not some random crime or accident of fate, then there was every reason to believe he might come after her. Yet the police had immediately assumed the crime was random, had never given her a guard, had done nothing, not a thing, to protect her. Anyone could kill her at any time.

She remembered, in the other parking lot, the odd procession of the dead she had seen—her father, her mother, her sister, and finally Rudd, not

dead, lagging behind, though when she had first seen it she thought it meant that Rudd too had died. Were she to open her door here, in this parking lot, would she see them again?

She tried again to drive the car, again could not bring herself to do so. A white haze hung before her eyes and even when she cleared the windshield again it was still there, and she was uncertain whether it came from outside or from within, or somehow both. She could hear, through the wind, the voice of her father, slight, almost indiscernible, yet somehow there. Or was it her father? Perhaps it was not him at all but the killer, or maybe just the wind. She raked the windshield wipers along the windshield again, saw nothing. There was nothing out there, she told herself, though she was uncertain as to whether she meant nothing to be afraid of or nothing at all. She put her hand against the windshield, felt the cold. She managed to engage the gear and then, unable to see, disengaged it again. Setting the defroster on, she steeled herself, threw open the car door.

The parking lot was covered with snow, her car the only one visible, everything else snow-bundled and shapeless, utterly silent. She didn't know whether to be relieved at not seeing the dead or terrified of being alone. The snow fell thicker and thicker. She climbed back into the car, turned on the headlights. A moment more and the windshield cleared and she could see out, her headlights cutting a few dozen feet into the snow, the flakes flurrying all about her. She forced the car into reverse and drove.

At home, a message from the detective involved with her parents' case. No news, he was sorry to report, but the boy, Rudd, had been deemed *sufficiently stable and noncomatose, I'm sorry, I'm reading off notes here,* and was now ready to be interviewed. Would she perhaps like to come as well? Perhaps he would say something to trigger something for her, a phrase the police might not catch. It would be a help if she came.

When she arrived, they led her to the interrogation room. The detective was inside, Rudd as well. She stood with several other officers behind the mirrored wall, looking in.

"You're the one who . . ." said one of the officers, a pudgy man holding a clipboard, as he pointed at her. "Your family was . . ."

"Yes," she said quickly. "That's me."

The sound out of the speaker was grainy, off-kilter. "And the last thing you remember?" the detective said.

"There isn't any last thing I remember," Rudd responded.

"Do you know him?" the officer beside her asked.

"Sort of," she said.

"Don't be silly. There has to be a last thing."

"I can't explain it. I was there on the slope, crouched, could hear voices but saw no one, and then some other things happened but I can't quite remember what they were. But I remember them happening. It's all a haze."

"A haze?"

"You know what I mean?"

"Sorry, it just sounds like something from TV. Would you be willing to be hypnotized?"

Rudd hunched his shoulders. "Sure," he said.

His voice was not what she, sitting beside his body in the hospital, had imagined it would be. Maybe it was just the loudspeaker. But his movements, too, were more nervous, jerkier than she had imagined. In the hospital, in her one-sided conversations with him, she had imagined certain gestures and sounds sitting like an armature on the template of his stilled body, but she had been wrong about them.

The detective asked Rudd if he knew Lyndi's father.

"No."

They showed Rudd a picture of her father.

"No."

"Ever see him before?"

"No."

"Not even the day they were killed?"

"Not even then."

"What about during the things you remember happening but you don't remember what they were?"

"I don't remember, but I don't think so."

"You saw who killed them?"

"No."

"You saw who tried to kill you?"

"No."

"Did you see anyone at all?"

"I saw no one."

"The voices you heard when you were on the slope: what were they saying?"

"I wasn't close enough to hear what they were saying."

"And that's your last memory?"

"I told you—there isn't any last thing that I remember."

It went on a while, circling always back to the same question and Rudd's odd refusal to acknowledge a final event. They would fetch a hypnotist, the detective said. But an hour later when the man was brought in, he couldn't get Rudd to go under. They tried a few more times in other ways, then he went away.

"Why were you up in the mountains?" the detective asked Rudd.

Rudd shrugged. "Recreation?" he suggested.

"But your mother says you're afraid of heights."

"My mother still thinks I'm five."

"You're not afraid of heights?"

"They take a little getting used to."

She herself, Lyndi thought, had once been afraid of heights. Once, when she was eleven and her father had stopped the car at a lookout going through the mountains on the way to Colorado, she had refused to get out of the car. She had lain flat on the back seat, a blanket over her head, shivering.

"Why do you think he chose you?"

"He who?"

"The killer."

"I don't know," Rudd said, pushing his hair back from his forehead. "How should I know?" There was a certain pained expression to his face. "Probably because I was there."

They kept talking. There was nothing, nothing, Lyndi thought. Sometimes the police around her would look at her after Rudd had said something, mentioned a name or a place, but each time she shook her head. The detective came out of the interrogation room, spoke to her briefly. She did nothing but shake her head. The detective sighed and went back in. Through the glass she saw Rudd take a handkerchief out of his pocket and begin wiping his neck. It came away bloodstreaked. They were wrapping it up, the detective's voice slower and more relaxed, Rudd claiming he wished he could have been of help. The policemen were moving off and down the halls, except the pudgy one, who asked her,

"You know the way out?"

"I think so," she said, and pointed around a corner.

"Go this way," he said, pointing in a different direction, "and you won't risk bumping into him."

"I don't mind running into him," she said.

The policeman saluted her with his coffee cup and left. She circled round the corner and down the hall. Behind her she heard a door open, then the sound of the detective and Rudd's tentative conversation. She half-turned, waved.

"Lyndi," said the detective.

She stopped, waited for them to catch up. "What is it?" she asked.

"Nothing," he said. "I was just saying hello."

She nodded. Rudd was holding his hand out to her. "In the hospital room, right?" he said.

"Yes," she said.

"My mother doesn't like you," he said. "Don't take it personally."

She nodded.

"You look like your father," he said. "At least like the picture of him they showed me."

Not knowing what to say, Lyndi said, "Thank you. About my father, I mean."

"You have a way home?" the detective asked.

"Scooter," said Rudd.

"It's snowy," said the detective. "Probably iced over."

"I can give him a ride if he'd like," said Lyndi. "You can pick the scooter up in the morning."

He looked at her, then shrugged.

On the way through the parking lot, walking slightly behind him, she kept expecting to see before him, through the snow, her dead father, her dead family. *What does it mean?* she asked herself, *that coming behind Rudd now comes not the killer,* as she had thought in that other parking lot might happen, *but myself?*

"What are you doing for Christmas?" he asked once she had started the car.

"I don't know," she said. "No plans."

"You don't have any other family?"

"Not around here."

He leaned over and smiled. "Maybe I'll try to visit you," he said.

"You don't have to."

"After all, you visited me."

She smiled. "o.k.," she said. "Drop by."

That was the start of it. Her doorbell rang early Christmas morning, waking her from where, again, she had fallen asleep on the couch. She stumbled to the door and opened it and there he was, bundled up so that only his eyes were showing, a present in one hand.

"No tree?" he asked.

"Couldn't see the point."

She opened the gift—a metal box of Almond Roca, something her father had loved but that always stuck to her teeth.

"Thank you," she said. "I wish I had something for you."

He smiled and ducked his head.

She got him a glass of orange juice, left him watching a parade on TV while she went upstairs, showered, put on jeans and a blouse. When she came downstairs, he described some of the floats she had missed, and they sat together on the couch, watching. After a while she got up and went into the kitchen, came back with two bowls of Corn Chex, a jug of milk.

They sat beside each other, crunching.

"You ever make that party mix?" he asked.

"No," she said. "My mom used to, though."

"Not my mom," he said. "But I had it this one time somewhere."

She went back into the kitchen, returned with the Chex box. There was a recipe for the mix on the side. Soon they were both in the kitchen, her mother's largest glass bowl out, mixing what was left of the cereal with butter and salt.

The phone rang and she went into the other room to get it. It was her aunt, first wishing her Merry Christmas and then berating her for not having come to California. "Thank you, I'm sorry, I'm sorry," Lyndi said.

"And then the neighbor?" her aunt was saying. "You know Mrs. Miller, not a neighbor exactly, but down the street, the colostomy woman?"

It was the latest installment in her aunt's life of grief and pain. Lyndi nodded and offered noncommittal sounds as the story droned along—Mrs. Miller and her colostomy bag and her swinging, cradle-robbing lifestyle, which seemed to consist, as far as Lyndi could tell, of her aunt having seen Mrs. Miller once give her paperboy a kiss on the cheek. "But, heavens, could you believe it," said her aunt, she had looked out the window, early this morning and there was Mrs. Miller, "bright as day and twice as ugly"—or as her aunt said it, "hugly"—"on the front steps, wearing hardly more than a bathrobe—"

"Aunt Debby," said Lyndi. "I have to go."

Her aunt fell silent. Lyndi stayed listening to the static. "Aunt Debby?" said Lyndi.

"Well," said her aunt icily. "If that's the way you're going to be, I suppose there's hardly any point in trying to bring you any Christmas cheer."

"Aunt, it's not that," said Lyndi.

"You have to want to heal," her aunt said. "But if you want to go through life with a gaping hole where your heart should be, far be it from me to—"

"—I have guests over," said Lyndi. "That's all."

Again the line was silent. On TV, Lyndi could see the parade winding down. She heard Rudd still rumbling about in the kitchen.

"Guests?" her aunt said in a tiny voice.

"Guest, really," she said. "A boy I know."

"Lyndi, you're dating and you haven't told me?"

"No," said Lyndi. It's not that exactly. It's just—"

"Would your mother approve?"

"Approve?"

"How old is this boy?"

"About my age."

"How much older? Some rapacious college senior, I suppose?"

"A few months younger, actually."

"You need a chaperone, Lyndi," said her aunt, finding her strength of voice once again. "You're clearly too young to be inviting teenage boys over for Christmas, and he's certainly too young to be accepting invitations from an older woman."

"We're not even dating," she said. "I hardly know him and I'm not looking for a boyfriend and, besides, he's shy."

"It hardly matters," her aunt said. "Every husband I had, I found by not looking. The shy ones are the worst. Now you get off this phone and hustle that boy out of the house this instant."

She hung up the telephone. She felt exhausted, drained. In the bathroom, she splashed cold water on her face, accidentally got some down the front of her blouse. She looked at her face in the mirror: it was her, she was fine, she didn't look that upset.

In the kitchen, Rudd had taken the Party Mix out of the oven, had put it on the stovetop. He was picking through, eating all the Corn Chex.

They poured the mix back into the bowl and carried it out to the couch, sat watching *It's a Wonderful Life*. A couple she barely knew came to her door with a plate of fudge, a note on it reading, *Happy Holidays, in your time of grief.* "Thank you," said Lyndi. "Thank you very much." The woman was trying to peer around her for a better look at Rudd. She kept it up until Lyndi, thanking her a third time, shut the door in her face.

After a few hours she made him some lunch. They talked about nothing, or nothing much. He was just out of high school, he said; he hadn't realized she was in college. They were nearly the same age, she said, so what did it matter? Her aunt called back to leave a vague but dire warning that filled up the answering machine tape. This was a *vulnerable time,* her aunt said, among other things, and *the world was full of wolves.*

"Your aunt seems a little bit unusual," Rudd suggested, but not unkindly.

She nodded, laughed. She got out Monopoly and they played through most of the afternoon. When it began to get dark outside, she went out to the garage freezer, looked through it until she found a honey-baked ham. She defrosted it in the microwave, began heating it up in the oven, made some mashed potatoes as well. They were lumpy, and there was not enough salt. "These are good potatoes," he said, and then told her how they had probably glazed the ham with a blowtorch.

Then dinner was over and he was awkwardly washing the dishes in the sink like dishes were something he had never washed before. She dumped the rest of the ham into the garbage and scraped the last of the mashed potatoes into the garbage as well. He was at the door, zipping his coat up to the neck, zipperhead glinting below his scar.

"Thank you for coming," she said.

"Can I visit you again?"

"I'd like that," she said.

He gave her a hug so awkward and crushing that it was clear his experience with women was entirely theoretical. And then, suddenly, he was out the door, gone.

5

L ater she could not remember how things became serious. There had been Christmas together and then she had seen him a few more times, and then he had fought with his mother and had shown up distraught, kissing her for the first time. And then suddenly he was living in her house without either of them really having talked it over. Both of them were chaste still and sleeping in separate rooms, but clearly on the way somewhere neither her aunt nor his mother nor the Church would approve of. By that time, trying to puzzle out how it had all happened, it seemed too late to turn back.

Besides, she was not sure she wanted to turn back. Left from her days in the hospital was the residual sense of connection to him, though in the first few weeks of living with him she realized she knew him hardly at all. There was an oddness to him, strange ticks, a tendency to lie about things that couldn't possibly matter, even at times a certain transient coldness she quickly began to classify as his *moods*. There were whole days she never saw him, days he spent completely out of the house or locked in the room he'd claimed, her sister's old room. Days too when she found him in the utility room staring at the clippings of the murders.

"Do you want me to take those down?" she asked, but he shook his head.

Other days, he was charming, sweet. He would make dinner with her, sit on the couch with her, take her tentatively in his arms and embrace her, but it never went further than a few awkward kisses. She wondered if there was something wrong with him, sexually. But he seemed normal enough in other ways. Maybe he was simply chaste. As a Mormon, she tried to convince herself, that was something she could admire and respect. Perhaps he was just saving himself for marriage.

They were mostly cordial to one another, polite even, even if at times he was a little abrupt. A few days after he moved in, she gave him a key to the front door, working it off a ring kept in her father's dresser drawer. He began to come and go at will, sometimes waking her when he came stumbling past the couch at three or four in the morning smelling of smoke or dirt, never explaining. After the first few times of not questioning him about it, she felt her chance to speak had passed. Instead she tried to train herself to wake up right after Letterman, go up to her own bed before he came in. It was easier sleeping in her own bed once someone else was living in the house.

"Do you miss your mother?" she asked him, a few weeks after he had moved in, both of them sitting on the couch.

"No," he said simply.

She waited for him to explain, but he didn't. They sat watching TV. "I miss mine," she finally said.

He turned the channel. "I might miss mine if she were dead," he said.

She didn't know what to say. She felt vaguely hurt but tried to push it out of her mind.

"What about your father?" she asked, and watched a strange, frightened look come over his face.

On TV: a small man and a tall man. The tall man was lumbering into things, slowly and ponderously. The small man kept darting through the tall man's legs and punching him in the stomach. There was a laugh track going. *Does he qualify as a midget or a dwarf?* she wondered. The small man was wearing a padded suit and a mask, so she couldn't say for certain.

She was doing homework for one of the two classes she was taking, her papers spread out across the desk, when he came in, dragging his backpack along the floor, abandoning it next to the couch.

"Good day at school?" she asked.

But he didn't seem to hear. Shrugging off his coat, he went into the kitchen.

"Rudd?"

She could hear him moving about, the refrigerator door opening and closing. She got up and went into the kitchen herself.

"Can't you hear me?" she asked.

"What," he said flatly, without turning around.

"What's wrong?" she asked.

"Nothing's wrong," he said.

She put up her hands and went out, confused. She sat down again with her homework, tried to go through it. She watched him come out again, pick up his backpack, shuffle down the hall.

She listened for the sound of his door opening and closing, heard nothing. She finished her homework and then sat at the table, staring at her pen, turning it slowly about in her hands. Finally she got up and went down the hall herself.

His door was closed. She knocked but had no answer. So she opened it, looked in. She uttered his name, inflecting the syllable upward, before realizing the room was empty.

Closing the door, she continued down the hall.

He was there, in the utility room, in front of the washer and dryer, staring at the clippings.

"What is it?" she asked. "What's wrong?"

He turned his head toward her, slowly, face slack, eyes dim. "Lael," he said. "What happened to Lael?"

"No," the detective said. "I'm sorry. No such person. No Lael Korth and no Lael anyone else for that matter."

"In Springville," Rudd said. "In the middle of town. I've been to his house."

The detective turned to her. "Does the name mean anything to you?" he asked.

Lyndi shook her head. The detective looked back to him and shrugged.

"But—" said Rudd.

"There's a Lyle Korth, roughly your age, lives in Springville. Mother by the name of Anne Korth. We contacted him. Says he doesn't know you, doesn't think he's ever met you. That's the best we can do."

"But his name is Lael," Rudd insisted.

"Then why didn't you mention it before?" asked the detective. "Where is this coming from?"

It went on like that, Rudd insisting there was a Lael Korth and that it was Lael Korth who had been with him the night of the murders—that was the real last thing he remembered, he said now: Lael's face beside his own, darkness coming on. Threading his fingers over his belly, the detective leaned back in his chair. He had been on a scooter with Lael, Rudd said, and then suddenly not on the scooter at all and instead both of them pushing their way up the slope, in the canyon somewhere, his breath coming hard, and something in his . . .

"What?" asked the detective.

"Nothing," said Rudd. "There was nothing. I'm starting to make things up."

"In his hand, you mean? What was he holding?"

"I was wrong," said Rudd. "That part I was wrong about."

"And his name?" said the detective. "Were you wrong about his name as well?"

Rudd shook his head. The detective got up to shake Rudd's hand and said thank you, he'd look into it, Rudd was right to come to him, but information like this, what was he to do?

In the car, Lyndi didn't know what to think. Rudd was beside her, looking ill and still going on about Lael, claiming now that Lael was in fact his half-brother, that they had that connection, that nobody had ever understood him except for Lael.

"Perhaps your mother would know where he is," she said.

No, he claimed, that was just it. Lael was his father's child, from a second wife, a secret wife—he had only learned of it himself by accident. There was no point in going to his mother.

"Surely," she said, "there's someone or something else you could—"

No, no, no, he said, his voice impatient. Lael had his own life in Springville but he hadn't been part of it, just as Rudd had had his own life in Provo and Lael hadn't been part of that either. If the situation were reversed, Lael wouldn't know who to ask either. *Rudd who?* people would probably say to him; there's no such person.

"Your name's not Rudd?" she asked.

"Of course it is," he said. "Rudd Elling Theurer. But if you called my mother now and asked to speak to her son she'd say 'Son? I have no son.'"

"Because you're living with me."

"She might do it even if I were still living at home," he said.

They drove a while and then she said, just to make conversation, "I didn't know your middle name was Elling."

"I don't have a middle name," he said, his face white with surprise. "And it's certainly not Elling."

"But you said—"

"I said nothing of the kind," he said. "Rudd Theurer, plain and simple."

She dropped him off at the house. He climbed out and tottered toward the door. He had said it, she thought. *Elling.* She had heard it plain as day. What point was there saying it if it weren't true? And, if it were true, what point trying to hide it? It was just a name. Do I hate him or love him? she asked herself. Do I know him well enough to do one or the other? No, she thought. And then, He needs someone to take care of him.

She backed out of the driveway and down the street, down past the church and the Baileys' brick house, then more houses and the Roberts' field and the second church, the one set back from the road, and Rock Canyon Elementary with the roadrunner on the marquee. There were kids playing on the playground. PTA MEET THURS 7, the marquee said, the "7" actually an upside-down "L." She reached the end of the street, turned left past the Missionary Training Center and the temple, on down Ninth East, past Allen's Grocery, *Closed Sundays* blinking on their sign, down past the university to Center street, and then past that too, the road curving toward the cemetery. Then left, out to the state highway, toward Springville.

The small house was on Third, a few blocks east of Main. It stood on a corner, red brick with peeling white trim, small and square. Built, she guessed, sometime in the forties. The door itself was odd, a grayish green more like primer than finish paint, flecked with yellow from a paint that either had been over it and was nearly scraped away or underneath it and was now wearing through.

She rang the doorbell. The plastic, cracked from exposure, scratched against the pad of her thumb.

Inside, a chime struck flatly like a battery somewhere was worn down. Some sort of song, impossible to say what it was.

She waited, was hooking her hair over her ears when the door opened.

A boy in his teens, blond and large, his skin pale, eyes green.

"You want my mother, I'm guessing," he said, and gestured back into the house.

"No," she said. "I'm looking for Lael."

"Lyle?" he said. "That's me."

"But you go by Lael."

"No," he said. "I go by Mark. That's my middle name."

"You've never gone by Lael?"

"What's this about?" he asked. "It wasn't you who called, was it? I mean, it was a man who called, but is that what this is about too?"

"Kind of," she said. "It has to do with my boyfriend."

She was surprised to hear herself use the word, *boyfriend*. True, he kissed her sometimes but it was distracted, passionless, infrequent, indifferent.

"—Lael," he was saying. "That's crazy."

She nodded. "Do you know Rudd Theurer?" she asked.

"Rod who? I already told the man no," he said. "Look, maybe if you have a picture, I've seen him or something."

"Never mind," she said, and walked back to her car.

The boy stayed on the porch while she got in, arms folded over his chest. There was something wrong, she thought as she drove back toward town. *A screw loose,* her father used to say of himself, joking, tapping one side of his own head, but with Rudd it seemed larger than that, not just a screw but a whole mechanism starting to grind itself up. Who was he? She hardly knew. But worse than that was that he himself did not seem to know either. *I should send him back to his mother,* she thought. But he hated his mother; it couldn't be any good for him to go back; she had to think of what was best for him as well as for her. No, she could not make him go back there, but he would have to leave her house. Surely there was a relative he could stay with, everyone has a relative. And then she thought, *No, I don't have one, not a sane one anyway, why should he?* But still, she was confused, she needed some distance. Mother or not, Rudd would have to go.

But when she got home she found him lying on the couch, wrapped in a blanket, only his face showing. He was asleep, face untroubled as cream. *No,* she told herself, *it can wait until tomorrow.*

She sat on the floor with her back against the couch. Whatever was wrong with him it was still good to have someone else in the house. She didn't mind taking care of him. Sending him back to his mother might kill him.

She had the TV on and the sound muted. She kept on slouching a little farther until finally she turned off the TV and undid the top button of her jeans, lay down completely, fell asleep there at his feet.

A day later or perhaps two, a Saturday, he had left for somewhere, hadn't said where, still hardly speaking to her, and she was going out the door herself, her coat on. Instead, she thought twice and went back inside, went to Rudd's door. She knocked once just to make sure, her gloves rendering damp sounds against the wood, and then opened the door and looked in.

It seemed an ordinary enough room, not far from the room it had been when her sister was still alive—same unmade bed, same walls, her sister's knickknacks piled on the three shelves to the right of the door. Rudd's own things, his clothing, stood in neat piles beneath the shelves.

Next to his clothes was a pile of never-returned school books, and then a box with crusted and brittle tape stuck along the open flaps. She opened it.

Inside were more old books, religious volumes: *Mormon Doctrine,* worm-eaten copies of the seven-volume *A History of the Church,* a *Doctrines of Salvation,* an old and tattered spiralbound typescript of something called *The Confessions of John D. Lee.* At the very bottom, freshly Scotch-taped to the floor of the box, was a Western States road map.

She put the books back, covering the map up. She picked up the books lying next to the box, each of them wrapped in brown paper so that she had to open the covers to tell what they were. Rudd had written his name in cursive, *Rudd Theurer,* on the title page of each, the names of the previous students there as well but crossed out, except on the title page of his English anthology where was written instead *Lael Korth* in a different hand.

She was dreaming and knew she was dreaming, but in the dream she was awake. She was lying in bed in her parents' room, the lights off, when she heard the door open and someone enter.

It was a figure that she could hardly make out for darkness. It hesitated in the doorway a moment and then glided silently in.

"Father?" she asked.

The figure didn't answer. She could hardly see it at all, a sort of ripple in the darkness as it slowly came forward.

"Mother?" she said. Then, "Rudd?"

And then the figure stepped forward and she knew, without knowing how she knew, that this was Elling.

She woke up on the couch, the TV nothing but static. There was above her a shape, crouched and not quite human.

"It's just me," said Rudd. "Nothing to be afraid of."

She sat up, wondering if this was still the dream, and brushed her hair out of her face.

"You startled me," she said. "Where have you been?"

"Out," he said.

"What time is it?" she asked.

"Late," he said.

"I want to know," she asked. "Who is Elling?"

"Elling," he said carefully. In the darkness, with the light of the TV behind him, he had a dark hole in lieu of a face.

"Or do you have a middle name after all?" she asked.

"I don't have one," he said quickly. "We've been through that."

"Elling? Lael? What's it all about, Rudd? Be honest with me for once."

"They have nothing to do with each other," he said.

"What are you hiding?" she asked.

"Stop it," he said. "Don't get like that with me."

She crossed her arms over her chest. "Maybe this isn't working out between us," she said. "Maybe you should leave."

"We'll talk in the morning," he said. He turned the TV off, started down the hall.

"I mean for good," she called after him. "I mean get out!"

"Good night," he said, and going into her sister's room, closed the door.

The next morning she felt guilty. *No, it was the dream, I was reacting to the dream, not to him. He's just a kid, even younger than me, and boys are less mature than girls anyway. I'm pushing him too hard, he's doing the best he can.* She had gone through a lot, true, this year, but he had gone through more, she had to remember that. She had to cut him a little slack. First his throat and chest cut open and then weeks in the hospital unconscious. He was still recovering, she told herself and then winced, thinking it precisely the sort of thing her aunt might say.

They had breakfast together and she was cordial, and neither he nor she said a thing about the previous night. At the end of the meal he came around to her side of the table and leaned down.

"You've been good to me," he said, and smiled.

For an instant it seemed like Christmas again. Maybe this was enough, she thought. Maybe it would be all right. Maybe it would all work out after all.

6

And then it was summer. She was in shorts most of the time now and things seemed largely better for him, his moods striking him less often. He was more affectionate, but still chaste, hardly going further than a few kisses or letting her lay her head in his lap. That was enough, Lyndi told herself, she could be happy with that.

But then he installed a lock on her sister's bedroom door, a simple latch that screwed into door and frame. He kept the room locked with a padlock when he was out. Perhaps he had figured out that she had come into the room, had been through his books. It didn't bother her, she told herself. It was her house and he wasn't paying any rent, but so what—he wanted some privacy, needed some. She could understand that. He would need that, wouldn't he, if he were to open up to her in other ways?

The detective called, inviting Rudd to go up the canyon, back to the murder site, hoping that being there again might spark something in Rudd's memory. No, Rudd said, he was forgetting that part of his life, moving on. The detective asked to speak to Lyndi. She got on the line and he asked her to please talk to Rudd, to try to convince him. The investigation was dead in the water, he said, no way around it, a killer was loose, months had gone by, they had a moral obligation, it needed to be jump-started. How strange, the detective said, to think of the two of them living together, and she said, living together but not sleeping together, just a question of loneliness and neither of them having anyone else to speak of. The detective was silent on the line for a long while, then said, "Not even sleeping together, if you'll excuse my saying so, it's even stranger than I thought."

She moved the phone to her other ear. "We're Mormon," she said.

"Of course you are," he said, but that was not what he had called about, was it? Only would she, please, see what she could do?

When she got off the telephone, she knocked on his door. He didn't answer.

"Rudd?" she said.

She put her hand on the knob and opened the door a crack. Inside, the room was dark. "Rudd?" she said again.

"Don't come in," he said. "This is my room. Never come in."

"But I just—"

"Shut the door," he said.

She pulled the door shut, stood outside, examining the grain of the wood. Finally she knocked.

"Rudd," she said. "We need to talk."

She pressed her ear to the door. She could hear him get up off his bed and move across the floor, the door creaking as he leaned against it.

"Talk," he said.

She moved her head back from the door. "Will you please come out?" she asked.

"I don't think so," he said.

"Look, I was talking to the detective on the telephone—"

"No," he said.

"But," she said. "The investigation. It's the only way—"

"No," he said.

"Rudd," she said. "Be reasonable."

"I don't want to go. It's a mistake."

Why, she asked, why a mistake? She could understand why he would be afraid of going back, but a mistake? Why? Perhaps in the long run it was something he needed, she suggested through the door, the victim returning to the scene of the crime.

"Why?" he said. "W-H-Y."

"Why are you spelling it?" she asked. "It's only three letters. That's so condescending." There was something wrong with his voice, a strain to it, nothing she could quite put her finger on. Perhaps it was just the muffling of the door between them, but it seemed more than that.

"It's the killer that returns to the scene of the crime," he said. "Not the victim. The victim keeps as far away from the crime scene as possible, otherwise it seeps up to stain the present."

"That doesn't even sound like you," she said. "That's something you read somewhere."

"You want me to go?" he said, yelling. "You want that?" He threw open the door, and she saw his face red and contorted, mouth quivering. "I'll go," he yelled, "but it's a mistake, beginning to end." And then he slammed the door and she was left, alone and hurt, in the hall.

They took the detective's car up to the campsite parking, walked the rest of the way. Rudd was pale, and looked helpless. She would protect him. She wouldn't let anything happen to him. She took his hand, found it clammy. He pulled it slowly away.

"Here it is," the detective said and then stood there, with his hands on his hips, watching Rudd. Rudd kept reaching out and scratching his throat, again and again until it began to bead with blood. The detective took out his handkerchief, polished his eyeglasses with it, then handed it to Rudd. Rudd took it, stared at it as if he didn't know what to do with it.

"Wipe your throat," said Lyndi.

He did, then drew the handkerchief away to look at it.

"I bet you were right here," said the detective, and pointed. "That's the hill you must have been talking about," he said, moving his finger slightly. He turned around. "Then the bodies, there, there, there, there."

"No," said Rudd. "Nothing is coming to me. I'd like to go home."

"You don't remember anything? Any little thing?"

"No."

"Which body was my father's?" asked Lyndi.

"There," said the detective, swiveling and pointing.

"And my mother?"

"There," he said again, then turned back to Rudd. "This *Lael,* you still insist he was here?"

"No," he said.

"No?"

"I don't know where that came from," he said. "Some sort of dream."

"Strange," said the detective.

"Surely there's something," said Lyndi. "How can you not remember anything?"

"I don't know," Rudd said, and looked at her pleadingly.

"Anything could be useful," said the detective. "Anything at all."

He stood. *Pretending to think,* she thought. He wiped his neck again. He wasn't even trying. It made her furious. "No," he said. "Nothing."

"All right," the detective said. "Worth a try. Let's go home."

•

In the car, he tied the detective's handkerchief around his neck, like a bandanna. *So fucking cavalier,* she thought, though she was not precisely sure if *cavalier* was the right word. He was smiling too—at least she thought so at first, but when she leaned forward found it to be more a look of terror than a smile. She hated him and felt sorry for him all at once.

"You've remembered something," she said, low enough that the detective in the front seat wouldn't overhear.

He looked at her—startled, she thought. "No," he claimed.

"I can tell," she said. "The way you were looking, your face."

"Stop it," he said.

"You're hiding something," she said.

"It's not me," he said.

"What?" she said, her voice growing louder. "Are you accusing me? Because there are only two of us back here, and if it's not you, who does that leave?"

The detective said, "Everything all right back there?" She turned to see his eyes in the rearview mirror. She slumped over against the door, away from Rudd, resting her forehead on the car window.

At home, he went straight to his room. She tried to follow him in but he held the knob from the inside and she couldn't turn it.

"What's wrong with you?" she cried. "Why won't you tell me?"

She kept trying to turn the knob but he was too strong for her. Finally, frustrated, she let go, latched the door, put the padlock on.

"There," she said. "Now you'll have to listen. You aren't going anywhere until you've heard me out."

She kept at his door through the day and into the evening, talking, accusing him of protecting her parents' killer, his own near-killer. What was he hiding? she asked. Why wouldn't he tell? Was it because it sounded crazy? Even if it sounded crazy, it could help, she said. Anything could help. She'd try to believe him, she said, she'd try to understand, certainly she wouldn't call him crazy. Hadn't she gone looking for Lael when the detective himself couldn't be bothered? And besides, he had to talk to someone—if not her, to whom? Certainly not his mother, who was nothing but trouble: he had said so himself. Lael? But that was a dream, or some twisted and inaccurate memory, *Lael doesn't exist.* She was quoting him, needless to say. *And who is there for you, Rudd?* Sometimes he made her so mad she just wanted to call the police and have him forcibly removed from her house, the locks changed, and that would be that. They would never see each other again.

How would he like that? Sad, but maybe that was what needed to be done, she was running out of ideas. She cared for him, she admitted, but some days she did not know what to do with him. What was expected of her anyway? Were they dating? Were they a couple? Was he even physically attracted to her? Did he like girls at all? Frankly she wondered sometimes if it was just her he found unattractive or girls in general—

"I don't find you unattractive," he said through the door.

—good, she said, good, there was at least that, God give her strength, maybe he better start showing it a little more. *I was with you,* she said, *even before I knew anything about you. I was sitting next to you and waiting for you to wake up, hours at a time, God knows your mother never did that,* God knows that she herself, Lyndi, hadn't had to, but she had, and God knew how things had managed to get to this impasse from that innocent-enough debut, God only knew that it wasn't her fault, not her doing, if anyone was to blame it was him—him Rudd, not him God—but she had tried to understand, he had been through a lot, both when he had been almost killed and then even before that. She was trying to understand that, to cut him some proverbial slack, but she had been through a lot too, in one sense not as much and in another sense perhaps even more, several strokes of a knife and she had been cut loose from all her connections with the world. All she wanted was for him to be honest with her, tell her what he knew no matter how crazy it must sound, open up to her a little instead of brooding and letting it eat away his organs one by one. She sounded like a self-help book, she knew, but that was the simplest way to put it—at least the simplest way to put it when you were forced to talk through a door. Really she did care for him, and she was pretty sure he cared for her, but he was going to go mad if he kept on like he was, holding it all in—cliché, she knew, but it meant something too—you have to let someone, at least one person in the world, know who you are—

"I've failed you," he said through the door.

No, she said. Well yes, but don't think of it like that, life's not over yet, and hadn't they had good times too? Christmas, for instance, he had been charming then, and times since then too? No, not a failure, he shouldn't think of it that way, but yes they could do better, yes they had some things to work out, but he should stop thinking *I,* it was not *I* but *we,* and those things could be worked out, she was sure, she wasn't innocent either though certainly not as guilty as he was. This was all new to her, she was still figuring out how to make a relationship work. They could work together, but that was it, they had to work together, they had to work things out, *you have to tell me what you think and know, and let's figure it out, who was involved, who was responsible, you can't have secrets from me, tell me what you know Rudd, tell me what you—*

"I can't hold on anymore," he said. "You don't know," he said. "If you knew, I promise you."

"What?" she said.

"I want to die."

"To die? Why?"

But he didn't answer.

"What are you talking about? It's not better for me or for you either, and who else *is* there? I don't want that, that's the last thing I want. How could you possibly get that out of what I've been saying?"

She heard him wandering about the room, sobbing.

"You're an idiot," she said. "A fucking idiot." She stood up, rushed from the door and into the front room, dialed 911. An ambulance was on its way, she was told. She dropped the telephone, running back through the house and pounding on the door. "Rudd," she called. "Rudd?" She tried the door and he was no longer in front of it or holding the knob but the goddam padlock was on, she had put it on herself. She moved through the other rooms, looking for something to open the door, the floor fluid and threatening to come up against her as it had when she had been first told of her family's death. She made it down the hall and into the utility room—washer and dryer, the photos and articles on the murder, tool chest in the corner. She opened it, grabbed a Phillips screwdriver, rushed back to Rudd's door. Four screws on the hasp the lock was attached to, she started on the first, the screw threatening to strip at first and then groaning and coming out slowly and cleanly, falling to the carpet.

"Rudd, don't," she said.

Then the next one, turning lazily: maddening to have to wrap all her energy into the turning of one tiny screw. Falling out and then the next started, the sound of Rudd inside the room burbling and dropping heavily to the floor, Lyndi's mouth making noises that she could not control, shrieking, it wouldn't come, wouldn't quite start, and she pushed her whole body against the handle of the screwdriver, and the screw finally groaned loose and twisted free. Then the last screw coming somehow smoothly and quickly and she turned the doorknob and pushed her way in—

He was lying on the floor, a Swiss Army knife in his hand, all four of its blades open. His throat was open and gurgling and blood bubbled up from it, the collar of his T-shirt bloody, blood now leaking down the sides of his neck as well. She put her mouth to his mouth and blew, hearing the air hiss out of the slit in his throat as he coughed blood into her mouth. She covered the slit with one hand, felt the air go in and stay in, blood welling between her fingers. He coughed again, and she tasted blood in his mouth, but he was still breathing, still breathing, and then paramedics pushed her aside, carried him away.

She had to wait. She kept sliding her chair forward until it was almost touching the desk and she could lean forward, examine the series of paperweights he seemed to have arranged as a barrier of some kind between where she was sitting and where he would be soon. When he came in, he shook her hand; she bumped a knee on the desk trying to stand. He sat down, busied himself with Rudd's file.

"He's stable," he said.

She nodded.

"His voice might change, depending on how the windpipe heals. The skin on his neck, though, at least some of it, has been traumatized too severely to do much with. It might bleed a little from time to time, leak a bit. We've done what we can, will eventually have to graft." He looked at her closely. "He's done this before, hasn't he? Tried to kill himself?"

She shook her head. "No," she said. "Someone tried to kill him."

"Oh," he said. "Perhaps I'll post a suicide watch."

"I'll stay with him," she said.

"His arms, we'll keep him strapped down for a few days," he said. "Just to be safe."

"All right."

He stood and left the room and never came back. Eventually a nurse came and got her, ushered her to a post-op room. Rudd was lying in a bed, unconscious, arms strapped down.

"Don't undo those," said the nurse, pointing to the straps. "They're for his own protection."

She pulled the chair closer, sat beside the bed, resting her hand on his arm.

"We're back where we started," she said brightly. "Ready to try again?"

In and out of consciousness. Awake, asleep, awake. *Bring me my robe,* she thought she heard someone say. A thin silver thread that resolved itself, slowly, into a bed rail.

He was awake, trying to move his hands, the bed rail he was strapped to groaning. She told him it was all right, and he looked over as if noticing her for the first time. His neck was bandaged, the pad soaked sufficiently with blood that she could make out the stitched flesh beneath.

"No," she said. "Don't try to speak."

He kept touching his index finger to his thumb again and again, until finally she realized he wanted to write something. She went to the nurse's station and got a pen, a pad of post-it notes as well. She loosened the restraint a little, but still had to hold the pad for him, nosing it along so he could reach both sides and finish his words.

I'm sorry, he wrote.

"Don't do it again," she said. "Promise me."

He nodded. *I love you,* he wrote.

"I guess I feel strongly about you too," she said. "I sometimes wonder why. God only knows."

Scratch my face.

"Where on your face?"

Whole.

She put her hand on his face, moving it, asking him *Here? Here?* until he nodded slightly. She scratched until he burbled, then went back to the pad.

Marry me, he wrote.

"Are you serious?" she asked.

Say yes, he said.

"You're an idiot," she said. "A complete idiot."

Then thought, *I would have someone for good then. I've made so many mistakes, why not risk one more? It's about time things started working out for me.* Yet he was unstable. *But aren't I good enough to save him?*

Please, he had written. The "s" and the "e" written small beneath the other letters because he could not reach the far side of the pad:

Plea
se

"You're an idiot," she said again. And then suddenly was so afraid of what it might be like to be completely alone again, so afraid of whatever else she might bring upon herself if she said no, that she took the pad and wrote, carefully,

Yes

7

"No," said her aunt on the telephone. "I won't have it, you're too young, absolutely not." Rudd's mother had said the same thing—*unacceptable*—which made Lyndi, who had been wavering herself, feel now that she had something to prove.

Her bishop was admittedly cautious, but not without optimism. "Well," he said, "you're young, true, but people have married young before and still made their marriages last. How old are you?"

"Nineteen," she said.

He looked a little shocked. "That's young. And how old is he?"

"Nearly nineteen."

The Bishop put his elbows on his desk, leaned forward. "That's even younger," he said. "Usually boys that age are going on missions."

"He's been through a lot," she said, "being almost killed and all. He's still working through it. I don't think a mission is the best choice for him."

"Have you prayed about it?"

"Yes," lied Lyndi.

"And he's prayed about it?"

"Yes," she lied. "We both feel it's the right thing."

"Good," he said. "And of course you plan to do it right."

"Right?"

"Temple marriage, I mean."

"Oh," she said. "Of course."

He came back from the hospital, his neck still wrapped in gauze. Every day, she helped him change it. She peeled away the dressings, smeared the surface beneath with a cream they had given her. The grafted skin was angrier than the rest of his neck, a blotched swath across his throat.

"How do you feel?" she asked.

"Good," he said, his voice odd and sunken from all his neck had been through, his intonation having acquired a certain flatness.

"Do you love me?" she asked.

"Yes," he said, same flat voice, eyes dull.

Wrapping his neck back up, she made him a bowl of runny oatmeal. He dribbled it into his mouth slowly, as if in shock.

"I was thinking a simple reception," she said. "Something in the backyard, if anything at all."

He nodded. "I don't know anyone," he said.

"That's true," she said. "We've already got a house full of things. Maybe nothing at all, then. We won't tell anyone. It'll be like eloping."

He said nothing. He continued to eat, spoon lifting slowly to his lips, oatmeal sliding in.

He was normal now, she thought, subdued. Having his throat slit a second time had made him tractable. He had, at least temporarily, become a good listener, would sit still as she talked, answer only if he was asked a direct question or given a cue. She had the upper hand for once, she thought, knowing it was a mistake to think of relationships in such terms but thinking in them anyway.

It was the end of summer and she had started back at college again, a light load. He was too ill for school, he told her, still having difficulties with his neck, which, despite the graft, oozed when he exerted himself. "Kiss me," she would say, and he would, blandly, his neck glistening.

The day before the wedding, he began to get anxious.

"Why the temple?" he said, as they watched TV. "My throat hurts." Indeed, his throat where the skin was grafted was a deep red. "Maybe we should think about this a little more. Maybe we should just get married civilly."

"*I* don't have any doubts," she said. "But if *you* do, fine, we can wait."

"No," he said. "I'm just trying to talk myself into it."

"I don't have to talk myself into it."

"Please don't be like that," he said. "All I'm asking is if you're sure."

"Sure as I can be," she said.

"Have you prayed?" he asked.

"Not exactly," she said. "But I have a good feeling."

"A good feeling? Why haven't you prayed?"

"Why haven't you?"

"It doesn't work for me," he said. "Not any more. God doesn't answer my prayers."

"Maybe he answers them in ways you don't perceive. Or maybe the answers are *no*."

"No," he said. "God has drawn a curtain between myself and heaven and there is no parting it. When I was growing up I sometimes felt him. Now, never."

"What did you do?"

"Do?" he said, suspiciously. "Who said I did anything?"

She went into the utility room, took a load of clothing out of the dryer, put it into a basket. It was still a little damp. She moved the clothing from the washer into the dryer. She carried the basket back into the living room and began folding it while he flipped through channels.

"You don't believe in the Gospel?" she asked him.

"It's not as simple as that."

She slid off the couch and sat in front of it, to be closer to the basket.

"You had a good feeling," he said, and laughed. "Maybe if you actually prayed, God would have plenty to say about me."

"He'd tell me to go ahead," she said quickly.

"Perhaps he'd tell you to stay the hell away from me," he said. "Or perhaps he wouldn't bother to part the curtain and take enough of a look at me to tell you anything at all."

He went to his room. When he came back from the hospital he had screwed the latch back into place, attaching another latch on the inside as well, so he could lock the door either from inside or out. She watched TV a while longer, then piled the clothes she had folded into the basket. Not knowing if the door was locked, not caring to find out, she left his clothes in two neat stacks outside his door. She went into the kitchen, leaving the dish towels on the counter, carrying the rest of the basket up to her parents' bedroom.

Stacking the clothes on her father's dresser, she put the basket outside the door.

She lay on the bed, hands above her head. It felt good to stretch. She was getting married tomorrow: surely there was something she should do. It didn't feel like she was getting married.

She got off the bed and went to the closet, took her mother's wedding dress out. She spread it on the bed, looked it over. It was simply cut, high-necked, sleeves down to the wrist and ankles, off-white, the fabric a little yellowed.

Taking off her clothes, she slipped the dress on, leaving the back unzipped. She stood looking at herself in the mirror.

You look beautiful, she told herself.

You're making a big mistake, she told herself.

You look beautiful, she insisted again. *You'll make a lovely bride. A blushing bride.*

But her face was pale. She slapped first one cheek, then the other, but it didn't look like she'd been blushing: it looked like she'd been slapped. Taking off the dress and hanging it back in the closet, she went into her parents' bathroom, applied a little rouge to her cheekbones.

She looked at herself in the bathroom mirror. *Garish,* she thought, *tomorrow I'll do it more carefully,* and then washed her face clean.

How much in life, she wondered, *can you press down, and how long can you keep it pressed down?* A risky thought, she knew, and then thought, *Why not pray?* There was one night before her wedding, it was not too late; why not correct her lie and pray?

She knelt down and rested her elbows on the side of the bed and stayed still, gathering herself so as to begin. It felt wrong to pray in her bra and panties. She got up and slipped into her clothes. She knelt down again, composed herself, began silently to call upon God.

Guide me was part of it and *in your inifinite wisdom* and *in the hour of my need* and *please, dear Lord, let me know if I.* A series of forms, verbal combinations imposed upon more transient thoughts. *Bless my family in death* and *if it be your will* and *I submit myself to you* and *Please God your child needs.* Her knees started to ache. Again, around in a circle, the same forms in a different order and *Please reveal your will unto me, dear Lord.*

She awaited an answer, shifting her weight from one kneecap to the other, but there was nothing, she felt nothing. It was just her with her eyes closed and nothing around her, two points of pain gathered in her kneecaps, the slight pressure of the bed against her forearms, but otherwise the rest of the world fled and God gone as well. She began again, more urgently this time, whispering audibly, yet more tentative as well. *I'm here?* she started and then *if it be thy will?* And *Please reveal? I am ready to listen? Show me thy will in regard to my life and I shalt obey? Give me a sign? Let me feel thy presence?* Still nothing, and more palpably nothing, and beyond that nothing, all suspended in a void. God had withdrawn utterly from her, and if she opened her eyes she would be thrown alone into the world to live by her own wits; it was just her, and in a way it was not even her but nothing pitted against nothing. In a panic she opened her eyes, still feeling the absence of God all about her. She fell down the stairs, fled down the hall, pounded on Rudd's door. "Rudd?" she heard her voice saying. "Please? I need you? Can't you let me in?"

8

She awoke in his arms, on her sister's bed, little memory of the night before beyond her blind flight from her parents' room. *I must not think about this too closely,* she told herself. When she got up she realized she was not wearing either shirt or bra.

She couldn't find her shirt. She found her bra under the bed and pulled it on, moving swiftly out the door and out of the room. In the bathroom, she looked at her face. Her hair was a mess. Her shoulders and neck, she saw, were colored with slight, almost invisible, streaks of blood. She looked over her arms and chest to find where she had been bleeding, but there was nothing—only on the back of one shoulder the distinct marks of teeth. But the teeth had not bitten through, had only left a bruise, blood couldn't have come from there. She looked at her legs and then lowered her panties, but there was no blood there either, *still technically a virgin,* she thought, but where had all the blood come from? And then she realized it must have come not from herself at all, but from Rudd's weakened neck.

She went upstairs to her parents' room. She washed herself from head to toe, scrubbing. There was nothing wrong, she told herself, nothing to feel guilty about, there was no bleeding and thus, unless she had been deceived, she was still technically a virgin, still technically chaste, still technically worthy to be married in the temple. In any case, she didn't remember any of it, so how bad could it be? Whatever had gone on, it wasn't *that;* perhaps things had gotten out of hand, but she had been frightened, incredibly alone, hardly herself. She couldn't be held responsible for what she couldn't remember, could she? They would go ahead with the ceremony, there was no point in putting things on hold. She would be married, she had the Church's approval to be married in the temple. She shouldn't have slept in his room, she shouldn't have taken her shirt off, but no harm done. Technically speaking.

She dried off, put on a floral-print dress, pulled the dry-cleaner's plastic over her mother's wedding dress and took it out of the closet. She went downstairs, draped the dress over the couch, and went back into Rudd's room.

He was still asleep, and she could see blood dried on his neck as if someone had been scratching at it. She could see too, looking closely, light streaks of blood on the sheets and even, here and there, on the white walls, though some might have been left over from the time he had slit his throat.

"Time to get up," she said. "Wedding day."

He stretched, smiled at her. "I thought I locked the door," he said.

"You opened it for me."

"If I had, I'd already be awake," he said.

"Not just now. Last night."

"Last night?" he said. "No, I didn't."

"You did," she said.

"You weren't here last night."

"I was," she said. "I slept right there," she said, pointing at the bed.

He looked at the bed. "I don't remember," he said. "I thought I slept the night through."

"No," she said. "You opened the door and then we talked a while, and then . . ."

"And then?"

"You don't remember?" She was thinking, *If neither of us remember, none of us can be held responsible.*

"No," he said. And then he said, furtively, "It's all starting to come back to me."

"You're lying," she said.

He lifted his hands, let them fall again. "Sometimes," he said, "things . . ."

"Things what?"

"Never mind," he said.

"No," she said. "What?"

"They escape me," he said. "Things escape me."

Things escape him? she thought, waiting in the kitchen for him to finish dressing. *Is it catching?* she wondered. Apparently things were beginning to escape her as well.

She poured herself a glass of orange juice. She could think it through, she told herself. If she wanted to, she could go back through the night and piece it together, all the way down to the bite on her shoulder. There were as well, she now realized, bringing the glass forward to drink, bite marks on her hands, hard to discern, a redness almost like a rash. Admittedly, there was a certain incentive not to piece things together. If she did, she didn't know if she could face being in the temple unworthily. But if she wanted to, she was almost sure she could.

He came out, wearing a pair of chinos, a white shirt, a sports coat she had chosen for him from her father's closet.

"How do I look?" he asked. He seemed very nervous. "Good enough to get married?"

She nodded, lips tight.

The day began to accelerate. They went to the garment distribution center and were fitted for garments. It seemed to take forever. There were no parking spaces left in the temple lot; they just kept driving around and around. It was an ugly building, Lyndi thought—the gold steeple, the white stone lozenges—from a distance a sort of third-rate wedding cake. They gave up and finally parked down below, walked up the steep hill, cutting across the grass. They started to run when Lyndi realized what time it was, then stood outside, panting, trying to catch their breath so as to walk in dignified.

She was assigned an escort and given a bundle of temple clothing.

The escort led her into a dressing room. They left her shoes on a rack just inside the door. "You're on holy ground now," the woman said. "No shoes." A woman standing guard at the stalls said, "Third on your left. New bride?" she asked, and smiled. "There now," said her escort from just outside the stall door. "Take off your clothing, please."

"What should I put on?"

"Just stay nude, dear," the escort said.

Over the top of the stall door, Lyndi watched her escort waddle away. She turned, looked at herself in the stall's mirror. *Nude,* she thought. *What am I getting involved in?* She took off her dress, hung it in the locker, smoothing it down. She removed her bra, then her panties, balling them up together and putting them on the locker's top shelf. She crossed her arms over her chest and stood there, cold, considering herself in the mirror, trying to look at ease. She rubbed her throat. Where was Rudd? she wondered. Was he nude as well?

The escort came back, a pile of thick folded fabric slung over her arm. She flopped it up and onto the stall door and Lyndi took it. It was heavy.

"Put this on," said the escort.

"And my underwear?"

"No," she said. "Just this."

Lyndi unfolded it. It looked like a cross between an x-ray vest and a heavy tablecloth. There was a hole in the center for her head to go through. She put it on.

The escort came, led her to a room containing two odd structures: eight aluminum posts arranged in a large square, with thin but opaque white curtains strung between them in place of walls. She entered and was ritually cleansed with water then anointed with oil, the hands of old women touching her forehead, then reaching in through the open side of Lyndi's robe to wet her back, her hip, her calf, each touch startling, a little burst of light. Then she was helped to step into her sacred garments and was led out.

Removing the poncho, she looked at her new undergarments in the mirror. She had to wear them now, forever, always under her clothes. She looked odd, like an old lady in an old-fashioned bathing suit. She felt the sacred marks with her fingertips, the slight raised embroidering over each breast, her belly, her knee, each mark hardly an inch long.

In her wedding dress now, garments underneath. Carrying under her arm the bundle—a gauzy case about the size of a pillow that held a pleated robe, a green apron with leaves embroidered on it, a sash, a veil.

She was hustled toward a small booth toward the back of the dressing room, another curtain. The curtain parted and she was ushered into the booth, where she was given "a new name, which you shall never reveal, except in a place that will be shown you hereafter." *What does this have to do with me?* she wondered. Lips were pressed to her ear. "The new name," the lips claimed, "is Rachel." *Never forget it,* she thought.

Then the curtain on the far side of the booth was parted; she found herself out of the dressing room and in a hall, an escalator ascending before her, her escort following her onto it. Up one floor and then around a curving hallway, through a door and into a chapel. A woman in white softly played a vibrato organ. Women were to one side, men to the other. Her escort took her by the arm, guiding her along the wall to the second row. Rudd was there too, dressed all in white. A man in white, near the organist, stood with his arms crossed. She turned and looked behind her. Row upon row of people in white, more coming in all the time, each carrying tiny slips of paper. *A gathering of ghosts,* she thought.

The men started to peel away to the left, the women to the right, meeting in a two-person-wide line at the chapel's back. *What was my new name again?* she wondered. *Raquel? No, Rachel.* And when would she have to use it? Would she know? There was a line of them out the door and then to the escalator, up the escalator and down another curved hall, down the hall and then toward a blockade of old men in white suits who diverted the line into an endowment room. The room was like a small theater. At the front was a temple worker standing behind a marble altar that seemed illuminated from within. Temple workers to either side directed the men to the right, the women to the left. She moved down her row and sat down.

She waited as everyone filed in. In the front of the room was a rich, blue curtain. She could not see Rudd though she craned her neck. The worker behind the altar stood unmoving. The doors closed behind her, the hinge clicking. The man at the altar reached down and pushed a button. A voice emanated from the ceiling somewhere. The function of the man behind the altar seemed to be to turn his head to look at the women when the disembodied voice addressed the women, to turn his head toward the men when the disembodied voice addressed the men. They were told that if any of them wanted to leave they should do so now. Nobody left.

The lights went down and the man behind the altar lumbered to a seat just in front of the blue curtain. A screen opened up. On the screen, she could hardly sort it out: some vague and cosmic images, eventually jump-cutting back and forth with scenes from nature. From the ceiling came voices rendered echoic and hollow, supposedly God and Jesus and the Archangel Michael. *I will go down,* Michael said, and by doing so became Adam, the father of all. Lights on, off, Adam and Eve in the Garden of Eden, bushes and branches conveniently placed to hide their privates. The appearance of the devil, identified by his dark beard. *It's a passion play,* she thought. Eve was given the fruit and ate of it. *Adam,* God called out. *Adam, where art thou?* There was a rustling in the bushes. Adam appeared.

I heard thy voice and hid myself, because I was naked.

Who told thee that thou wast naked? Hast thou partaken of the fruit of the tree of knowledge of good and evil, of which we commanded thee not to partake?

The woman thou gavest me, and commanded that she should remain with me, she gave me of the fruit of the tree, and I did eat.

The lights came on and Lyndi was taught what they called a sign and a token, and was made to open her bundle and put on the apron that represented the apron of fig leaves Adam and Eve had made to cover their nakedness. *But I'm not naked,* Lyndi thought. The movie came on again, Adam and Eve wandered the lone and dreary world, God appeared as a floating, glowing, venerably bearded old man. God kept sending people down to Earth to provide Adam *further light and knowledge.* Each visit, she was made to put on more clothing or to rearrange the clothing she already had on. She took off the apron, put on a gauzy robe, a veil, a sash, then put the apron on again. She moved the robe from left shoulder to right. She was given tokens and signs, certain handshakes and gestures—the sign of the nail, the sure sign of the nail—and with each received also a certain name.

She was being shown, the disembodied voice told her, the signs and tokens that she would have to use in the afterlife, presenting them in proper sequence and order to those angels who stood as sentinels along the path to heaven.

They moved from the signs and tokens to the penalties—promises that one would never reveal the signs and tokens, even at the peril of one's own life. If you were put in a position where you were forced to reveal the signs, you were apparently supposed to kill yourself. She was made to draw her hand across her throat as if it were a knife. She was made to pull her hand across her chest and then let both hands fall, as if she had opened her chest to let blood spill down her ribs. Later still, the back of her thumb traveled symbolically from one hip to another, slitting open her loins.

This was, she suddenly realized with a shock, the way her family had died, the three significant gashes, though they had not taken their own lives but had had them taken by someone else. She looked about for Rudd, searching the rows, and caught a glimpse of him beyond other heads, extremely pale. It wasn't, she told herself, the temple's fault. Anyone could pervert anything; the temple ceremony was pure. But why were the penalties needed?—not only the promise not to tell but very specific means of self-slaughter associated with each token and sign?

And what, she wondered, if her father had been killed because he had revealed the signs and tokens? Was this beyond the realm of possibility? No, she said to herself, as she made motions to slit open her belly, this couldn't be. Besides, what about her sister? Like Lyndi, she was too young to have been in the temple. She knew nothing about the temple. There would be no point in killing her.

They were made to lift their arms high above their heads and, while lowering their arms slowly, to chant aloud the words "Pay Lay Ale." This, according to the disembodied voice meant "O God, hear the words of my mouth." Several couples were invited to come forward and enter into the true order of prayer. Since it was their first time, both she and Rudd were required to come. Rudd was pale. He looked decidedly ill. His neck was seeping slightly, she saw, from where he had drawn his finger across it while representing the first penalty. In the circle, they repeated all the signs and tokens they had learned, then joined hands with the person next to them using the sure sign of the nail, raising their free arm to the square and resting their elbow on the shoulder or arm of the person beside them. Her arm, raised high, started to ache, and she worried that she was resting it too heavily on Rudd's shoulder. And then the prayer was over and the circle was breaking up, the man at the altar slowly getting up. She squeezed Rudd's hand, watched him stumble, dazedly, back to his seat.

The disembodied voice was well pleased. It commanded that they be *presented at the veil.* The rich blue curtain rose, and behind it, at a little distance, was an opaque but thin white curtain, with periodic openings, aluminum posts visible from time to time.

A man with a pointer approached the curtain and held a section of it smooth. She could see distinctive marks, the same markings as those on the garment she now wore under her clothing. The disembodied voice began, from above, a discourse on the significance of the marks, the man with the pointer gesturing to each one. The mark of the square, over the right breast—exactness and order, uprightness in thought and deed. In the curtain it was not just a mark but an opening, something big enough to slip your arm through. She imagined a tiny disembodied hand reaching through the mark on her own chest, right into her lung. The mark of the compass, also an opening—left breast—suggesting that Jesus Christ would serve as a compass to guide one to eternal life. The navel mark, an open slit—acknowledging the nourishment we need, not only physical, but the spiritual nourishment of God's words. The knee mark—the only one on the curtain that was a mark instead of a hole—symbolizing that every knee shall bow and every tongue confess that Jesus is the Christ.

They were to come to the veil, a temple worker would be there to assist them. On the other side, behind each section of the curtain, would be another worker, this one representing God. They would come to the curtain, offer through the veil their given name and their temple name, exchange signs and tokens, and by so doing be admitted into the presence of the Lord.

The disembodied voice ground to a halt and a balding man wearing glasses with flashing gold frames ushered them up. Women to the left, men to the right.

She joined a line waiting for a section of the veil. Her escort plucked at her sleeve. "Not yet," she said.

"Why not?"

"When you get married, your husband takes you through the veil."

"He does?"

She nodded. "He'll go through himself," she said, "and then they'll set him up on the other side in the role of God so he can guide you safely through."

She stood back a little, waiting. She watched God's hand reach through the navel slit, grasp the hand of someone who wanted to pass through. How odd. She thought of the garment she was wearing, hands reaching in or reaching out through the marks, who was to say which? It was as if God were curled up inside and waiting to reach out to others that approached one's body. Hands reaching through slits in her breast, her belly, embracing someone, drawing them in beneath the flesh, as if the presence of God were subcutaneous.

She could see Rudd at the curtain, God's arm pushing through the mark of the square to wrap around his back. Rudd's own arm was thrust through the compass, the other arm hidden somewhere in front of his waist. His mouth was speaking into the fabric, the veil shivering. And then the embrace was broken and Rudd was ushered through, the veil slowly falling still again.

She looked at the marks, remembered again the graphic rendering of the murder site from above, the bodies at each point, and wondered at its symbolism. She began to think of the bodies not so much as bodies, nor as marks, but as openings, slits in the veil, each murdered body a way of opening the surface of the earth itself and passing through it, endowing the earth with spilled blood. Or perhaps, as a perversion of the temple ritual, it was an attempt to defile, an attempt to close the curtain between God and this Earth, a gesture toward apocalypse. In either case, it suggested why Rudd had not been killed—he had represented the knee mark, found below the others, and there was no opening on the curtain for the knee mark, nothing reached through the knee. It was just a mark, not a hole. He had been on the hillside as a mark but not as a hole: Rudd had never been meant to die.

Too quickly she was being taken to the veil, still thinking of her dead family, and when, after being called, Rudd extended to her his hand through the navel mark, it was as if he had pushed his hand through her father's corpse. She was short of breath. She could not remember the words and her escort had to whisper them to her. It was odd hearing Rudd's voice playing the role of God, his voice muffled through the veil and already flat besides. She took his hand, resting her thumb over one of his knuckles, and gave him her given name through the veil.

Their hands separated and locked into the next grip. "What is that?" his voice asked and she gave him the answer, and when asked the name of the sign, she told him it was her new name. "Will you give it to me?" he asked. "I will through the veil," she said, and leaned forward and spoke her new name, "Rachel."

She moved back, tried to release her hand for the next clasp, but he kept his grip.

"That's not right," he whispered through the veil, and she said, "What?" and her escort shushed her, and Rudd said, "Give me the right name," and she said, "That is the right name, Rudd," and she heard, through the curtain, whoever was serving as his escort say, "Didn't she say it right?" and Rudd, beginning now to raise his voice said, "No, she was wrong. The name was *Elling*. Elling," he said, quite loudly, and he was shushed and corrected by his own escort. He let go of her hand and her escort led her away from the curtain. She felt horribly confused and ashamed. "What do we do?" she asked the escort, and the escort shrugged and said, "Why don't we just start from scratch?"

She was led again to the veil, God was summoned by means of a mallet on the side of the aluminum post between sections of curtain, the veil parted and God asked, "What is wanted?"

"Eve," said her escort, "having been true and faithful in all things, desires further light and knowledge by conversing with the Lord through the veil."

Rudd's/God's voice: "Present him at the veil, and his request shall be granted."

"Her," she heard his escort correct him.

"Present her at the veil, and her request shall be granted," Rudd said.

The veil closed and Rudd's hand snaked again through the navel hole and they negotiated the first clasp and her own given name and then she gave the clasp associated with her new name. She leaned forward to whisper the new name to him. "Rachel," she said, and felt his grip tighten until it hurt. "Say it," he hissed, and she leaned even farther into the curtain until she could feel his ear with her lips, and she whispered, almost inaudibly, "Elling."

Later, they sat on two plush chairs in the room behind the veil, the celestial room, waiting to be taken to a sealing room to be married. It was filled with men and women in temple clothing, some circling about, some sitting, some praying. Everyone conversed in the verbal equivalent of earth tones. An enormous chandelier hung from the ceiling. Rudd was smiling in a way that looked like he was about to go mad.

"What's wrong?" she asked.

"Nothing," he said.

She straightened her apron, smoothed it over her belly. "You don't feel any different?" she asked.

"Different?" he said. "Of course I feel different. I've just played God. That would have an effect on anyone."

He stopped to straighten his hat. "Did you hear?" he asked.

"Hear what?"

"Pay Lay Ale," he said. "His name is in that."

"Whose name?"

"Lay Ale," said Rudd. "Lael."

"Stop it," she said, covering her eyes with one hand. Her head hurt.

"Pay him," he said. He was speaking too rapidly. "We have to pay him. It doesn't mean, 'O God hear the words of my mouth.' It means just what it says."

"Look," she said. "About what you did at the veil—"

"It's Elling," he said. "Your name is Elling. I named you and you accepted the name. We've pulled a fast one on God."

"The name wasn't Elling," she said. "That wasn't my name."

"No, we changed it," he said, nodding.

"I don't want to marry you," she said.

"You don't?" he said, and seemed genuinely confused.

She looked away from him, back toward the veil. The temple workers were standing near it, talking softly.

"Who's Elling?" she asked.

"You are," he said.

"But where's the name from?"

"Nowhere," he said, and turned away.

"Why did you want to give it to me?"

"I had to do it," he said. "Because of the new name I was given."

"What name?"

"I can't tell you," he said. "I can know your name, but you can't know mine."

"Was the name Lael?"

He shook his head.

"You're crazy."

"You still believe that you're living out your own life," he said. "But you're not. All of this," he said, gesturing around the celestial room, "giving you a new name, having you play a role, is to thrust another life onto you."

"Don't, I'm not—"

"Listen," he said. "What's it about if not possession? I play God at the veil, and God lives through me. For a moment, I become God. We're told to open ourselves to the spirit of the Lord, we act under inspiration, having breathed in the life-breath of another. That's the message of the Gospel: anyone is subject to possession, but only the holy open themselves to it willingly."

"That's wrong."

"Exactly," he said. "And that's why we're taking charge. We don't want to be vessels that the Lord can fill. We've taken on names other than those He tried to give us, and now we're going to let them stick in our craw and never get out of us."

She got up and walked nervously around the room. Finally she sat down in a chair on the opposite end. She knotted her fingers together, closed her eyes, tried to pray. Her head was throbbing. *Dear Lord,* she began, then stopped.

"You're here under false pretenses, Elling," she heard Rudd say. "Prayer won't work for you."

"Get away from me," she said.

"I'm the only one left to you," he said. "Without me you have nothing at all in the world."

He padded back to the other side of the room, sat down, arms folded. He stayed watching her.

•

She felt frightened. Her head ached. She had rushed everything and now she had given herself over to a man hardly more than a boy, insane. It was all a mistake, but what else was there for her? It was meant to happen, it had to happen, it had happened. She had set something in motion and now there was no stopping it.

A man was saying something to her, his glasses so thick she could hardly make out his eyes at all.

"Excuse me?" she said.

"You're," he said, looking at a clipboard, "Melinda . . ."

"Yes," she said. "Lyndi. That's me."

"If you'll just come this way please."

She stood, confused, and followed the man. Rudd was there, she saw, beside her. She felt utterly bereft.

"Where are you from?" the man asked.

Neither of them said anything.

"Nervous?" the man asked. "No reason to be," he said, and smiled broadly. "You only have to do this once."

Do what? Lyndi wondered. Her head ached so much she could hardly see. They were at the escalator and going up and then she was moving again around a circular hall. They stopped outside a room with a large altar at its center, a knee rest all around it, mirrors on all the walls, chairs around the walls as well. There were two men on chairs to either side of the altar, another man sitting behind the altar as if it were a desk. She felt like she was going to the slaughter.

"Oh, no," she said at the door. "I don't think so."

"Excuse me?" said the man at the altar.

"It's all right, Lyndi," said Rudd, holding onto her arm, his voice and manner suddenly gentle. "You don't have to go through with this."

"No?" she said.

"No," he said, and his voice seemed actually kind. "We can go home."

"But then," she said. "What?—"

"You decide. It's up to you."

He let go of her hand and took two steps into the room. Her headache was worse, casting a strange mist over everything. He was there, standing just inside the door, stretching out his hand to her, the men inside craning their necks to look at her, beaming. *Let her enter,* she thought. Closing her eyes, she stepped forward into what she was certain would be a disaster.

9

First month. She awoke to finally find her head clear and him lying beside her, both of them crammed into her sister's twin bed, her sacred undergarments strange against her body. He was sleeping, his face serene. She got out of bed, trying not to wake him, and went into the kitchen.

She poured a glass of milk, made scrambled eggs, slightly runny, two pieces of white toast, diagonally cut. She brought them to him on a tin TV tray painted baby blue.

"Good morning," she said. "Breakfast is served."

He rolled over, opened his eyes, stared at her.

"I made eggs and toast," she said, "and I poured this milk."

"Thanks," he said, and sat up enough to get the plate onto his lap. She lay down next to him, on her side, her shoulder nudging the edge of the tray. She caressed his hip beneath the sheet. "What's the occasion?" he asked.

"First week of marriage."

He grunted. She watched him move food from plate to mouth until he was done. He reached over and settled the tray on the floor beside the bed.

"Kiss me," she said.

He obediently and awkwardly did, then flattened himself back into the bed, closed his eyes.

"Maybe," she said. "I was thinking, why don't we move up to my parents' room?"

He shook his head.

"That bed's bigger," she said.

"I like it here."

"But the bed," she said. "And the rest of the room is small as well. I don't know that I can fit all my things here."

157

"I don't think they'll fit," he said. "You should keep your things where they are."

"But we should live together. That's what married people do."

"We are living together."

"Share a bed I mean. A room too."

"This is my room, Elling," he said. "I'm not going to give it up. You can visit me sometimes, but it's mine."

"Don't call me that."

"Why not? It's your true name, isn't it?"

She turned in the bed, away from him. "I don't want to be married to you," she said.

She listened to him fluff his pillow.

"Thank you for breakfast," he said. "Now please let me sleep."

A certain pattern settled into place in the second month, with Lyndi feeling that her life had returned largely to what it had been before. School kept her occupied, mostly. She could never tell from day to day how Rudd would be. There were times he would almost seem like an ordinary person, caring and loving, but other times he was caustic, his behavior hurtful. He knew how to get her into a discussion, the conversation building quickly into an attack.

"You don't know when to stop," she would tell him, eyes burning.

"I know when to stop," he claimed. "I just never stop there."

It had been a mistake to get married, she told herself, she should get out. But it wasn't as easy as that, and he knew what he was doing: every time things seemed almost unbearable he softened, his face changed, and she was given a few days to recover.

In his worst moods he would call her Elling, knowing it would set her off. He suggested to her that without the temple her parents would still be alive.

"The temple can't be blamed," she said.

"It makes people crazy," said Rudd. "You saw. Finger across throat, breasts, stomach. It's a lesson in bleeding a human body dry."

"It's symbolic," she said.

"Blood sacrifice," he said. "Ever heard of it?"

He explained it to her, even though she didn't want him to: letting a man's blood spill onto the ground as a way of baptizing the earth, redeeming a lost soul. Mormons had done that in the nineteenth century; it had clear ties to the temple ceremony; the temple rituals, the so-called symbolic rituals, were founded in blood, on the bodies of the slaughtered—

"Stop it," she said.

She didn't care to talk about it, he understood; it was easier not to think about it, wasn't it? If that was the way she wanted to live her life, that was fine with him. Ignorance, he suggested, a certain comfort in—

She went upstairs and into her parents' room, slamming the door after her.

Third month. He was wounded too, she told herself, and that was why he tried to hurt her. He was colder now; they hadn't slept together since the middle of the second month. He was more withdrawn, less antagonistic toward her. Sometimes, walking by his room, she could hear him talking as if he were having a conversation with someone, but when he came out later, there was just him.

She began to realize that he was seriously disturbed, perhaps a great deal more seriously than she could even imagine. There were times his eyes would flutter oddly, his speech lodging in his throat and coming out as if there were another throat hidden within. He took to staying in the house, often hiding in his darkened room the entire time she was at class or out shopping. Sometimes he would greet her briefly when she came in; other times, he wouldn't even unlock his door, though every third or fourth day he was waiting for her out on the couch, apparently cheery. She would, when she saw him, speak cautiously to him, waiting to see how he would react.

Once she was reading a leatherbound Book of Mormon and he came, sat on the couch, looked over her shoulder.

"What's that?' he asked. "A diary?"

She looked around for what he might mean. She lifted the book slightly. "This?" she asked.

"That."

"The Book of Mormon," she said.

He drew closer, squinted. "Don't lie to me," he said. "I can see perfectly well the pages are blank."

She thought at first he was joking, torturing her in some new way, but soon realized that he literally couldn't see any text on the page. As the month went on, she realized that a selective blindness extended not just to the Book of Mormon but to words or phrases in the newspaper, to things said on television. There was no pattern she could see to it, and four days after believing the Book of Mormon to be blank he picked it up, read a passage from it, seemed to recognize it perfectly. It came and went. There were objects too that he could not perceive and times too when she spoke to him that he did not respond. At first she thought he was ignoring her, and sometimes he was. But confronted more and more often with his blank and placid face, she began to realize it was something he didn't control.

When she brought it to his attention, he seemed terrified. "There are holes," is how he phrased it, but then refused to discuss it beyond that. Indeed, only a few minutes after she first brought it up, discussion of his condition joined the ranks of things he literally could not hear. *Holes,* she thought, and imagined how that must have been: going through life with gaps springing up, things that read as blank and empty spaces, as if the world were unfinished. Did he see people that way as well? She wondered if there were times when he saw her face as only a smooth white plate, anonymously threatening. She would watch him, she told herself. She would help him all she could.

Fourth month. He was hardly ever psychologically abusive to her now, but he was beginning to deteriorate, his personality giving way. *Elling,* he kept calling her, and it was not to needle her, but because the name kept welling to the surface of his consciousness. *Hooper,* he called himself once, in her hearing (*Let's just see about that sandwich, Hooper,* he said to himself while waiting for lunch), but when she mentioned the name, he blanched. "No," he said. "Don't call me that."

She swallowed hard and called his mother, asked her if she knew either a Hooper or an Elling.

"Who are you?" Rudd's mother asked.

"I'm Lyndi," she said. "I married your son."

"I'm sorry," said Rudd's mother. "I'm no longer speaking to my son." She hung up the telephone.

"I'm Lael," Rudd started saying. "Call me Lael, Elling."

"Stop playing, Rudd."

"I need Lael back," he said. "Bring him to me."

"We can't find Lael," she said. "We don't know where he is."

"I'll have to find him," said Rudd.

The next day he began mailing letters, general delivery, to Lael Korth, three or four a day, addressed to different towns throughout the West. On the third day she took one out of the mailbox, carried it up to her parents' bathroom, and opened it up. It read:

lael nd'd asap STOP rudd nds hlp STOP
why hst thou frskn me STOP pls cm STOP

She tore the letter into tiny pieces, flushed them down the toilet. She debated taking the remainder of the letters out of the box, destroying them as well and then, considering, decided they could do no harm.

When she went back downstairs she found Rudd in the bathroom, staring at himself in the mirror.

"That's not my face," he was saying. "Who took my face?"

"Rudd," she said. "We have to talk."

"Not until I find my face," he said. He kept ducking down, springing up in front of the mirror again, but he never seemed able to find what he was looking for.

By the fifth month he had discovered the wooden shed in the backyard, the one her father had used as a junk shed, and had taken everything out of it, piling it all along the back fence. That was a good sign, she decided; he was taking an interest in something, he was actually leaving the house.

She still knew it would be a good idea to call someone, get some help, but it was harder to do than it should have been. She often opened the yellow pages, flipped through the appropriate listings. There were too many names, no indication of who was good and who wasn't. Besides, if his condition were revealed, they would take him away. She was afraid of what was happening to him but was also afraid of being left alone.

There were a number of minor incidents, or at least incidents which, because of the oddness of his actions over the previous few months, now seemed minor. But there was one that she classified as major. She came home one day to find him wandering around the backyard wearing nothing but his sacred garments. She pulled him quickly inside.

"What is it, Rudd?" she asked. "What's wrong?"

"The earth," he said, grabbing the skin of his chest and tugging at it.

"That's flesh, Rudd."

"This is the earth, Elling, and these," he said, touching each of the garment marks in turn, "are the dead. Father, mother, sister. Me."

"But you're not dead," she said.

"I mostly am," he said, and drew his hand across his throat, hard. She watched the skin fluster, waited for it to start to bleed.

"You're going crazy," she finally said.

"Of course I'm going crazy," he said. "I'm wearing the dead."

She found him a few hours later in the kitchen, cutting the marks out of all his garments with a pair of utility scissors. He was holding a garment shirt up, examining the holes.

"Rudd?" she said.

"I know," he said, regarding her through a hole, terrified. "I've only made it worse."

He paid more and more attention to the backyard shed. By month six he had removed the locks from his bedroom door, reinstalling them on the door to the shed, one inside, one outside. What was he doing in there? she asked him. "Nothing," he said, and then, "it's my little house."

"Can I come in?"

"No," he said. "Not yet."

There was only one window and he had packed mud against it from the inside so she could not see in. She walked around the shed looking for cracks, but the few that were there had been filled with dried mud mixed with grass, and she worried that if she pushed it through, he would notice the dirt on the floor and become furious. He moved an old, broken-down refrigerator from the garage into the shed. He would not say what it was for. Things began to go missing from the freezer, things like frozen meat.

One day when he was in the shed, she chose to enter his now unlocked bedroom. He had moved all his own things out of it to leave it exactly as it had been when her sister had been alive, except the bedding was missing. She waited that night for him to come in, but he never came. When she wanted him, she had to knock on the door of the shed. He would come to the door and ask what was wanted, and when she responded, she would hear a scraping sound. When he opened the door the rest of the room would remain hidden behind a sheet he had strung onto an old laundry line. It did not smell good inside. He would squeeze his way out, shut the door and lock it, and only then, outside, would he converse with her.

"What are you doing in there?" she asked.

"You'll see," he said. "You'll see."

•

Seventh month. She woke up one Saturday morning and looked out the window to find him locking his shed. He kept shaking the locks to make certain they were secure.

She got up and went down to the kitchen, put two bowls on the table, poured some cereal for herself and for him. He came in, looked at the table a few seconds, then went into the living room. When she followed him, she found him with one hand on the doorknob.

"Where are you going?" she asked.

"I have to buy something."

"Do you have any money?"

He put his hands into his pockets, then took them out again. He reached into the pocket of his coat, pulled out his wallet. It was empty.

"No," he said.

"How are you going to buy it?"

"I don't know," he said.

"Do you need to borrow some money?"

"Yes," he said. "I need some money."

She began to put on her coat. "I'll drive you," she said.

He went out the door. When she went out she found him in the back seat of the car.

"Don't you want to sit in front with me?" she asked.

"I'm buckled in," he said.

She started the car, pulled out of the driveway. "Where to?" she asked.

"Antique store."

"Antique store?"

He nodded. She drove him around downtown until they found one that seemed acceptable to him, a shop with an old desk in the window, license plates from all fifty states tacked up just inside the door.

"Help you?" said a man in overalls, sitting behind a counter on a tall stool.

"Yes," said Lyndi. "Rudd?"

"I need a hitching weight."

"A what?"

"For a wagon. A hitching weight."

"Now what in the world you after a hitching weight for?" the man asked. "For hitching?" When Rudd said nothing, the man said, "Not much market for those."

"No," said Lyndi. "I suppose not."

"Then again," he said, "no harm looking."

He got off his stool and ambled to the back of his shop, waving for them to come along. He stepped over a pile of old sewing machine parts, a stack of fifties pinups wrapped in dusty plastic, then rounded the corner into a small boxy space, a sort of large closet with the door removed. There was horse tack on the walls, most of it cracked; an old nickel-plated camp shovel in one corner; a trowel; an odd spiked ball hanging on the end of a leather strip; a plaque upon which were mounted five strands of barbed wire, the names of each burned into the wood beside it; a picture of an adobe hut with a sign on its side reading *J. James, notorious outlaw, slept here;* a fist-sized box of horseshoe nails; a scattering, along the floor, of rusty horseshoes, one still attached to a taxidermied hoof and foreleg. On a double-thick shelf were lead sinkers and plumb weights, a bullet mold, a jumble of loose, broken-toothed gears.

"What exactly does it look like when it's at home?" the man asked. "This hitching weight of yours."

"I don't know," said Rudd.

"You don't know."

"Don't you?" asked Rudd.

"I never had to know," said the man. "Until now."

They tried the other dealers in town, without success. One had a wagon in its front yard and the owner went out to take a look at it, thinking it might have a hitching weight attached, but no. They drove home, Rudd increasingly moody.

"What do you need it for?" Lyndi asked.

"Weight," he said.

"What are you weighting down?"

"Nothing yet," he said.

She waited for him to say more, but he said nothing. When she tried to query him further, he said, "Quit asking, Elling," and then, growing hysterical, "Where's Lael? What have you done with Lael?"

At home, he went immediately into the shed, shut the door. He came out once, near evening, to take from the kitchen several packages of frozen hamburger, a jar of peanut butter, and a loaf of white bread. It was days before she saw him again.

Eighth month. When he did finally come out of the shed, he no longer seemed to recognize her. He navigated the house strangely, as if it were an unfamiliar place, as if the floorplan were shifting with each step he took. He called her Elling almost exclusively now, but she was glad to have him say anything to her at all. He committed acts he didn't remember, would eat lunch and then a few minutes later ask for lunch. He asked her questions, and a few minutes later asked the same thing again.

"How are things in the shed?" she asked.

"Good," he said. "Good. It'll care for itself for a while."

"Perhaps you should see someone."

"Elling," he said. "Rudd's feeling just fine."

"No," she said softly. "He isn't."

She called her bishop, explained the barest details of the situation, asked for advice.

"Oh," he said. "Goodness." He gave her the number for LDS Social Services, the Church-sponsored clinical program. She called and was put on hold; eventually they hung up on her. She called back and after fifteen minutes was given someone to speak to—a licensed therapist, she was told.

"Well," said the man. "I've got an opening three weeks from yesterday."

"Three weeks? Can't I arrange for anything sooner?"

"I'm sorry," he said. "We're understaffed. It's the best I can do."

"But he's bad," she said. "It's a real problem."

"You could check him into the hospital," he said. "But I'm sorry, that's as soon as I can manage."

She made the appointment, informed Rudd of it. Would he go, she wanted to know. Was he willing to give it a chance? *A good honest-to-goodness counselor,* she thought, hearing her aunt's voice in her head. *Grain-fed.*

"Sure," said Rudd. "Unless Lael comes back first."

She caught him looking into the mirror, speaking to his reflection. "I don't have anyone," he said. "I don't even have me."

"You have me, don't you?" Lyndi asked and came forward, put her arms around him from behind.

He just kept looking into the mirror.

"No one," he said. "No one at all."

With a stick, she pushed out the mud between the cracks in the shed walls. Inside, it was dark. She could see nothing, nothing at all. There was a stench seeping out. When she put her ear to the hole, she heard a strange, slight hissing.

What's next? she wondered. She contemplated having him committed, taking him to the hospital, but no, she wanted to talk to someone, she wanted to speak with someone first.

She began to chart his behavior, thinking that the statistics might be of some help later. There were certain consistencies that she might not have noticed otherwise. For instance, he always checked the lock on the shed eight times after he locked it, banging the lock each time. He called her Elling between twenty and thirty times a day, but never more or less. When he was committing acts he would not remember later, he would hold his face slack, looking almost like a different person. He would speak to himself while regarding his reflection in the mirror, but when he looked directly at his hand, he seemed to think it belonged to someone else. He consistently disliked being touched, not only by her, but by his own hand.

She consulted a lawyer about getting the wedding annulled. Was it possible? It was possible, he suggested, if both parties agreed or if there was some indication the wedding had taken place under coercion, but it was not the usual thing. Was she Catholic? If not, why not opt for a simple divorce?

But it was too much to even think about: barely twenty and already divorced, her life for all intents and purposes over, at least in Utah where a premium was still put on the virginal. Her parents had had difficulties, had even struggled; her father had been obsessive-compulsive, her mother distracted; it was not always such a good combination. But they had weathered it out; they had stayed together until they died. Rudd was sick. He didn't know what he was or who he was, and she didn't know either. *If he could get better,* she thought. And then, *He never will.*

10

She had been sleeping but was dreaming of water, the smooth glassy surface of Lake Powell, her body speeding across it just over the surface. She plunged down suddenly into the water and traveled along beneath, scraping the bottom, and when she tried to get to the surface she couldn't. She struggled and awoke, found a hand clamped tightly around her neck, cutting off her breath.

"So, Elling," Rudd's voice said. "We kill her?"

She could see only his dim outline in the darkness, his body straddling her hips. She struggled. *No,* she tried to say, but couldn't speak. She could hear the blood grow loud in her head, beating slower and slower. She shook her head as much as she could, managed to scrape together something of a breath.

"Elling?" Rudd said.

She worked her hands free of the blankets, began to dig her fingers into his arms. He seemed not to notice. She tried to reach his throat.

"Elling?" he said again.

"No," she mouthed.

The blood was slowing in her ears again, and slowing as well, she felt, were her hands. She could hardly move them. There was a boiling in her ears, the room losing first the quality of its light and then fading altogether.

When she became conscious it was morning. She could feel sunlight on her but could hardly move. She got up and locked the bedroom door, fell back on the bed. Her throat hurt. When finally she got up for good and looked in the mirror, she saw her neck speckled with neat ovoid bruises. She swallowed, as best she could. Her nails were broken, she saw, her hands bloody on the tips with not her own blood but Rudd's. She washed them, washed her neck as well.

When she came out of the bedroom she was holding her mother's hair dryer like a gun before her. She went from room to room. Rudd was nowhere to be found. She left the hair dryer on the mantel, took up the fire poker, went out into the backyard.

"Rudd?" she called, standing beside the shed, then realized it was locked.

She went back into the house, sat at the kitchen table. On it was a postcard showing a cityscape, the words *Nueva York!* printed along the bottom in purple letters. She turned it over.

> *Dearest Rudd,*
> *Am having a wonderful time here in the Big Apple.*
> *Wish you were here.*
> *Join me?*
> *Lael*

The postmark, she saw, was local, Provo, dated the day previous. The card was clearly written in Rudd's own hand.

She put it down. Taking the poker, she went out to the shed.

She worked the poker's blunted nub between the door and the frame, pried opened the door. It was warm inside, the smell horrific, and when the door opened there came as well a swarm of black flies that whirled about her head, butting against her lips, her eyes. She shooed them away.

There was the sheet hung as a curtain just inside the door and she could see when she got closer that he had made slits in it, versions of the garment marks though backwards:

⌐   V

—

—

Carefully she reached out, tugged the sheet off the clothesline. Behind it, he had torn up the wooden flooring, heaping it splintered and jagged against one wall, exposing the bare earth beneath. He seemed to have worked the earth, for it was loamy and when she stepped onto it she sunk up to her ankles. In the middle, on its back, sunk almost to the lid, was the old refrigerator.

There were, she could see, flies creeping in and out of it through a tear in the rubber seal of the door. She put her ear closer to the tear, heard a dull hissing within.

She went to the mud-caked window and broke it out with the poker, to get the smell out a little, to get more light in. She looked around. In one corner lay a pile of filthy bedding, stained and frayed. Next to it, the box he had kept in his room, sitting directly on the dirt, mold creeping up its side.

She opened it, saw again the church books. She removed them one by one and dropped them atop the torn-out flooring. Taped to the bottom of the box was the map, but she could see now, from the way it stood out in the tired light, that there was a raised rectangle in the map's center, something hidden.

She peeled the map from the box's damp bottom. Underneath were several sheets of paper, folded, words typed on them. The first began:

> "The Murderous Existence of William Hooper Young"
> by Rudd Theurer
> For my decade I chose the 1900s and the year 1903 but some of this happened in 1902 too. The most important part in fact (the murder). . . .
> In 1902 William Hooper Young was involved in killing a woman named Anna Pulitzer and dropping her body in a drainage canal. The body was "nude and lying in slime." I said "involved in killing" on purpose: certain people think that he might have had some help from someone named Charles Elling. . . .

Oh Christ, she thought. It went on like that, giving the facts of the murder and the trial, speaking too of the hitching weight Young had used to weigh down the body, some sort of high-school project that seemed to have infected Rudd's life. The ritual nature of the murder that seemed, at least slightly, to foreshadow the murder of her parents. No wonder Rudd had gone mad, she thought; he had written about a murder and then had almost been killed in a similar fashion—it was as if he had raised the dead. More disturbing, she thought, he had begun to see her as Elling, for Elling, it turned out, was the partner in crime, the one on whom Young tried to blame the murder when caught by the police, the one the police could never find. *Like Lael,* she thought, and then, *In what sense for Rudd was I his partner in crime?*

At the end of the essay was a single sheet of paper. She tugged it out. There, written in Rudd's hand, in tiny script,

SUNRISE IN HELL

BY WILLIAM HOOPER YOUNG

Verse 1st: Some sins are not to be forgiv'n
Our Savior's blood doth not wash clean
The devil bars the path to heav'n
And to our Lord we are unseen

Chorus: Else shall we face sunrise in hell
The devil he shall broil us well
Much better shorten our own lives
Than, after death, the devil's knives

Verse 2nd: Yet God has offered us in love
A means of holy murder true
Baptis'd by one's own spilt blood
The taken life shall life renew

Chorus: Else shall we face sunrise in hell
The devil he shall broil us well
Much better shorten our own lives
Than, after death, the devil's knives

Verse 3rd: To kill the sinner is to save him
Before he doth besmirch again
The devil he will but enslave him
Unless the knife forthwith is giv'n

Then there was a gap, a blank expanse, at the very bottom of the page an additional verse in Rudd's hand:

Final Verse: So call yourselves to action brothers
Take for yourself the heavy knives
Take up fathers daughters mothers
Take them up and take their lives

Her hands, she could feel, were shaking. *I am surprisingly calm,* she told herself and indeed in her mind she was, despite the strong tremors of her body. Her hands let the papers fall. She saw herself step toward the refrigerator door and bend down to take the handle. She popped it out of its lock and then, in a single movement, wrenched the door open.

Inside, the stink of putrid meat, the box filthy. A cloud of black flies, thousands of them, a tremendous symphony of them, bouncing against her arms and face and spinning about the room. Covered with flies, she realized she knew that it was Rudd who had murdered her parents, and knew as well that she had known this deep down for some time. The flies swirled about her and out the door, and in little more than a moment she felt herself adrift again, irrevocably and utterly alone.

But the feeling did not last. What, she wondered, was that stirring, there, in the box, rising up, now that the flies were gone?

When a messenger comes saying he has a message from God, offer him your hand and request him to shake hands with you. . . . If it be the devil as an angel of light, when you ask him to shake hands he will offer you his hand, and you will not feel anything. . . .

—*Doctrine and Covenants* 129: 4, 8

The category through which the world manifests itself is the category of hallucination.

—GOTTFRIED BENN

PART III

HOOPER, AMUCK

It took him a long moment to understand where he was. At first there was only a gray space, featureless, unlit, as tight upon and around him as a coffin, which slowly began to congeal, if congeal was the right word, into something else. The space opened itself up, fled back and away from him until he felt he could sit up, and perhaps even stand—though he remained motionless, unmoving, the relation between his body and his mind perplexed.

He was, he could see, in a room, but a room washed out as if seen mostly in darkness. There, the edge of a cabinet, glass-fronted and snug against a wall. Furniture draped with a light tapestry, fringed at one edge. He could begin to make out the wooden frame of a bed, its stain chipped away along the edge that touched the floor, just below the tapestry's fringe. He was lying on a plank floor that had been, he could smell, recently waxed. He turned his head and saw the gryphon-pawed legs and base of a swivel chair done up in dark leather, its back dimpled and puckered with rivets. It was sitting near a fireplace of white brick. Two narrow pillars, perhaps marble, perhaps a finely painted plaster, ran from floor to mantel. The grate was not free but rather tiled over with ceramic, the casement for a cast-iron burner bulging like a blood blister in its center. The stove was warm, he could feel from the floor, and the chair could be rotated, or swiveled rather, to take full advantage of the heat. Though at the moment the chair was facing the bed. It was conceivable, he thought, that he had fallen out of one or the other, chair or bed. More likely the chair than the bed, since he was fully clothed.

When the room seemed to have gained a certain consistency, a certain rigor, he moved his hands, which had become, in his fall (if there had been a fall), trapped beneath his body. They were tingling, and one was beginning to ache. His nails, he saw, were jagged, broken, and he wondered if he had bitten them down himself. Was he the sort of man to bite his nails down?

He pulled himself up to sitting, turned to his knees and, groaning, pulled himself into the chair. The heavy spring squeaked, squealed.

From the chair he could see someone in the bed, a young woman, turned on her side and away from him, atop the tapestry but beneath a coverlet. Her shoulders were bare and uncovered, her hair streaming along the bolster.

He looked about. Had he been here before? Yes, he thought he had been there before. Was this his room? No, surely not. But how did he know it was not his room? He knew. Yes, but how did he know? He simply knew; wasn't that sufficient?

It is my father's apartment, he thought, and for a moment this seemed the right answer, but then a moment later, *No,* he realized, *my father is long dead. A suicide.*

Then whose room? The girl's? How could he tell if he did not know who she was? Yet something stopped him from walking around the bed and looking her full in the face. Perhaps simply the fact of her bare shoulder. Was this a woman he knew, perhaps intimately? It was not simply his wife, of that he was certain. He had not seen his wife for some time and the terms upon which they had parted could hardly be considered amicable. One does what one can but one occasionally makes mistakes, even errors that acquire a certain difficult gravity. Yet what was a wife for if not to understand one, to accept one despite one's foibles, to help one strive for betterment?

Or was he in fact correct? Why was he having such difficulty, then, remembering not only his wife's face, but her name?

He cleared his throat. The woman in the bed did not shift. He cleared his throat again, louder this time. She was a sound sleeper.

He allowed his gaze to wander the room. A very simple moulding near the ceiling, a runner of painted wood interrupting the flatness of the upper wall, above it a slight curve, a rounding, just at the jointure of wall and ceiling itself. It relaxed the eye. Lower, a closed, narrow door leading perhaps to a closet. An open doorway, leading into a kitchen, a tiled floor, one edge of a skirted sink.

"Miss?" he said. He cleared his throat, stared at the back of her head. "I fear I find myself in something of an embarrassing predicament," he said. "My memory has deserted me. I must admit I am unsure of where I am or even of who you are."

The woman still did not respond. *Perhaps,* he thought, *she is deaf. Or perhaps she is doing this purposefully as a means to punish me or drive me away.*

"If I do know you," he said. "Might I ask you to turn toward me and pay a little heed? I have no doubt that the right word or phrase, the right gesture from you, will propel me to a speedy return of my senses."

When the woman still did not respond, he began to be very afraid.

He stayed still for a moment, regarding her back. Then carefully he reached out and with a finger and thumb took hold of the top edge of the coverlet, tugged it carefully up and over her shoulders. The woman seemed to settle slightly against the bolster, the movement almost imperceptible but enough to cause him to withdraw his hand. In pulling the coverlet up, he saw, he had freed her foot, which lay sole upward at the extreme of the bed, curled. *Like a dead fish,* he thought.

He made his way slowly around the bottom of the bed, stooping forward and skew to see her face. Yet even before he was all the way around he could see that he had been right to be afraid. He could see through her hair something wrong with her forehead: blood matting together strands of her hair and puddling in her eye socket.

He turned the coverlet down and saw she was naked to her waist, then folded it to render her bare from head to toe. With the flat of his hand, he pushed her shoulder, turned the body face up. The skin was lukewarm and rubbery and it held the imprint of his hand where he had pushed. Beneath the body the tapestry was stained dark with blood and he could see her left temple caved in and soft, dribbling both blood and brain. Her belly too was neatly slit, the gash almost long enough for him to slip his fist into, he thought, and then wondered, *Why would I think a thing like that?*

So, he thought, *not her apartment. At least no longer.*

Shocked at himself, he reached out and touched her neck, though he already knew she was dead. On the bedside table was a vial, empty. There was a knife on the table as well, an ivory-handled stiletto, its blade sword-shaped and sharp on both sides. *Why,* he wondered, *do I remain so calm?* He reached out and brushed the woman's hair back and tried to recognize her, despite her broken skull, and thought perhaps he did but could not force a name onto her. Picking up the knife he examined it more closely, the blade four or five inches long and well-milled, its bevel even and careful. *No,* he thought, *I should not have picked that up, the police shall want to see that and just where it lay.*

And then thought, suddenly, *Suppose the murderer is still here?*

•

Carefully he made his way to the smaller door in the room. He turned the handle with little noise then threw the door open with a single, taut gesture. Save for shirts and coats, a top shelf of starched collars, the closet was empty. The rest of the bedroom too. In the kitchen, the space under the skirt of the sink was bare save for a small tin of white powder that he took for lye. The cabinets were empty as well. A sitting room just off the kitchen was equally empty.

Still carrying the knife, he went to the apartment's front door, opened it. It led onto a landing paneled in dark wood, a white honeycomb tile lining the floor, a set of stairs descending to a street door. Only when he saw the street door did he begin to hear street noises, muffled, as if they hadn't existed before the door had been perceived. There was another apartment on the opposite side of the landing, a door identical to his own. To the right, the open door of a bathroom.

Leaving the apartment door ajar, he went to the door across the landing and listened, holding his ear close. There was a dull murmur from within. He knocked and the murmur ceased. After a brief silence, it resumed. He knocked again, louder, and the murmur stopped again, followed by footsteps, the creaking of floorboards. Realizing he was still holding the stiletto, he slid it into his pocket.

"Who is it?" a voice asked.

He cleared his throat. "It's me," he claimed.

Was "me" enough? In any case he could hear the door rattle and a moment later it was cracked slightly open to show a man in a cravat and a tweed topcoat.

"Ah," said the man, and opened the door wider. "It's you, William. Why didn't you say so?"

"Call me Hooper," he said. "Yes. It's me."

"Well," the other said. "What is it, Hooper? Everything satisfactory? Do you care to come in?"

"Satisfactory?"

"Across the hall," he said.

"What," he said slowly, "is there to be satisfactory or not across the hall?"

The man regarded him oddly. "The apartment, of course."

"Oh," he said. "Yes, of course."

"Are you certain you feel well?" the man said. "Please, come have a seat."

Confused, Hooper stepped deeper into the apartment, allowed himself to be seated on a horsehair sofa. Close by, in a wing chair, sat another man in cravat and shirtsleeves, his coat laid across his knees. Upon it was an open book.

"Hello," the man said.

"Hello," said Hooper.

"We were just reading aloud," said the man. "The Scriptures." He smiled. "Begin the day with the word of God and end it with such."

Hooper nodded. "It is not my apartment, is it?"

"Which?" he said. "Why, what an odd question."

The other man came back in to offer Hooper some water. It was tepid. He drank it slowly.

"Elder," the seated man said. "William just asked me the oddest question."

"He's not feeling himself, Elder," said the other. "And he prefers to be called Hooper. Perhaps he just awoke and hasn't yet a foothold, as it were."

"Perhaps not, Elder," said the first. He turned to Hooper. "In answer, no it is not your apartment. It belongs to your father. As does this apartment, as does the house as a whole. As you well know."

"My father?" said Hooper. "But my father is dead."

The two men exchanged glances. "Nonsense, Hooper," the seated one said. "He is only abroad."

"Abroad?"

Both men nodded. "In Europe. You occupy his apartment until his return."

"Ah yes," Hooper lied, shaking his head. "I remember now. I don't know what's been wrong with me."

"Are you certain you're all right?" asked one of the two.

"There hasn't been anyone coming and going in the house today, has there?" asked Hooper.

The standing man shook his head. "Not to my knowledge. Only you," he said.

"Do I live alone?"

"Hooper, have you been drinking?"

Back in the apartment, he draped the corpse with the coverlet, arranging it so that no portion was visible. He sat down on the chair but found the stiletto to be needling through his trouser pocket and into his thigh. He stood and plucked it out and put it again on the bedside table just as he had first found it.

Only me, he thought. And then added, *Hooper.*

And only then did it occur to him to be surprised at the name. Hooper? If he had been asked if that were his name he would not have said so. It did not feel altogether the right name for him. But it was the name his tongue had uttered, in preference to the other name the Elder had offered. *William.* His father too, named John, that didn't sound right, and Young not right as a family name, or as part of his own full name: William Hooper Young. Why was it he felt so alienated from his proper names—names that his tongue could give, apparently out of habit, as correct, even if he could not get his mind around them. And his father alive? He had been certain that his father was dead, his mother had said as much, over and over, he had seen his father dead in his coffin, but no, no, why had he thought that? He had gotten confused; he had made that up: it was apparently his father who was alive and his mother, not his father, who was dead.

And this woman, what was he to do about her? This corpse in his bed, in a bed that technically belonged to a vanished father, dead. Certainly it was understandable that his mind was running a little ragged. He should be, he thought, even more distraught than he was. Perhaps it was even worrisome that he was not.

Only me, he thought again. *Then perhaps I am the one responsible for this poor creature's death.*

But why? he wondered.

But even if I'm not, he thought, *it may appear to others as if I were.* Though he realized his mind was taking a turn into dubious territory he could not stop himself. He was sorry that the woman was dead but he did not know her; how could he be responsible? And yet the police, he knew, were likely to ferret out the easiest solution to the problem, and the easiest solution to the problem, particularly with the Mormon missionaries across the hall claiming that nobody had entered the house, was the inhabitant of the apartment: he himself. The missionaries would not be blamed: there were two of them, it was not their apartment. They would support each other's witness. No, if anyone were to be blamed, it would be he.

He sat on the bed. Reaching out, he stroked the woman's hair. Did she look familiar?

But perhaps if I speak now I'll at least have a chance, he thought. For what else was he to do? Hush up the crime? Take charge of the body himself and dispose of it? This would serve not only to cover the crime and protect the murderer but, if the disposal of the corpse were ever to be traced back to him, implicate him. No, he must speak with the police, lay down for them all he knew, all he understood, and then allow them to do as they would. At least his conscience would be appeased, and perhaps his forthrighteousness would do much, or at least something, to convince them of his innocence.

He was still, he realized, stroking her hair, as if she were a lapdog. He took his hand away, and stood, pacing into the kitchen and back again. At last he tightened his coat and, feeling in his waistcoat pocket for a coin, left the apartment.

Yes, he thought, he would choose the righteous thing. He left the landing and started down the stairs. There was nothing else to be done and this way at least his conscience would be gratified. He would be at peace with himself rather than at variance and with his mind moving two ways at once. He would open the door, find a willing boy, send him along to the police.

Yet when he opened the front door there was a man on the step, his face seeming at once old and young. Hooper looked at him, holding the door ajar.

"Hello, Hooper," the man said, and nodded once.

And suddenly Hooper remembered what he was meant to say.

"Elling," Hooper said. He opened the door wider. "Would you care to come in?"

Upstairs, Elling stood in the kitchen. He removed his gloves, working them off slowly, finger by finger. When he was done he went to the sink, peered beneath its skirt. The gesture struck Hooper as odd; he had the strange sensation that he had seen it done before.

"She isn't here," said Elling.

"What?" said Hooper. "No. She's on the bed."

"Certainly you should hide her," said Elling.

"But why would she be there?" asked Hooper. "I said nothing to suggest that I'd put her there. And how is it that you know that she is in such condition as demands being hidden?" *Unless,* he thought, *she was brought to it by your hand.*

"That's where she goes," said Elling, and now seemed again young. "Goddammit, how many times do I have to tell you? Bloody sheets in the closet, body under the sink. Can't you do a goddam thing right?"

Something's wrong, Hooper thought. "I'm sorry," he said.

"Shall I go out?" asked Elling. "Shall I go back out and begin again?"

"What do you mean, begin again?"

He had his head in his hands now and was sitting on the edge of the bed. The room around him, what he could see of it through his hands, was beginning to fade, going gray. He watched the walls before him waver, as if underwater, as if coming asunder.

"Shit," said Elling. "Pull yourself together."

Hooper nodded. He reached out and touched the bed, pushing his palm down against it until it felt sturdy, authentic, real. He could feel the texture of the tapestry pressing into it. When he lifted his palm away, he found it pebbled from the fibers.

"We'll start again," said Elling.

Hooper nodded.

I t took him a moment to understand where he was. At first there was only a gray space, featureless, unlit, but it opened itself up, began to acquire variance, contour. A room, then. An apartment. He was sitting on a chair beside a bed and in the bed was a woman, facing away. The coverlet was stripped back and he could see that the woman was nude and soaking in her own blood.

Oh, Christ, he thought.

He stood and tugged the woman onto her back, put his hand against her throat. He could not feel a pulse and her neck had grown stiff, as had her other joints. The skin was growing cold and felt rubbery, holding the imprint of his fingers. One side of her skull was fractured and blood had pooled in her eye socket, but most of it had spilled out when he moved her. Her other temple was broken as well, leaking both blood and brain. Her belly was neatly slit, the gash almost long enough for . . . for what? He didn't know. It was a longish gash in any case.

Where am I? he wondered. Was this his room? No, he didn't think so. Did he know this woman? No. But how could he say for certain? Perhaps he knew her; she looked familiar but it was hard to say with her skull broken as it was.

Who did this? he wondered. And then, *Was it me?*

His first impulse was to hide the body, move it out of the house somehow, or out of the room, or at least off the bed so he did not have to look at it while he tried to think, tried to remember what had happened. He could hide her in the closet, or perhaps under the skirt of the sink, or perhaps some other place. He could cut her up and place her piece by piece in the stove and burn her until she was gone, but what would his neighbors think of the smell of burning flesh and bone and hair? And could he himself stand it? Wait, were they *his* neighbors? Was this even his apartment? Perhaps it would be better to simply leave things as they were and slip out and then, at a little distance from the place, try to sort it out. No one need know he had been here. Unless it was here that he belonged.

He had the vague impression that all this had happened before.

Or perhaps, he thought, it was better to go directly to the police and tell them the truth. Say he had returned to his apartment and found the girl dead in his bed but that clearly he had nothing to do with it. Yes, of course. He had seen her lying in the bed, realized suddenly she was dead and then from the shock had passed from consciousness. That too would explain where his memory had gone. And explain too why he had felt at first that he had not known where he was. His consciousness had been returning and he was still muddled and confused. He would go to the police and make a clean breast of it—

Or not, he thought. Would the police be likely to credit his story? And what if he told the story and it *wasn't* his house, wasn't his apartment at all, but the girl's? How, then, to explain his own presence to the officer?

"Your relation to the deceased?"

"None."

"Then how is it you came to be in her apartment?"

"Was it her apartment?"

The officer would look at him sternly. "This one," he would say to his recorder, "he's not telling what he knows. Make a note of it."

"But I *am* telling all that I know," he would protest. Yet by then it would already be too late.

And then, sitting in the chair, staring at the unmoved body, he realized that it would be already too late long before that. Indeed, it would be too late the moment after the officer sat down at the table across from him and said:

"Name?"

What was his name? That indeed was the first thing. And the second, he thought, is like unto it: Was this his apartment or was it not? And finally, Who was this girl?

He covered the body with a coverlet. This did not make him queasy and this indeed surprised him; he was made of stronger mettle than he would have believed.

He left the apartment, crossed the hall to knock on the door opposite. But this too, he realized, was probably an error: were this not his apartment, he should not be seen.

He could hear footfalls on the parquet on the other side of the door; lithely he crept back and away and closeted himself in the bathroom on the landing between apartments, leaving the door ajar so as not to give himself away, standing in the dark.

The door opened and he heard a man's voice.

"Hello?" the voice said. "Is anyone there?"

He tried to see the man through the crack between door and wall, but the angle wasn't sympathetic and he saw nothing. He heard the man call out again, then heard him cross the landing, knock on the other apartment's door.

"Hooper?" the man called. "Are you there?"

Hooper? he thought. As good a name as any other, and one he was vaguely willing to accept as his own. Was it his apartment, then?

He stayed in the dark room until the other man had left the landing and gone back into his own apartment. Then he crept down the stairs and out the front door.

The day outside was bright and slightly cold. He stayed as he could to the walk, to avoid the puddles that at times were splashed up by the passing wagons—

Wagons? he thought. *Can that be right?*

Yes, he thought, *that's right.*

There was, he could see, on the other side of the street, a boy, possibly twelve years old, leaning against the wall. His face looked somewhat familiar. The boy was looking at him from under his hat, tossing some trinket up in the air and catching it in his palm. As he came closer, he saw that it was a rabbit's foot on the end of a length of thong.

"You get luck out of that?" he asked the boy.

The boy nodded. "Never did bad by it," he said. "You need luck? I'll sell it to you cheap."

Hooper shook his head. "Superstition," he said.

The boy smiled. "What's wrong with superstition?" he asked. "Who says it don't work?"

Hooper took a coin out of his pocket, held it between himself and the boy. "This coin is for you if you fetch the police," he said, "bring them back to that house over there."

"Yeah?" said the boy. "And what if I say the coin's for the rabbit's foot."

"Pardon me?"

"I'm not going to any fucking police," said the boy, his face growing red, contorting. "The last thing you need right now is police, brother. What you need is a little luck."

"Are you asking for a fight?" Hooper started to say, but even as he said it the boy folded over and then seemed to gather himself like a bird. When he unfolded again he was big, taller than Hooper, with a face that looked simultaneously young and old.

"Goddam it, Hooper," he said, "don't you remember the fucking sequence? I'm not even supposed to be in this part of it."

"Lael?" Hooper said.

"No, you shit, Elling. It's Elling now."

"Oh," said Hooper. "Elling. Right."

Elling took him by the hand, began to walk. "Listen carefully. You don't go to the police."

"I don't?"

"That's the last thing you want. You've got to stop screwing this up."

"But—"

"I mean it," said Elling, leading him up to the stairs and into the house. On the landing, he motioned for Hooper to be quiet, didn't speak again until they were behind his door. He said, "And the other thing: I didn't do this. Don't blame me."

"Do what?"

"The girl. I didn't do that. You did it, friend."

"I did?"

"Don't you recognize her?"

"Should I?"

The room around him, what he could see of it, was beginning to fade, going gray. He watched the walls before him shiver, and began to feel there was something underneath—

Elling put a hand on either side of Hooper's head, staring into his eyes. "Focus, Hooper, focus."

"Oh," said Hooper, confused. "All right."

"Look," said Elling. "We'll leave you clues or something. Notes. Will that help?"

Hooper looked at him, confused. "It can't hurt," he finally said.

"Right," said Elling. "Third time's the charm."

For a moment he was not certain where he was. There was at first only a gray space, unlit, without features, closed in tight around him like a coffin. Yet after a moment he could see that some portions were not uniform, and began to make out simple planes that became more complex, more intensive, shades of lighter and darker gray. A moment later he could not understand how he had seen it as gray at all, for he now could see a high variance of both color and contour.

He was, he could see, in a room. He was sitting on a chair beside a bed. No, no, he was lying on a plank floor, beside a bed, beside a chair. Carefully he pulled himself up, into the chair. His body felt weak, his limbs hesitant to accept his commands. His hands ached.

From the chair he could see someone lying in the bed, a young woman, turned on her side and away from him. She was lying on top of a thinnish tapestry, but partly beneath a coverlet. Her shoulders were bare, her hair tangled and spreading wispily away from him.

His hands tingled. He looked down at them. They looked as his hands had always looked. Yet there was something odd about his sleeve. Attached near his wrist was a perfectly square piece of paper with some writing on it. The paper was colored an oddly uniform and pale yellow, unlike any paper he had ever seen. It was resting on his sleeve and clearly affixed, but he could see no pin affixing it.

He reached out and touched it, tugged it. It came away in his hand without much effort. Yet when he pressed it again to his sleeve it affixed itself again. He removed it again and found a strip on its underside to be covered with a gummy substance not unlike glue.

Ingenious, he thought. He stuck the slip onto his sleeve again, and it held! He removed it, then stuck it to the back of the chair. It stuck there too, equally well. He removed it, saw that it left no residue. *Incredible!* he thought. *So simple and yet—*

For a brief moment he saw flash up before him a quivering and angry face, simultaneously young and old. It startled him, confused him, and when he turned back he found that he had been mistaken about the paper. It was a simple piece of ordinary paper, machine milled, a pin through it. He sat staring at it a long moment before thinking to read what was written on it:

Your name is William Hooper Young. You go by Hooper.

Of course it is, he thought. Of course I do. But why bother to write this on a piece of paper and pin it to my arm?

When he lifted his head he realized there was a scrap of paper pinned to the girl as well, fluttering on the end of a straight pin stuck lightly into her back, just to one side of her spine. He reached out, took hold of the pin, carefully worked it free. The tip of it was red and slick, but no blood oozed from the hole it left. He pushed the pin into the bed frame, read the note.

Anna Pulitzer. An acquaintance and a sinner.

He crumpled the paper up and dropped it onto the floor.

"Anna," he said. "Wake up, Anna. While you've been sleeping someone's been pushing pins into your back." He began to reach for her, to prod her bare shoulder, but did he know her well enough to do so? What was the degree of their intimacy, if any? An acquaintance, the note had said. What was she doing nude in this bed, and he himself fully clothed?

She did not move. He cleared his throat. She still did not move. He cleared it again, louder this time. She was a sound sleeper.

"Anna," he said again and reached out to take her shoulder. Her flesh was cool to the touch.

He began to be very afraid.

He stood and leaned over her. He could see through her hair something amiss with her forehead; blood was matting together strands of hair. When he brushed the hair back he saw blood puddling in her eye socket, starting to coagulate and film over. With the flat of his hand he rolled her off her side, turning her face up. Beneath her the tapestry and bedding were stained dark with blood, and he saw her left temple caved in, slowly leaking blood and brain. Her belly too was neatly slit, the gash almost as long as his hand, slightly puckered. A scrap of paper had been wound into a tight scroll and inserted into her belly button. When he removed and unrolled it, he saw that it read:

Deceased. Murdered.

Sweet Lord, he thought. And then thought, *Who is leaving these notes?* The handwriting was small and spidery, nearly illegible. Was it his handwriting? He did not think it was. But he wasn't certain.

But there, didn't he just see the body's eye blink? Anna's eye? No, it was impossible. Anna was dead, the note said as much. But there again, the eye, blinking. But how could he even see the eye, filmed as it was with blood? And weren't her lips moving?

Am I going mad? Hooper wondered. And there was, he now saw, a note on the bedside table, two notes in fact. One folded around a knife, saying:

Your knife.

Another, lying flat on the bedside table:

Stay focused, Hooper.

Focused? he wondered. But on what exactly?

He crumpled the note and dropped it to the floor. When he looked up he saw that there were notes everywhere, on the walls, on the doors, on the floor. How he had not noticed them before, he did not know. He began to be very afraid. *Please help me,* he thought, and made his way slowly through the room and toward the front door. He tried not to step on any notes, but by the time he reached the front door he found notes pinned to his arms and legs and the front door too was bristling with them. He reached out for the knob, and they began to flutter all around him.

Son of a bitch, he thought.

What was going on exactly? He needed to relax, to focus, to stay focused. The note had said as much. Calm down, relax, stay focused. But how was that to be done exactly?

When he took a few steps back from the front door, the notes settled, and the breeze, if it had been a breeze that had so motivated them, died out.

And when he took a few more steps back the notes seemed to melt away into the door.

He turned back and went into the bedroom. Anna was still lying on the bed, same position, still dead, still winking at him. *Stay focused,* he told himself.

There was, he saw, a note on the bedside table, beneath the knife. Why he hadn't seen it before, he couldn't say.

Hide the body, you fool, the note said.

Ah, he thought, immediately feeling calmer. *Now we're getting somewhere.*

He wrapped the body in the sheets and the tapestry, then dragged it off the bed, the body sliding all at once into a heap. He dragged her by the feet across the floor and opened the door that was marked with an unusual-looking square yellow piece of paper—or rather (what was he thinking?) an ordinary scrap of paper—*closet.*

The small room was empty, the walls a cheap pasteboard, cracked in places. He pushed her in, leaned her against the wall, tucked the sheets in with her. He closed the door, stepped back for a look.

There was something underneath the note. He reached out and pulled the note away. Beneath was another note.

Not safe enough, the note said.

No, he thought, *not safe enough.* Anybody could come in and open the closet door, catch sight of the body. Not that people normally did come into one's house and open one's closet, but still. What if they did?

Not safe enough, not safe enough, he thought. He was getting anxious. He looked at the closet door. *Where is the note?* he wondered.

What note? he wondered.

Oh Christ, he thought, holding his head in his hands, *stay focused.*

What was it he was supposed to be worrying about? Yes, the body.

No, the closet was no good. But what then? He couldn't put her under the bed, the bed had a box frame, so there was no *under* to the bed. The closet might be good if there was something else in the closet, something he could hide her body under or beneath. The pantry? Same problem as the closet. Under the sink?

Yes, he thought, *under the sink.* Would she fit?

He dragged her out of the closet. Carefully he dragged the mass of bedding and body out of the bedroom and into the kitchen. He parted the sink and looked under it. Was there enough room? Well, not with the bedding perhaps, but the body, yes, if he folded it over, perhaps so. Was it too stiff to fold? No, it seemed supple enough. Probably she had not been dead for long.

He took the body under the neck and knees, folded her so her knees were touching her breasts. Turning her sideways, he forced her back-first under the sink. He had to hook her ankles behind a pipe to get her to stay in place.

He stood and admired his handiwork. When he dragged the sink's skirt into place, she could not be seen at all.

And what about the bedding? He carried it around the kitchen and through the bedroom, finally dropped it in the closet, turning it round so the bloodstains and gore could not be immediately seen. It looked ordinary, like any other heap of soiled bedding.

He returned to the kitchen, poured a glass of silty water from the sink, drank it down. She was there, he thought, a few inches from his feet.

Why am I not anxious? he wondered. And why too was he doing this, hiding a dead body, a murdered body? *What, if anything, do I have to do with her death?* And these notes, who was writing them, and why was he paying attention to them? *No,* he thought, getting anxious again, *something is wrong.* Something didn't click, something was out of joint. He would be well served to figure out what it was.

He began to pace back and forth.

At last he put his water glass down on the table, dropped wearily to his knees, and with the back of his hand parted the skirt surrounding the sink.

The girl was there, still folded up. There was, he realized, a rag stuffed into her mouth, filling it. Had that been there before? He didn't remember it. He reached out and very carefully tugged it free. It kept coming and coming.

"Please," the dead girl said, once it was completely free of her mouth. "You don't have to do this to me. Untie me."

"But you're not tied up," he said. "You're just folded up. And you're dead."

The girl was silent a long moment. "I want you to listen," she finally said. He could hear her words clearly but somehow did not see her lips move. "See these? These are ropes. I want you to untie them."

But see what? he wondered. She hadn't moved, not at all. What did she think she was showing him? It was like fingernails or hair, he thought, growing on after death. Her voice didn't know she was dead yet.

"This is some sort of trick," he said.

"No," the body was saying, and went on about the ropes. But what was that, fluttering, on her shoulder?

"You're having a bad dream, Anna," he told her, and reached out and took from her shoulder a small perfectly uniform piece of yellow paper.

Do not hold converse with the dead, it read.

Good advice, he thought.

"Anna?" she was saying. "But who's Anna? I'm—"

But luckily he had already begun tucking the rag back into her mouth. Soon the skirt was hanging properly again, and she was nowhere to be seen.

2

What he needed, he realized, was a trunk. A large trunk. He would put the body in that and smuggle it from the house. No one would be the wiser. He would get it out of the house and then they would have no way of implicating him in the crime. Or Elling either. Where was Elling? He had thought it would be, considering Elling's own proclivities for men, safe to leave him with the girl—he and Anna had been alone before, never to disastrous result. But apparently he had been wrong. Elling had killed the girl, who admittedly was a sinner. *An acquaintance and a sinner,* he wanted to say for some reason. They were never that close, despite what Anna herself had hoped for. But he had not killed her; Elling had killed her. Or at least that was what, if asked, he would tell the police.

What was the truth of it? The truth was that he couldn't remember. Better then not to go to the police. Better simply to divest himself of the body and continue on as if nothing had happened.

The trunk, then. Easy enough to acquire. He simply stepped out into the street and spoke to a boy who struck him as oddly familiar. A few coins were exchanged and moments later the boy came back down the street, lugging an empty trunk behind him.

Inside the apartment, boy dismissed, Hooper opened the trunk and looked in. *It will do,* he thought. He could tuck her in and carry her out; she was small enough to fit, if he bent her right, if she wasn't stiff yet. He reached his hand in past the sink's skirt, felt her. No, she was still warm, not stiff yet. She must not have been dead long.

Should he put her in the trunk now? No, he thought, better to hide it in the closet out of sight and wait for nightfall.

•

He sat on the bed, staring out the window, waiting. The sky, he could see, was going slowly dark. He felt drained, physically exhausted. He sat and stared.

When it was fully dark he drew the curtains and got the trunk out, dragging it across the bedroom floor and into the kitchen. He had just begun to tug the body out from under the sink when someone spun the ringer of the door.

He stopped, stayed still, holding the girl's legs in his arms. After a moment's silence, he tugged her the rest of the way out. He had just lifted her off the floor and was beginning to push her into the box when the ringer spun again.

He steadied her on the lip of the box, tried to decide what he should do.

"William?" said a voice through the door. "Is it you, William?"

"Who is it?" he called. It was awkward holding her, crouched over the box as he was. He let go of her head and her torso fell into the open box, her legs still hanging over the edge. Her body was much suppler than he imagined it would be, this long after death. And her eyes were blinking at him again.

"It's me," the voice behind the door claimed. "May I come in?"

Me? he wondered. *Me who?*

He lifted her legs and forced them into the trunk, let the lid fall. He went to the door, opened it a crack. A man, well-groomed, stood there.

"Yes?" said Hooper. "Can I help you?"

The man shook his head. "What a strange thing to say, William," he said. "Don't you recognize me?"

He looked at the man a long moment, his thin face, bright eyes. "Elling?" he said.

The man laughed. "Not Elling, William. One of the elders. From across the hall."

Behind his back, Hooper could hear a dull thumping. He half turned, saw the lid of the box give a leap.

"Yes," said Hooper. "I go by Hooper."

"Ah," said the elder. "As you wish, Hooper. Aren't you going to invite me in?"

"Can't," said Hooper. He glanced quickly behind. She had gotten one foot mostly out. What would it take for her to realize she was dead?

"Can't?"

"Indisposed."

The other man regarded him quizzically. "Indisposed?" he asked.

Hooper nodded.

The elder nodded. "Well," he said. "I can deliver my message from the doorstep, as it were. My companion and I wanted to invite you across the hall to join us for dinner. Do you care to come?"

In just a moment, he thought, *she will start screaming.*

"Can't," he said.

"Can't?" the man said.

Hooper shook his head. "Indisposed," he said. "Terribly sorry."

"Ah," said the elder. "Indeed. I wish you the best, then."

"And I you."

The man started to say something more but Hooper was already closing the door. He turned and went back to the trunk, forced her foot back in. He closed the latches and bound the straps, then sat down on top of the lid to smoke. His hands, he realized, were shaking.

Some time later he heard a sharp rap at the door. Like a man in a trance, he found himself moving to it, watched his hand turn the handle.

The door slid open. It was a man who looked neither young nor old, wearing gloves. "Charles," Hooper said.

"Hooper," said the man. "You didn't imagine I'd abandon a friend in need, did you?"

"I admit the thought had crossed my mind."

Elling came in, peeling off first one glove then the other, then held them like a bouquet in one hand. "She's in the trunk?" he asked.

"Who?" asked Hooper.

"The woman," said Elling. "Mrs. Pulitzer. You didn't leave her in the closet again, did you? I thought we talked about that. I thought you'd understood."

"No," said Hooper. "She's in the trunk."

"Good," said Elling. "Why didn't you say so from the beginning?"

He went to the trunk, opened it up, stared in. The girl was inside, knees folded up near her chest.

"What exactly do you have to do with this?" asked Hooper.

"Me?" said Elling, turning. "What makes you think I have anything to do with it?"

"Come on," Hooper said. "Why did you kill her?"

"Kill her?" asked Elling, smiling. "But I didn't kill her, Hooper."

He turned back around and fastened down the trunk. Putting his gloves on again, he took one of the handles of the trunk. "Give me a hand with this, Hooper. A cab is stationed below."

He sat beside Elling on the driver's board, listening to the horses' hooves. The trunk was behind them and inside the closed cab. *Did I kill her?* he wondered. He had no memory of doing any such thing. But if he hadn't killed her, why would Elling suggest he had?

Unless he wanted to protect himself.

He turned and regarded the man beside him. He was wrapped in his coat, barely visible. How well did he know Elling? He couldn't remember.

"Where are we going?" he asked.

The wrapped figure turned slightly, regarded him. "To free ourselves of this awful burden," he said.

Before long they reached the outskirts of the city, and soon too they had arrived at a drawbridge. Elling called out for the bridgeman, who came down and held up his lantern. Hooper turned his head away, and saw that Elling was doing the same.

"Where are you going?" the bridgeman asked.

"Across the bridge," said Elling, his voice strange and hoarse.

The man kept his lantern up a moment more and then turned. He went to his wheel, worked the drawbridge down.

They crossed in silence. "We shall return a different way," said Elling.

They followed the road west down to where it crossed a canal over a stone-sided, wood-slatted bridge just wide enough for a narrow road and a brace of trolley rails.

"As good a place as any," said Elling.

Hooper swallowed. "I suppose," he said.

Elling smiled. He tied the reins back and stepped down from the cab. Hooper followed him. They opened the door of the cab and dragged the trunk out.

"Do we throw the whole thing in?" asked Hooper.

"No point wasting a good trunk," said Elling.

He put his hands under the girl's arms and pulled her out. "Take her legs," he told Hooper, who did so. They carried her onto the bridge and rested her on the wall to one side.

"We need something to weigh her down," Elling said. "Otherwise she'll float."

Hooper stood dumbly.

"Go find something, Hooper," Elling said. "And hurry."

Hooper nodded and turned away. What was there? A stone from the walls of the bridge? They were, it seemed, mortared in place. Was there anything in the cab? No. But on the floor of the cab was a square of yellow paper and on it, he could just make out in the moonlight, the word *under*.

He stooped down. And he could see, hanging between the horses and the cab proper, a hitching weight. It looked absurd and in flux in the darkness, as if its shape had yet to be determined. Even after he had unhooked it and taken it in his hands it remained troublingly protean.

He carried it back to Elling. "Will this do?" he asked.

Elling regarded it, nodded. "A lodestone," he said. "To be slung around the neck." He fished a leather strap from one pocket and threaded it through the weight, then tied it around the woman's waist.

"I thought you said neck," said Hooper.

"Manner of speaking," said Elling. "Up we go then, brother Hooper."

He took her again by the shoulders, waited for Hooper to grab the legs. Together they lifted the body over the side of the bridge, and let it fall into the canal below.

It hit with a hard sound, like a stick striking rock, and was quickly swallowed up. It was too dark in any case to see much of anything.

They walked together back toward the cab, climbed in. They sat in silence for a moment, unmoving.

"Well, that's that," said Hooper.

"Don't be too sure, friend," Elling said, regarding him with a piercing eye. "Don't be too sure."

It was nearing light by the time they got back to Young's father's apartments. There was already the bustle of noise and bodies in the streets, torpid still, just a few figures here and there, but growing.

Elling pulled the wagon up short. Holding the reins in one hand he reached over to clasp Hooper's hand with the other.

Hooper took the hand dully, then slowly climbed down.

"And the wagon, then?" asked Hooper, looking up.

"Rented," said Elling. "I'll drive it about the streets a few hours and then return it."

Hooper nodded. He turned and walked to the street door, which he opened with a key he discovered in his pocket. When he turned about again, the street was empty, the cab gone.

He climbed the stairs as quietly as he could, crossed the landing, and went into his apartment, locking the door behind him. Inside it was dark, a little dim light flitting through the windows. He felt his way through the kitchen and into the bedroom, let himself fall on the bed, fell almost immediately asleep.

When he awoke, it took him a moment to understand where he was. At first there was only a gray space, featureless, unlit, as tight upon and around him as a coffin, which slowly began to congeal, if congeal was the right word, into something else. There, the edge of a cabinet, glass-fronted and snug against the wall, there a television, its screen lit and sound oozing—

"Not a television," said Elling, behind him. "Wrong place. No such thing as a television yet."

"What?" said Hooper. "How did you get in? How long have you been here?"

But Elling was nowhere to be seen. Had he been imagining things? He sat up in bed, examined the room more closely. It was, he realized, his father's room, in New York. He knew exactly where he was, exactly.

But why had he slept in the bed where Anna had been killed? It made his skin crawl to think about it. He got up and brushed off his clothes. Her clothes, he realized, were still there, in the apartment, bundled in the closet with the sheets. He should have dumped them into the canal along with her corpse, shouldn't he have? No, perhaps not. They wouldn't have sunk like the body had.

In any case, it was too late. He would have to dispose of them separately now. He would have to ship them away, somewhere far.

Like Chicago, maybe.

Why Chicago?

No reason. Why not?

He gathered the sheets from the closet and carried them out into the kitchen, stopped dead. In the middle of the floor was a trunk, lid thrown open, empty.

But he hadn't brought the trunk in. It was still in Elling's rented cab.

But perhaps Elling had realized and turned the cab around and brought the trunk back to him.

But the lock was still on the door. He had locked the door and the door was still locked. How was it possible for the trunk to be here? It was as if he were missing something. Like he was having those blackouts again. He glanced at the cuff of his shirt, expecting to see it stained and spattered with blood.

Wait a minute, he thought. *What blackouts?*

"Lael?" he called.

There was a slight nickering laugh. *You have to try better than that to keep your friends straight, Rudd.*

He reached out and took the closet door handle. Still sitting, he turned it, pushed. The door slid slowly open to reveal a large room with perfectly straight walls and regular angles, a carpet on the floor that stretched from wall to wall to wall without gap or seam. A large bed with a woman on it, her ankles tied together with duct tape, her arms hidden behind her back. Her mouth was gagged and she was looking at him with fierce and determined eyes, trying to speak through her gag.

He shut his eyes and kept them shut tight. On his knees he moved far enough back into the room to feel out the door handle and pull the door shut again.

For a while he could hear, through the door, the noise of the girl, the sound of her thrashing. He tried to slow his breathing, tried to focus on the real world, tried to see the streets of New York, his father's apartment. After a time he felt sufficiently himself to open the door again. This time he found only a closet, the girl gone, bloody sheets draped over the trunk and ready to be packed and shipped. Everything was as it should be.

He dragged the trunk out of the apartment, leaving it on the landing as he turned around and locked the door. When he turned back, he could see one of the elders peering out of the other apartment, watching him.

"Greetings, William," the man said.

"Please, Hooper," said Hooper.

"Hooper it is and shall be," the elder said. "You're going away, I take it? Traveling?"

"No," said Hooper.

"Oh. I just assumed, the trunk and all—"

"Not at all," said Hooper. "Just a few things to be shipped to a friend."

"Can I be of service?"

"No," said Hooper. "I can manage, thank you."

"Well, then," said the elder, somewhat stiffly, touching his hat. "A pleasure speaking with you."

When he was gone, Hooper dragged the trunk to the bottom of the stairs and out the front door. A boy was there, just across the street. He looked vaguely familiar. Hooper gestured to him and he came over.

"Sir?" the boy said.

"How'd you like to earn a little pocket money, lad?" asked Hooper.

"Yes, sir," said the boy, and then stopped and looked at Hooper askance. "For doing what?"

"Just grab a handle and help me lug this trunk to the station."

The boy smiled and took hold. They started off down dusty streets, past brownstones, along the boardwalks.

"Sir," said the boy, half-turning.

"What is it, you little scamp?" asked Hooper.

"Did you hear word of the murder, sir?"

Hooper stuttered in his steps but went on. "What murder?" he asked.

"A woman, sir. Killed and then abandoned in a canal. Only the killer didn't realize the canal went dry at low tide. A trolley man saw the body first thing this morning."

"I see," said Hooper.

"Grisly, sir," said the boy. Turning, he half-looked at Hooper as he continued to shuffle forward. "What do you suppose drives a man to kill?"

"Do I know you?" Hooper asked the boy. "I must confess you look familiar to me."

"No, sir," said the boy. "I don't suppose you've ever seen me in your life nor ever shall again."

Hooper nodded. They kept on, heading west, toward the train station.

"Shouldn't you hire a cab, sir?" asked the boy.

Hooper shook his head.

"Well," said the boy. "You know best, sir. It isn't very heavy in any case. What's in it, sir, if you don't mind my asking?"

"Personal effects."

"What's meant by that, sir?"

"Just a few things to be shipped to a friend."

"There can't be much in there," said the boy. "Not that I'm complaining."

It was suddenly becoming dark. Around them, the apartments and brownstones had begun to give away, opening up onto houses set back from the curb and from perfectly manicured lawns. Hooper could see a man, at the far end of the sidewalk, coming toward them.

"This isn't the way to the station," said Hooper.

"I've just been following your lead, sir," said the boy. "I'm not to blame."

The man was coming toward them, walking slowly. Hooper looked about for a street sign, saw not the usual wooden post but on the corner a pole with a flap of metal painted green and lettered white. Timpview Drive, it read.

Timpview Drive? he wondered. *Where is that in relation to Penn Station?* He was very lost, he realized, though a moment ago he had known exactly where he was. And now, he found, he was not even sure from which direction he had come.

He turned to the boy, but he was gone, the other end of the trunk resting on the sidewalk. And it was not a trunk, he could now see, but a suitcase ingeniously wheeled at one end, a square of yellow paper reading *trunk* attached to it.

The man was already there, nearly on him. Hooper looked up, smiled. The man nodded, squinting into the darkness, then stopped a few feet shy.

"Nice evening," the man said.

"Yes, indeed," said Hooper.

"Not too hot, not too cold."

"That's right," said Hooper.

"You're a block over, aren't you?" said the man. "Mrs. Theurer's boy. Rudd. Married now, aren't you?"

Hooper began to shake his head and then stopped. Rudd Theurer. Did he know anyone by that name? "Yes," he said. "That's right. Rudd."

"Thought so," said the man. "I have a way with faces. Mel Johnson," he said, extending his hand. "You've got your father's face."

Hooper took the hand, smiled. "You know my father?"

Mel Johnson nodded. "Quite well before he died. A shame, that."

"But my father's not—" Hooper started to say, but then stopped.

The man, in any case, wasn't paying much attention. "What's in the suitcase?" he asked. "Traveling, are you?"

"No," said Hooper. "Just a few odds and ends."

"Where are you living now, then, young Rudd?" asked the man.

"A few blocks away."

"What street?"

"Over there," said Hooper. "Just a few blocks that way."

"Just off Canyon Road? And what's that on your suitcase? A post-it note?"

"I have to go," said Hooper. "I'm sorry."

"All right, then," said the man, smiling. "Off you go. Nice to see you again."

Rudd passed the man and walked on, dragging the suitcase down the sidewalk. He would just keep walking, he thought, until he recognized something. If this Mel Johnson were questioned by the police, he would only say he had seen Rudd Theurer out pulling a suitcase down the sidewalk. And now he, Hooper, had a false name he could use. Perhaps others would mistake him for Rudd Theurer as well. If the police were to sniff out his trail, they would not find him at the end of it but only Rudd Theurer. He himself would be left safe and sound.

And suddenly he began to recognize the buildings, was again in a part of Manhattan that he knew. And what he had thought was an ingeniously wheeled suitcase was not a suitcase at all but a trunk, and the boy who had abandoned him was with him again.

"Well?" he asked the boy. "Where have you been?"

The boy shrugged.

They kept on. Up ahead, Hooper caught a glimpse of the train station. Soon the trunk would be safely on a train somewhere. Where? Who knew, anywhere, the first train out. And then he would be home again, and safe as well.

3

He bought a copy of the *Times* on the way home, from a boy that struck him as somehow familiar, and sat on a bench to read it. He discovered that yes, they had found the body. The canal had been tidal, the water rushing out at low tide. He and Elling had made a mistake. The article spoke too of the hitching weight they had tied to her waist and described it as being "of peculiar make." What did that mean exactly? Could it be traced? Had Elling rented the wagon under another name?

He folded the paper under his arm and continued home. A few blocks away, he ran into the elders from across the hall, each carrying the Book of Mormon, walking together. He stopped and lifted his hat to them.

"Just going home, William?" one asked as they both stopped.

He nodded. "Hooper," he said. "I go by Hooper."

The other smiled. "Of course you do," he said.

They stayed looking at each other for a long moment. At a loss, he felt the paper tucked under his arm. Holding it out, he said, "Would one of you like to take it? I've finished with it."

"Thank you," said one of the elders. He reached out and took the paper, then looked at his companion. "Shall we tell him, Elder?"

The other elder hesitated, shook his head.

"Tell me what?"

"The police," said the first elder. "They came asking after you."

The other elder looked at the first sternly.

"The police?"

"He gave us a newspaper, didn't he?" said the first to the second. He turned to Hooper, patted him on the arm. "Watch out for yourself, Hooper."

•

He spent nearly an hour outside the building, across the street, watching. It seemed safe. If someone was watching the building, they were discreet enough that he couldn't identify them.

When it began to grow dim outside, he ducked his head and crossed over the street. He darted in the door.

He made his way quickly to his apartment, fumbled the door unlocked, closing and locking it behind him once he was in.

For a moment the room seemed wavery, as if underwater. He took a deep breath and rubbed his eyes and again it was just an ordinary room.

He left the entrance hall and went into the kitchen. He was tempted to look under the skirt of the sink, but resisted the temptation, instead making his way through and into the bedroom.

The room was empty, the closet door slightly ajar. Had the police been in the apartment? He opened the door of the closet, immediately saw the blood staining the closet floor. He began to pace the room. Undoubtedly they had not been inside, he thought, or they would have stayed waiting for him. But how had they known to come looking for him in the first place? And how much time would he have now? Perhaps they were already on their way back to look for him again. No, he must leave, as quickly as possible.

But where? he wondered. *Where shall I go?*

He let his hands stray through the clothes in the closet, finally choosing both a shirt and coat that looked well-worn, on the verge of shabbiness. He took off his own shirt and put the shirt and coat on, found them oddly too big. They were his, weren't they? Whose else could they be? Was he himself growing smaller somehow? In any case there was an advantage in them being too large; it would make him seem more of a tramp. He would be incognito.

Going back into the kitchen, he searched through the drawers and cabinets. In one he found a boning knife, meant to be held with one's thumb pressed to a smooth spot dimpled on the guard. He made a few passes through the air with it, stowed it in his pocket. The other pocket he filled with cayenne pepper, loose handfuls for use as a defense.

There was a sound, like a bell striking, though not a bell exactly. He stopped moving, one hand still in his jacket pocket, and listened. The police?

But no, surely not, just a horse bell or the bell of a dray or a clock striking. There was no bell attached to the door of his house, only the ringer, and no one had knocked on the door.

The bell that was not exactly a bell struck again, then struck a third time.

He took his hand out of his pocket, out of the cayenne, and brushed it off on his coat. It was a doorbell, he had to admit, and now began to see—through the furniture, the wood floor, the fireplace, the simple bed—other shapes, other objects asserting themselves more insistently. A carpet that stretched from one wall to the other without seam. A television set. A less simple and larger bed with a slatted headboard upon which lay a woman, bound hand and foot, just barely moving, her eyes glazed and dull.

In the hall mirror, he pushed at his hair. But was that him in the glass? He hadn't shaved or bathed, he realized, in a number of days.

The doorbell rang again. He moved down the hall, starting down the stairs toward it.

"I wouldn't do that if I were you," said a voice behind him.

He turned and saw there, behind him, his half-brother.

"Don't worry," he said. "I can handle it."

"Please," said Lael. "You overestimate yourself. Don't you want me to come along?"

He stayed a long moment looking at Lael. The doorbell rang again. "All right," he said, "come if you want."

He turned and without looking behind him to see if Lael followed, he continued to the bottom of the stairs. What had been the name the man on the street had called him? Rudd? Would that work here as well?

The doorbell rang again before he reached the door. He opened it, looked out.

On the steps was an older woman, her hair carefully cut and streaked, trying to look younger than she really was. She had a suitcase to either side of her.

"Well?" she said.

"Excuse me?" he said.

"You must be Rudd," she said. "You're filthy."

"Hooper," he started to say, then corrected himself, stopped. Behind him he heard his half-brother's voice. "Tell her you've been working on the car," Lael said.

"I've been working on the car," he said.

She looked at him, narrowing her eyes. "But the car's right here," she said, pointing to the driveway. "And the hood's down."

"Right," he said. "Just finished."

"I suppose your beard grew while you were fixing the car as well, eh? Cleanliness, not beardliness, is next to Godliness," she said. "Aren't you going to invite me in?"

"Invite you in?" he asked. "But who are you?"

"This is bad, Rudd," said Lael, behind him.

"I'm Lyndi's aunt, silly," she said. "Here to meet the new in-law. You."

"Why didn't you call?" he asked.

"I did," said the aunt. "I called and called. Nobody ever answered. So I just came."

"Invite her in," said Lael. "Then kill her."

"Are you kidding?" asked Rudd, half-turning to Lael, trying to see him there behind him.

"No," said Lael.

"No," said Lyndi's aunt. "Maybe there's something wrong with your phone? Where's Lyndi? And what's that post-it on your shirt? 'Hopper.' What does that mean?"

"Invite her in," Lael said.

"Lyndi's not here," said Rudd.

The aunt shrugged. "I can wait," she said, and took a step toward the door. Rudd quickly closed it further, peered at her through the crack.

"I don't think that would be all right," he said.

"Where is she?" the aunt asked.

"Don't be a fool," said Lael, hissing now in his ear. "Invite her in. Be cordial. Offer her a glass of water. Slaughter her."

"Would you like a drink?" he asked.

The aunt nodded. "Why can't I come in?" she asked. And then asked again, "Where's Lyndi?"

"Just a moment," he said. "One drink coming up," and shut and locked the door.

"You're going to ruin everything," Lael was whispering all the way back down the hall. "Everything." He sat leaning against the counter, his arms crossed, watching Rudd's shaky hands pour a glass of water.

"If it's so important," Rudd said, "why don't you do it?"

Lael smiled. "It's not as easy as that," he said. "Our relationship has changed."

"How has it changed?"

"For one thing, there are four of us."

"Four of us? Where are the other two?"

"It's not as simple as that."

"I don't understand what's going on here. I want to be back in New York."

"No," said Lael. "That's not the problem. Don't lie to me. You understand all too well."

Rudd was already starting back toward the door, hands still shaking, trying to ignore his half-brother's voice. He managed to get the door unlocked. He passed the glass of water to her, spilling some on her hands.

"Thank you," the aunt said, and took it. She took a long drink.

"Should have poisoned it," said Lael.

"Shut up," hissed Rudd.

"Excuse me?" said the aunt.

"Nothing," Rudd said.

The aunt put her knuckles against her hip, her elbow swiveled out. "Young man," she said, "I want to know what's going on here. Where's my niece?"

"She isn't here," said Rudd.

"Then where is she?"

Rudd stared. "New York," he finally said.

"New York? What business would she have in New York?"

"Vacation," whispered Lael.

"Vacation," said Rudd.

"Vacation?" said the aunt. "But why would she go on vacation without you?"

Rudd shrugged.

"There's something funny going on here," the aunt said.

"You see?" said Lael. "You should have listened to me."

"Would you like to come in?" asked Rudd, and opened the door wide.

She looked at him warily, took a step back. "I don't think so," she said.

"But you wanted to come in before," he said.

She stepped all the way off the porch, began backing slowly away down the drive.

"You've got to catch her," said Lael.

"Wait," said Rudd. "I'm not going to hurt you."

"Throw the pepper in her eyes," said Lael, but by the time he said it she was already out to the sidewalk.

"What about her bags?" asked Lael.

"What about your bags?" asked Rudd.

"I'll leave them there," she said. "You can take them inside if you like. Or not. I'll come back for them." She set the water glass down on the cement. "Here's your glass," she said. And then she was off, down the sidewalk and away.

"Now you've done it," said Lael. "Now you've really done it."

They went back into the house, Rudd shutting the door behind him, locking it. He started down the hall and toward the stairs, his half-brother coming close behind him.

"She'll be back, you know," said Lael.

"I know," said Rudd.

"And she won't be alone."

"I know," said Rudd.

"Don't you care?"

Rudd shrugged. He started up the stairs. Had he been walking that slowly, for them to have such a conversation over ten feet of hallway?

"Don't you love me?" asked Lael.

"Excuse me?" said Rudd.

"Don't you love me?" Lael insisted. "Don't you care for your half-brother?"

Rudd paused on the stairs and turned. There was his half-brother behind him, hesitating, pale as a ghost.

"I think I hate you," said Rudd.

Lael smiled. "Close enough," he said. "Same difference."

They were standing on either side of the bed, Lyndi lying bound and gagged between them. Her eyes were closed. She looked pale. How had she gotten out of the trunk and back on the bed? He did not remember carrying her, or tying her up for that matter.

"Which one of us tied her up?" he asked Lael.

"Whichever," Lael said. "What difference does it make?"

But it does make a difference, Rudd thought. *It must.*

"Well," said Lael, sighing, "are you ready?"

"Ready? Ready for what?"

"To get back to it," said Lael. "To get on with it. To finish." He cracked the knuckles on one hand, then cracked those on the other. "But we should do something about Lyndi first."

"I thought we already did something about her," said Rudd.

"We did," said Lael. "Or rather Hooper and Elling did. But that was a different girl. Anna."

"We should bring it to a stop," said Rudd. "Whatever we're doing, it's time to stop."

Lael laughed. "It's too late, Rudd. You couldn't stop now even if you wanted to."

Rudd turned and made for the door. He passed through it and went down the stairs and out the front door, which somehow opened again into the same room, Lyndi on the bed, Lael standing beside. He went out the door and down the stairs again and this time into the kitchen, only it was not the kitchen but again the same bedroom.

"Change of heart, Rudd?" asked Lael. "Little late for that now, isn't it?"

"I'm not the person you think I am," said Rudd.

Lael chuckled. "Who is?" he asked. "But you're not who you think you are either."

"Want to bet?"

"No time for a fight, Rudd," Lael said. "In fact, time's running out altogether." He gestured toward Lyndi, whose eyes were open now. She was dully struggling. "You've got to kill her," said Lael. "Kill her and we'll get on with it."

"I don't want to."

"You want me to do it?"

"I don't want anyone to do it."

Lael shrugged. "Whatever, what do I care? After all, brother, it's your life."

Lael turned around and faced the closet, took a wool jacket and a fedora out of it.

"Put these on," he said to Rudd.

Rudd took them. "What's this for?"

"It's time to leave," said Lael.

"Where are we going?"

"New York."

Rudd slipped the hat on. *New York?* he thought. He put the hat on his head, held the jacket in front of him, looked at it.

"Come on, Hooper," said Lael. "We're in a hurry."

The jacket seemed too big for him until he had it on, but then seemed to fit just right. *How odd,* he thought.

The room was changing around him, the carpet pulling away from the walls and becoming a rug of oriental design. The girl on the bed, he saw, had gone pale, all the color draining out of her, as if she were becoming a ghost. He looked up at Lael, saw him the same way, devoid of color and substance as if one could reach through him. His own hand, he saw, was still fleshy and solid.

"Aren't you coming with me, Lael?" he asked.

"I'm Elling now," the man said. And indeed as Hooper looked at him he could not understand how he could have mistaken Elling for anyone else. Who had it been now? "You're on your own, Hooper," the voice said, "at least for a while." And then Elling and everyone around him seemed to fade, and his own mind went dark as well.

4

It was time to leave. It would not be long before the police would be back; he had already spent too much time in his father's apartment as it was. He slipped out of the door of the apartment and down the stairs, changing his walk to crouch a little, ambling like a tramp, swaying a little on his way down the street.

A block away from the apartment he passed a brace of policemen moving the opposite direction. He ducked his head and gave them a wide berth. Both of them, somehow, looked vaguely familiar. Neither one paid him any heed. After they had passed, he slid into a doorway and watched them covertly to see where they were going. Did they turn into his doorway? He shielded his eyes from the sun with one hand. Yes, perhaps. He couldn't see clearly for the sun and crowds, but they were, in any case, now gone.

He kept on down the street to the corner and then turned, went down a block, cut up again to less busy streets. Four or five blocks away from his father's house he straightened up, straightened his cap, and headed for the railroad tracks.

He had gone a few more blocks when he heard a voice behind him calling his name. It sounded vaguely familiar. He kept on walking, hunching his shoulders slightly and picking up his pace.

"Mr. Young!" the voice called behind him. "Mr. Hooper! Wait!"

He cast a quick glance back over his shoulder, saw only a young boy. He slowed down a little, never quite stopping but still letting the boy catch up.

"What is it?" he asked once the boy was beside him, panting. It was the same boy, he saw now, who had helped him with the trunk. "Speak up," he said.

"It's just," the boy said, and then looked shrewdly at Hooper. "I know what you did, sir. I read it in the paper."

"What have I done?" asked Hooper.

"And," said the boy, "it seems to me it might be worth something to you to stop me from calling attention to you."

Hooper swerved toward the boy and struck him hard in the temple. The boy stumbled and cursed, went down.

"Don't threaten me," Hooper said, and kicked the boy in the throat with the tip of his shoe.

The boy gave a strangled cry and gripped his throat and then, as Hooper watched, he began to change, his body stretching in every direction until he was fully a man.

"Lael?" said Hooper.

"Elling," said the man, still holding his throat, his voice rasping.

Yes it was Elling, thought Hooper. But how was that possible? "What are you doing here?" he asked. "Where do you come from?"

"You've gone too far," said Elling. "Can't you see this is just a game?"

"A game?"

Elling nodded. "Pay the boy and get on with it," he said.

"Why?" said Hooper.

"And," said Elling, ignoring him, "you forgot to mail the note."

"The note?"

"Jesus," said Elling, "don't you remember anything? 'Search in vain; have killed myself.' Does that ring a bell?"

Hooper shook his head. "I don't have any paper," he said.

"Ask the boy," said Elling, still rubbing his throat, which, Hooper saw, was now smeared with blood.

"What boy?" Hooper asked. He reached down and touched his own throat and brought his hand away to find it bloody as well.

"Brothers always," he heard Elling say. But when he looked up, Elling was nowhere to be seen, in his place a small boy holding out his palm.

He shook his head to clear it, then reached into his pocket and absently removed a coin, pressed it into the boy's hand. Then he started past.

The boy stopped him. "There's something you're forgetting," he said.

"Forgetting?" said Hooper.

"Something you wanted to ask me."

"There is?"

"Don't you remember?"

"It must not have been very important," said Hooper, and brushed past.

But there was a larger hand on his shoulder and when he turned he saw not the boy, but a pale-eyed man, hawk-like and older.

"Lael?" he said.

"Elling, goddammit! Can't you keep something straight in your head for three goddam seconds? No wonder you have problems!"

"Problems?"

"Problems, yes, problems!" Elling slapped him hard in the face. "All right," he said. "I'll write the note," he said. He took out a pencil and a square of paper, a tiny envelope such as those made for visiting cards.

"Search in vain," he said slowly as he wrote, "have killed myself. H. Young." The signature, Hooper saw, was his own. "I'll post it as well," he said. "I'll do all the goddam work. Now go," said Elling. "Board the train and go."

Confused, Hooper stumbled off. He looked back over his shoulder and saw Elling having a conversation with himself. Where was he, Hooper, going? Yes, the train.

He climbed aboard the first train leaving, bought a ticket from the conductor. The latter gave him a long look through his thick spectacles but sold him a ticket and passed on.

There were two others in the compartment with him. One an older lady who kept her hand always on a carpetbag in the seat beside her, the other a gentleman about his own age, starched collar, well-dressed, who was reading a copy of the *Times*.

Young cleared his throat.

"Where is this train going?" he asked.

The woman just gripped her bag more tightly. The man moved his paper down slightly, looked at Hooper over the top of a pair of spectacles. The man looked vaguely familiar, Hooper felt. So, for that matter, Hooper realized, did the woman.

"You don't know what train you're on?" asked the man.

Hooper looked at him. "I believe I might have climbed aboard the wrong train," he said.

"Well," said the man, folding the printed sheets over and laying them in his lap. "What train were you trying to get on?"

"What train is this?" asked Hooper.

"Why didn't you ask the conductor?"

"I didn't think to," said Hooper. "Please, there's no reason not to be civil."

The man picked up the paper again. "Upstate," he said from behind it. "We're traveling upstate."

"Thank you," said Hooper. He looked back, stared at the empty seat across from him. *Upstate,* he thought. He would travel a few more stops, step down once he was a little distance away from the city, and then hide, "tramp it," as it were, live incognito and by the rough a few weeks until it was safe, until he could think of what to do.

He closed his eyes and felt the slow rhythm of the train. Yes, he thought, he would hide. He would start his life over. Everything would be all right. He was nearly asleep now, his eyes closed, occasional light from outside passing over his lids. Everything, he told himself, would be all right.

He heard a sound at a distance, like a bell. What could it be exactly? Like a bell but not a bell. Something was shaking him, had been shaking him, he realized, for quite some time.

"Hooper," a voice was whispering. "Hooper!"

He rubbed his face. He opened his eyes and saw beside him, in the seat that had been occupied by the man with the newspaper, his half-brother, Lael.

"How did you come here?" Rudd asked.

"I'm like the Holy Ghost," said Lael. "I'm always here."

He heard the sound again, the pitched vibrations after it. The train seemed to ripple as if underwater, but then kept on in its steady, rocking motion.

"What is that?" he asked.

"What?" said Lael. "The doorbell," he said. "But no reason to answer. They'll be here soon enough."

Rudd struggled to get up, fighting against the motion of the train. "I should answer," he said. "It's impolite not to."

"Doesn't matter if you do or don't," said Lael. "It's too late."

Rudd made his way out of the compartment and into the companion-way. It was louder out there, the motion and movement of the train all around him. He began to make his way toward the front of the train.

"Time to say good-bye," said a voice behind him.

He turned and looked to see Lael, his head poking out of the compartment door.

"Good-bye?" Rudd asked.

"You won't see me again," said Lael. "At least not for a long while."

"But you're like the Holy Ghost," said Rudd. "You're always here."

Lael nodded his head. "That's right," he said. "But how often do you catch a glimpse of the Holy Ghost?"

Rudd started to speak but the doorbell rang again and the train shook and was gone, and Lael along with it. He was in a hallway. The hallway of his house, Lyndi's house. He felt bereft and adrift.

He went back to where the train compartment had been, where there was now a door. Opening it, he went in. It was a bedroom. On the bed was a girl, hands tied, mouth gagged, eyes closed. Was she dead? He got closer, bent down near her face. No, she was breathing.

He loosened the gag and pulled it down around her neck. Immediately, she opened her eyes.

"Rudd," the girl said, keeping her voice even, looking at him with an unwavering gaze. "Don't you know who I am?"

He stopped, nodding. Who was she? She looked familiar, didn't she?

"I'm Elling," she said.

"Elling?" he said.

"Yes," she said, "don't you remember? You gave me that name, didn't you? In the temple?"

In the temple? he wondered. Yes, he thought, the name had been Rachel, but he had changed it, he had pulled a fast one on God.

"But if you're Elling, who's the other one?"

"The other one," she said. At first he thought he'd found her out, that she didn't have an answer. "The other one," she said finally, "is an imposter."

An imposter? But how had it happened? How had he let it happen?

"Rudd," she said, this new Elling said. Or was it the old Elling? "Let me go."

He looked at her a long time. "All right," he finally said.

Her legs, loosely tied, came quickly free. In fact, he couldn't understand why she hadn't gotten free of them on her own. "I'm sorry," he said. "I didn't mean to kill you." He started back to work on the knots around her hands. They were very tight, her hands he could see curled and dark, perhaps permanently damaged. What did he feel? He did not know what he felt. No, he felt hemp cord, rough, tightly coiled.

The doorbell rang again.

"Hello?" he said. "Just a minute," he said. The ropes weren't coming loose. "I'll be right back," he said.

"No," she said. "Untie me first."

"I'll hurry," he said. "I just have to answer the door."

"But—" she said.

"I'll be right back," he said, going out. "I promise."

Looking through the peephole he saw the girl's—Anna's? no, that wasn't quite right, what was her name?—aunt, two uniformed officers behind her. He opened the door a little way, peered out around it.

"Yes?" he said.

"I demand to see my niece," said the aunt.

"She isn't here," said Rudd. "I told you that already."

One of the officers took a slight step forward. *Officer Etting,* his tag read. Did he look familiar? Rudd wasn't quite sure. "Sorry to bother you, sir, but this woman has a suspicion that something untoward has happened to her niece. Would you mind if we came in?"

"Officer Elling?" asked Rudd.

"Etting," the man corrected.

"She's not here," said Rudd again.

"Where is she, then?" asked the aunt. "Where is she?"

What was it he had said before? What was wrong with him that he couldn't remember? He looked behind him for his half-brother, but nobody was there. He was alone.

"Well?" said the aunt. "Well?"

"Lael?" he called out.

"Excuse me?" said the other officer on the porch.

"If we could just come in a moment and look around," said Officer Etting. "Just to reassure her."

"No," said Rudd. "Absolutely not." He started to close the door but the officer already had his foot wedged in to block it.

"There's nothing to be afraid of," Officer Etting said soothingly. "Just let us come in, just for a moment, and then we'll leave you in peace."

Rudd looked at him for a long time. Did it matter if they came in? What mattered anymore? He wasn't sure. "I have too much to do," he said.

"We don't want to have to call for a warrant," said the one who wasn't Etting.

"Who said anything about calling for a warrant?" asked Etting smoothly. "You're going to let us in, aren't you?"

"I'm not," said Rudd.

"Sure you are," said Etting. "You want to cooperate."

He tried to force Etting's shoe out of the door but it wouldn't go. "Lael?" he called again, but there was no response. He began to grope around for something to help force the shoe out but found nothing; he was in the entrance hall, he had nothing but himself, but then, he realized, there, in his coat pocket—

He opened the door wide, reaching into his coat pocket at the same time, bringing out a fistful of pepper.

"There," said Etting, "that's more like it."

He threw the handful of cayenne pepper into the policeman's eyes. The man stumbled back, shouting, rubbing his face. Rudd slammed the door shut and bolted it, rushed up the stairs and into the bedroom, closing and locking that door too.

His heart was beating hard. The girl, he found, had managed to get up off the bed and was on her way, swaying, into the closet. He took her by the arm and pulled her out, pushed her onto the bed and tumbled on top of her, knees straddling her hips. Below, downstairs, he could hear someone pounding on the door and the door beginning to give. They would be through soon, and he was not, he realized, even quite sure what door it was or what place it opened into. There is so much more, he thought: his father's face at the trial, his temporary cell, the testimony of witnesses, his rabbit's foot, the rush of the crowd toward him and their attempts to kill him, and then finally his own jail cell and twenty years of peace. But no, he thought, he didn't have a father, his father was dead, he had no father, that had been the trouble all along. But at very least, someone's father's face at a trial, someone's holding cell, the testimony of blank-faced witnesses, someone's rabbit's foot, the rush of a crowd toward someone and their attempts to kill him, and then finally someone's jail cell and twenty years of peace. But not his. In any case, so much more. But no more time.

These painful moments of lucidity, an affliction. What can we do but wait for them to pass?

They were through the door downstairs, and he could hear them going through the house, shouting, making their way in. Where was his half-brother now, now that he needed him? He shouted his names, but there was no response.

Only me now, he thought. He felt the girl beneath him swallow, her throat shuddering against the web of his thumb. *Only me,* he thought. And as he did so she faded from beneath him, disappeared. So she had gotten away after all, he thought. *But how?*

He stayed there, motionless, his hands still clenched where her neck had been, trying to bring her back. He waited for someone to tell him who to be next.

I was Mormon when I started writing *The Open Curtain*. By the time I finished it, years later, I had left the Mormon Church of my own volition, first by gradually ceasing to participate in the ceremonies of the Mormon temple, then by tapering back my participation in weekly church services, and finally—finding neither of these to give me sufficient distance from a culture that objected to my first book of fiction on moral grounds— by formally requesting, in 2000, to be excommunicated. The book itself was an integral part of a movement from a position of faith to a position of unbelief, a movement that the book itself charts in a real and palpable way.

The novel began when I, much like Rudd himself (though I was years older than he at the time), stumbled across an account of William Hooper Young's early-twentieth-century murder of Anna Pulitzer. I was intrigued by early newspaper speculation that the murder was related to the Mormon practice of Blood Atonement, a doctrine that the Church has actively denied ever existed despite a great deal of (admittedly shadowy) evidence to the contrary.

Young's crime reminded me of a ritual murder I hadn't thought about in a long time: fundamentalist Mormons Ron and Dan Lafferty's double killing of Ron's wife and young child in American Fork, a town a few minutes away from where I grew up. The murder had occurred just shy of my eighteenth birthday and somehow became firmly imprinted in my mind as I moved into my college's dorms and became for the first time semi-independent of my family. At the time, I felt like the Lafferty murders revealed a part of Utah culture I'd never known existed.

Thinking of these two ritual murders with eighty years between them, both of them committed by Mormons on the fringe of their faith, I began to feel that the undercurrent of violence in Mormon culture really hasn't changed, that the conditions that made violence well up in earlier Mormon culture are still very much present today. Violence, as Jon Krakauer has suggested in his *Under the Banner of Heaven: A Story of Violent Faith,* a book that focuses on the Lafferty murders, has always been a largely suppressed and unacknowledged part of Mormon culture. This notion of the continued relation of violence to Mormonism became the basis for trying to understand Rudd's obsession with Hooper Young's crime, as well as the basis for the temporal confusion that takes place later in the novel.

A few years after the Lafferty murders, the Mormon temple endowment ceremony was changed in significant ways. The most significant changes to my mind involved the deletion of the "penalties," a portion of the ceremony in which each temple participant mimed out stylized ways of being killed if they were to reveal temple secrets. Many temple-going Mormons saw this as a positive step: I tend rather to see it as a further repression of Mormonism's relation to violence. Changing the ceremony hasn't changed Mormonism's underlying violence; it has only hidden it.

Since the Mormon temple and its ceremonies are so integral to Mormon experience—and are also the most hidden part of Mormon culture, I felt that any book that spoke in any detail about the relationship of Mormon culture to violence needed to acknowledge the connection of the temple ceremony to violence. To do that, I would have to talk, at least a little bit, about the ceremony itself. I have tried to limit my discussion of the ceremony largely to one chapter in the second section of the book, and have tried to signal it in such a way that Mormon readers who hold the temple ceremony sacred will be able to see it coming and will be able to avoid it if they so choose. I've tried as well to be as respectful as possible and to focus on portions of the temple ceremony that are no longer practiced. I think this information is essential to non-Mormons who don't know anything about the ceremony itself, but may also be important for Mormons who came to the temple ceremony after it changed in 1990. I give a great deal less information away, by the way, than one can find in a two-minute search on the internet.

The newspaper articles are actually from the *New York Times* and are quoted for the most part verbatim, with ellipses indicated where a portion of the article has been removed. I have in one or two instances made changes in spelling or corrected an error, but every attempt has been made to preserve the accuracy of these articles.

As the newspaper articles suggest, Young did write a piece called "Sunrise in Hell," which he published in a newspaper called the *Crusader*. I tried to find this piece with the help of several different researchers, but though we located other issues of the newspaper we had no success finding the issue in question. I suspect no copy is extant, but would be delighted if I can be proven wrong. The poem that ends the second section is meant not to serve as Hooper Young's actual work but as Rudd's attempt to recreate the poem as a kind of Mormon hymn.

I intend for this to be my last Mormon-themed book, at least as far as fiction is concerned. It is my departure from Mormonism both as a person and as a writer. Mormonism is a culture that nourished me as a person and as a writer growing up; without it I would not be who I am. And yet at the same time I feel remarkably comfortable having left it and am not sorry to be free of it. Or at least as free of it as one can ever be of a culture whose rhythms of speech and ways of thinking one still finds oneself to lapse naturally into years later. I suspect those rhythms are sufficiently burned into my brain that they'll stay with me until I die. But that relation to language, to me, is the best thing about the culture.

COLOPHON

The Open Curtain was designed at Coffee House Press, in the historic warehouse district of downtown Minneapolis. The text is set in Garamond.

FUNDER ACKNOWLEDGMENTS

Coffee House Press is an independent nonprofit literary publisher. Our books are made possible through the generous support of grants and gifts from many foundations, corporate giving programs, individuals, and through state and federal support. Coffee House Press receives general operating support from the Minnesota State Arts Board, through an appropriation by the Minnesota State Legislature and from the National Endowment for the Arts, a federal agency. Coffee House receives major funding from the McKnight Foundation. Coffee House also receives significant support from: an anonymous donor; the Elmer and Eleanor Andersen Foundation; the Buuck Family Foundation; the Bush Foundation; the Patrick and Aimee Butler Family Foundation; the Foundation for Contemporary Arts; Stephen and Isabel Keating; the Lenfesty Family Foundation; Rebecca Rand; the law firm of Schwegman, Lundberg, Woessner & Kluth, P.A.; the James R. Thorpe Foundation; the Archie D. and Bertha H. Walker Foundation; Thompson West; the Woessner Freeman Family Foundation; the Wood-Hill Foundation; and many other generous individual donors.

This activity is made possible in part by a grant from the Minnesota State Arts Board, through an appropriation by the Minnesota State Legislature and a grant from the National Endowment for the Arts. MINNESOTA STATE ARTS BOARD

NATIONAL ENDOWMENT FOR THE ARTS

To you and our many readers across the country, we send our thanks for your continuing support.

Good books are brewing at coffeehousepress.org